D1825091

A story of despair and redemption in the baseball offseason.

Dedicated to my son Ben, who suffers with me; and with thanks to Maggie and Ben for their help and encouragement.

'All my players are someone's son.'

Felipe Alou, in his Expo days.

John Young
November 2011 to April 2012

1. The New GM

Peter was so sick of Ben Cherington. It was not as if it had been an earth-shaking decision. The Red Sox were hardly capable of earth-shaking decisions. Market pressures. The whole Red Sox Nation thing sucked. Bunch of overpaid kids sitting there drinking beer and eating fried chicken and the whole city thinks it has the answer and Cherington interviews all the guys Theo rejects in Chi.

The mound of claims on his desk had grown again this afternoon and he was discouraged. He usually hated this time of year. Take today, no chats on ESPN and the free agents would be posturing with guys like Boras claiming guys like Willie Bloomquist are worth millions. But today Baseball America was releasing the Nats top ten prospects. Over-hyped Harper would be top, of course, but the rest would be interesting.

Anna was coming over with more claims. She was a decent youngster. Not bright, but pretty enough to pull a husband in the next few years. Probably have half a dozen affairs before that. In many ways watching the social scene was the most interesting aspect of working for a huge insurance company. Not that the social scene was all that interesting. Not for him as a spectator. But for the young ones, especially the singles. Best advice he could give a decent-looking youngster who wanted to get married was to find a job in a big insurance office. Or even if they just wanted to get laid regularly. Or occasionally. Or just be sociable. Even Peter still often went out for a drink with a colleague, although he preferred to walk over to the Bistro du Midi or Teatro Bar on his own. All the younger guys tried their boring line of chatter on Anna. She liked him, he knew that. He was so hopelessly unthreatening. Once when he was teasing her she had giggled and asked if he was coming on to her. He had laughed and said that it was entirely possible she could do better than a sixty year old bald man. She had responded by saying that it was amazing how much worse she could do in this dump. He knew they all tried to pick her up. She had that look. The 'I can be picked up look'. Also the 'I may just put out look' and then there was the 'and the one night stands work for me if you buy dinner' look. She would do well in insurance.

Peter was stupid enough to think the Expos would win the World Series in his life-time but not stupid enough to think Anna wanted to get into bed with him even if he bought dinner. Not that the Expos existed anymore, but his loyalties had followed them to Washington. Washington, of all places. Selig should be shot. Giamatti's death may have been the worst thing to happen to the Expos. After Rick fucking Monday.

Anna told him that some of the claims forms were getting urgent. Stuart didn't like it when the forms were in the office for more than a week. Some of the ones on Peter's desk would remain there for a month or a year if he didn't just move them on unread. Mostly he just stayed late and moved them to another desk. Usually Bert's or Michele's. Bert was a prick and Michele would have been if she could pass the physical. Maybe she could? Whatever was in those pants was likely to remain her secret for a very long time. Sometimes he just wrote approved across a claim and sent it to accounts.

Most claims came in through electronic mail, of course. The advantage of this was that he could spend his afternoons on the baseball chats while people thought he was processing claims on the computer. The disadvantage was that when he forwarded claims to his colleagues, they could trace the sender. Bert had caught him out twice, so he had stopped forwarding things to him electronically. Michele was still fine. And Beryl and Zainab were perfect. Beryl was as old as him and, like him, was really not brilliant on the computer. So she questioned as few things as she could because she was terrified to get fired. Zainab was an immigrant. Lucky to have a job, so she kept her mouth shut. Probably a Muslim. Sad really, the way she was treated because she was a sweetheart, despite the head scarf. Everyone in the office was suspicious of her, or seemed to be. He had asked her to join him for a drink a few times after work. Well, coffee, of course. She had a couple of teenagers. Probably ten years older than she looked. Whizzo on the computer. In fact best claims adjuster in the office without doubt and no chance of promotion unless she joined the Unitarian Church after a masterful sex change operation. The best career path for a woman was still the one Anna was taking.

*

How could Aaron Fitt have put Matt Purke in the list? Mind you, he fit Rizzo's profile perfectly. Lots of potential but unlikely to play more than five games because of injury. Still there was no more Wily Mo Pena. Or Elijah Dukes or Lastings Milledge. And Nyer Martin was gone. He would read what Fitt wrote. In fact, compared to the egos over at ESPN, they were all pretty sane over at BA. God, he hated Keith Law. Who fucking cares how he beats his eggs for an omelet. Might as well tell us how he beats his meat. And now Bowden was over at ESPN as well. Both those two heads wouldn't fit into one room. Not that they would want to after some of the things Law wrote about Bowden; between his cooking tips and reading list.

He stretched. He'd better call Marianne. With the prospects list released he would stay late. Good chance to transfer some claims to the saps when the office was empty.

Aaron Fitt was really pretty good. Really, all the BA writers were decent and answered questions as if they respected the poor bastard asking the question, even the ones from fans who may know a little less about the game. Fitt sort of made him feel good about the Nats as well. That was the point; fans should be encouraged to feel good about their teams. Not like Law: Morse can't hit, Desmond can't field, Espinosa a strike out machine. The only guy he likes is Harper, another big head. Peacock maybe a middle reliever. Milone strictly AAA. Hope Rizzo read Fitt and trades Desmond for something good, let Lombardozzi have a chance and if it doesn't work there is always Rendon. Maybe he would drop by The Junction for a beer on the way home, just to think about 2013.

*

God, poor Wilson Ramos. All the potential, all that money, all that talent but really he is just a kid with a family from a poor country wanting a life. Sometimes you forget.

*

One thing going for the Boston fans, they weren't all jerks. Not as good as St Louis maybe, but better than the Yankees. He had overheard a comment about Cherington again last night and what a cool GM he was and how he would take his time choosing a manager because he was not the type to panic and all that.

Again. Doing his 'I'm as cool as Theo shit'. Again. Anyhow, this guy in a work shirt leans in and asks how the fuck they can worry about fucking Dale Sveum when a kid like Wilson Ramos is going through hell. And his family. And they all shut up. Just like that. Decent lot really. Then talked real soft about the whole thing and two of them even passed on the next round and went home.

*

Red Sox fans remember Dan Duquette and are laughing about him already. Assholes. Duquette did a brilliant job for the Expos. Only problem is that he has such a horrible personality. Real prick, as if that would stop him being a good GM. Anyhow, with Angelos and Showalter in Baltimore they could confuse Duquette for Albert fucking Schweitzer. He could easy win Miss Congeniality over there. Maybe he should write BA about a new award for the sweetest guy in baseball. Duquette could be as brilliant as he likes, of course, because in a division with Tampa, Boston and the Yankees, he can forget success. Mind you, if ever three guys deserved to be in a leaky boat together it was those three in Baltimore. Maybe throw Angelos' sons in for good measure.

God it was deadly in the office. Anna had a skirt on, Zainab was off sick. Or maybe it was one of her kids was sick. Stuart was out of the office at some committee meeting. That was bad; he would come back with a new idea. Actually, a re-cycled idea. And expect everyone to froth with enthusiasm. Even Keith Law wasn't doing a chat this week. Now that Neyer was gone, Law was probably the most reliable. Probably just liked to write belittling comments to the fans. Neyer was much nicer. They are all much nicer. Shit, Dan Duquette is probably nicer than Keith Law.

Word was Rizzo was interested in Oswalt. Perfect. Maybe pick up Marquis again and try and get his five starters all on the 60 day together. With Roche and Zimmerman. And then Purke and Rendon. Christ, they could open a hospital. At least Rosenthal thinks they are more interested in Buehrle. Better boring than injured. Serve fucking Obama right if the Nats got Buehrle. Christ, how can the president of the fucking country support the fucking White Sox when he lives in Washington? Maybe not for long, poor bastard. What a crap job. Better working in insurance. Wonder if he really thought the Republicans would give him half a chance? Still, he looks quite distinguished with his grey hair, if a bit tired.

Friday night and not much doing. Maybe drop in at the Bistro then walk up to Copley to catch the bus. Even have one or two in The Junction. Nothing much is going to happen on the weekend. Even next week, not until after the twenty-third. Still, he would drop in for a few drinks and see what the bar talk was.

By the time he got home he was ready to go straight to bed. Friday nights could be like that. Marianne tended to work late and have something simple then just want to read. Stupid night to work late. Why would people want their teeth drilled on Friday night? Just to enjoy the pain? That was cruel, because Marianne was brilliant. He wouldn't go to anyone else. She had tried to convince him that no one should ever get any sort of medical attention from a close relative except in an emergency. He had just told her it was urgent that whoever stuck a drill in his mouth better not hurt him or he would let all his teeth rot and she was the only one he trusted. His teeth were pretty strong, so once a year she cleaned them and he rarely needed any other work. Other patients had their teeth cleaned by the hygienist, but he insisted on Marianne. He really was terrified of all dental work.

He stuck his head into the study to tell her he was off to bed. She said she would read for a little. That was code for I will read until I go to bed in the other room. That suited him as when he had too much to drink and had eaten something based around French fries and coleslaw, sleeping alone was an excellent idea. Between pissing and farting, he was not an attractive prospect. On his sober nights he was not an attractive prospect, but on nights like these he was pretty much a boozy slob. Which is what Marianne had called him on occasion.

Not much had been going at The Junction, more talk about Penn State and The Patriots than baseball. Boring really. He never liked football much. Never knew why. And as for the mess at Penn State, well, there was little you could say, which is why so many people were saying so much. Missing the real point, which is if people are allowed to think they are too important, they can begin to think the rules don't apply. No one even mentioned Wilson Ramos, which was also too awful to think about.

*

Good for Jamey Carroll. God, why didn't the Nats at least try to keep hold of a guy like that? Plays the game right. And going to the Twins. Good organization that, especially with Terry Ryan back. Poor Bill Smith. Ryan was an impossible act to follow. Cherington caught a break with the Sox imploding this year; makes Theo seem human and fallible. Mind you, Cherington's looking even more fallible now. Never made an offer to Papelbon. Oh yeah. Maybe Theo told him it was a waste of money. Still, Papelbon in Philadelphia was a marriage made in heaven. Peter hated Papelbon, hated the Phillies, and as a bonus, the Red Sox fans were pissed off. Can't beat that for all an all round good move.

And Wilson Ramos was found. Hard to believe the Venezuelan Police managed that on their own. Probably Chavez had him tied up in a garden shed somewhere. What a country. Should get all the ball players out. Certainly all the Nats. Bet the Nats had to pay something. Probably to the police. Good old Rizzo, though, just shut up and got on with it. He was no Jim Fanning, of course, but he was doing all right. If he just manages to sign someone who isn't injured. Maybe Mark Buehrle. Hope they just let Ramos alone now so he can get his mind right for next year. Needs his mother and family more than baseball and reporters. Jesus, the thought of Jesus being number one again. Another of Rizzo's hospital evacuees. Ten games and then the DL. And no Pudge. He won't be back.

Fucking Loria has made offers to Buehrle, Pujols, Reyes, Cespedes and probably
Ty Cobb. He is such a shit. Why would anyone play there? What he and Selig did to the Expos was criminal, took the bats, balls, and Beinfest and sent the poor bastards who were left off to Puerto Rico. Selig promises him Florida and he helps try to close down the Expos. Bastards. Now it's the Miami Marlins with their new stadium no one will come to because they wouldn't even watch them when he bought a World Series. Probably Selig asked the umpires to treat them kindly because he was so close to good old Jeff. Pricks. Fucking Marlins always beat the Expos. Nats too. Man, it would be terrible if Albert went to Miami. Couldn't be that stupid. Never once read that Albert was stupid. Just jacking up the price and Loria gets to look like he is a big man. Well, Albert will go back to St Louis and you'll still be short, fat and bald, Jeff. Hope he gets Reyes as he has been linked to the Nats. Another member of the Disabled List. Wish Rizzo would wake up to the fact that these guys are more valuable when they actually play. Well, maybe not Werth. Still, Werth plays and doesn't moan

so don't knock him. Hope he has a good year. He liked guys who played the game right. Like Jamey Carroll.

Cherington is high on Sveum, must mean Theo is going for Maddux. And Francona looks like he will be out of work. Do him good. Few people realize he was an Expo, but he was. Great hitter if a bit fragile. Maybe needed pain killers way back then. What great teams they were. Cherington could learn from Fanning. Everyone could have learned from Fanning. Every new GM should study the life and times of Jim Fanning and the Expos. BA loved them back then. What wasn't to love? Fucking Rick Monday.

*

Sunday was always a bit a lost day in the off season. Always worth reading what Cafardo had to say but really it was usually just a light on all the rumors already out there. Sure to have a comment about the closer situation and Big Papi. Papelbon has done Ortiz a favor if he wants to stay. No way Cherington wants to have it look like a leaky ship over at Fenway. Nothing from Zuckerman or Goessling on the Nats except about Ramos. Leave it alone. It's over. Little thing on Purke. Why bother? Headed for the DL. Maybe a lifer on the DL. Poor kid.

Still there was nothing much going down. At least Lannan wasn't pitching against the Phillies later. Great when the highlight of your Sunday was the fact that Lannan couldn't pitch against the Phillies in the off season. Why was it that every second Sunday during the season, Lannan seemed to pitch against the Phillies and get clobbered. The other Sundays were generally taken up with the Marlins. He always watched Sunday games on MASN and had the feeling the

Nats won about one in ten. Always a great way to finish the weekend. Especially if the Red Sox won. Depressing.

Marianne always went out for the day on Sunday. Worked well in the season but in November it just meant killing time for Peter really. Usually he had lunch in a bar. And a few beers. He hated talking about the Pats but at least they had taken a few hits lately. And the whole NBA was mercifully in a labor dispute. Best thing that could happen to basketball. And the Bruins were trying to win the Stanley Cup by boring everyone to death again. Even talking baseball was pretty hopeless in Boston where even those who had heard of the National League, had never heard of the Nationals. Strangely enough, lots of them had heard of the Expos. Peter would have bet that BS, Before Selig, the Expos would have been the favorite National League team in Boston. What wasn't there to love? Red Sox fans sort of liked the Expos. Fucking Claude Brochu.

*

So the Sox would give Sveum a second interview. Now there's a big story. Could have hired him a week ago. Of course asshole Selig insists on them interviewing minority candidates. Like the Red Sox are going to suddenly embrace civil rights. Maybe in the outfield if you can hit .300, but not the manager. Maybe hire Minyana once Cherington is done. Have to ask Theo. Meanwhile the Red Sox will pretend to be deep in contemplation over the new manager to be hired by the new general manager. Nice if Duquette did a bang up job in Baltimore and the Red Sox finished last. Whatever happened to Yaz? Lonborg and Champagne? They had a soul back then.

Nothing doing in Nats land. Almost sacrilege to sign someone until all the Wilson Ramos shit is behind them. Great to have him back but do we have to

11

spend all this time hearing about who was the most upset, who supports him most, who hates Chavez most. No one giving up gas in the car or boycotting Venezuelan oil. Kilgore did a little piece on the GM meetings which sort of said Rizzo ain't telling just now. Kilgore's okay, though. In fact, Nats writers are all okay. Love to watch Chase Hughes knee working overtime on Beltway Baseball. Nice youngster. Best of the lot was still Bill Ladson. Only because he remembered the Expos. And liked them. Must send him a question. Was old Woody as cool as Livan?

*

Another Blue Monday. No chats on ESPN. Maybe he should push through a few claims. No lack of them on his desk or on his computer. Stuart was back today. And Zainab. Zainab looked worried. Stuart looked peeved. Zainab always looked worried. Stuart always looked peeved. No wonder he loved his job. He had used the fact that Zainab was away to forward her half of his computer backlog and also managed to rid himself of over half his paper claims to Michele. He was saving Bert for the annual meetings in December. God, Zainab had tears running down her cheeks. Hope it's because her kids are sick. He didn't want to be the cause of the grief with the extra work.

Anna came over, smiled at him. Whispered that Michele seemed to have an awful stack of work and giggled. Then she said that he admired his style and smiled again. So Anna knew more than she had let on, but it seemed fine. She walked over to Bert's desk and dumped some claims, then turned to Peter and winked. Good girl. She would do very nicely.

As he moved towards the coffee machine, Stuart told him he had to talk to him. Not now, not now, tomorrow morning first thing. He still looked peeved. Maybe worse. What could be up? Oh well, tomorrow would be soon enough.

No chats. And he was not really interested in claims. Of course, he was never interested in claims. Read one this morning about some guy with a family of five kids. And a bloody dog. The stupid things people write in the section about other information. As if anyone cared about his goddamn dog. Peter didn't really care about his goddamn kids much less his goddamn dog. Or his goddamn wife who was in the goddamn hospital. Hopefully getting a goddamn hysterectomy. Five kids. They don't deserve a roof. Still, the claim was legitimate enough and in the end he marked it approved and urgent. What the hell. Guy could hardly write. Thing was done in pencil.

Zainab was pretty upset. Maybe looked like she wanted to talk to him. Kept sort of looking over. He'd have to be careful. He didn't mind exchanging greetings with his colleagues but that was about it. Most of them were jerks, like Bert and Michele. He knew a few were interested in baseball but he avoided talking to them as well. Probably Red Sox fans anyhow. But he thought the less he said about baseball the better. If he drew attention to his interest, the fact that he spent four or five hours a day chasing information on the computer might be noticed. All he needed is some smart ass like Bert asking a lot of dumb questions or making comments that were supposed to be witty. He might try to forward some work to Bert. Zainab looked so upset. If she broke down with too much work his little trick might be revealed. He must avoid talking to her.

It would help him if the company hired a couple of new people for the office. He might be able to forward them work for a few months before they caught on.

Company was so damn cheap though. All they did was talk about cuts and making economies. Surely it was important to process claims quickly to develop a reputation for being fair and efficient. Good marketing, really, just common sense.

Poor Zainab, look at her. Careful. Don't look at her; she might catch your eye.

Nice little thing by Kilgore about a Cuban kid called Soler. So much better idea than that other Cuban who was twenty-nine. Rizzo should get his act together. He was aiming for 2013, not 2012. And with real bodies, not some fantasy World Series based on your DL. Kilgore should be the GM. Better than Cherington, anyhow. Even Rizzo. Some dink rated the GMs and placed Theo right up there. Sure, had a great year did Theo. Turned his complete failure into the presidency of the Cubs. Always had a soft spot for the Cubs until Soriano went there. Not that anyone wanted him in Washington.

2. The GM Meetings

God, Stuart was a pain. So there were a few claims that went through by mistake. He had a point about that arson thing. He had made it sound so much like a threat, especially the bit about recording it on his file and doing spot checks. He was surprised that they had found that many. Mind you, he processed dozens, well no, hundreds without reading them. But when he did read them it seemed like almost all of them were okay. He would have to use Bert and Zainab more. And Michele. Maybe try it with Rachel and Abby, but they were pretty sharp and also pretty aggressive. That's the trouble with hiring kids.

Zainab still looked awful. So sad, he peeked over and she was crying. He looked away quickly but she came over to his desk and apologized. Hoped she wasn't upsetting him. Hard to deal with that so he just sort of grunted a 'no'. Don't engage.

Still no chats today. Probably waiting for the meetings to get going. They had started, but they were scratching around for rumors. Dierkes was good, did all the hard work for him. Mind you, left sort of an empty space in the day if he didn't try to dig out the rumors himself. Maybe not a bad idea. He should read the claims before approving them. God, was Bert smirking at him? What a jerk.

Hey, he had forgotten about Schoenfield. Never much bite in his chats and he had struggled with the software at first, but it beat claims. Fuck Stuart. Not that Schoenfield had the decency to answer one question of interest. Justin Verlander was of no interest to him. Nor was he interested in Yu Darvish. Half Iranian. Likely to be locked up as a terrorist if he pitches badly in this country.

He should certainly avoid Texas. Verducci was right about him, two year shelf life. Like Dice-K. And now the Sox and the Yanks were talking about Buerhle. He'd be a fool because for the sort of money he could get, they'll expect Whitey Ford and he's no Whitey. Stick with the Nats. Come on Rizzo. Nothing immoral about being healthy. We already have Wang for the DL. Get one who actually pitches.

Maybe he would stop for a drink at the Teatro, wash the taste of Stuart out of his mouth. He liked the Teatro when he wanted to be alone and, to be honest, Stuart had scared him a bit and he needed to think.

*

He had decided not to tell Marianne about the meeting with Stuart. She tended to be very impatient about his career. Career, oh yeah. When he was being treated he admired her skill but he had to admit he resented her success, especially when compared to his own limited success. Or was it controlled failure? Mind you, how could anyone want to work inside other people's mouths? Once, after an argument; not really an argument, they never really argued probably because Marianne did not think it worthwhile. Did not think he was worth the trouble. Sad, that. Anyhow, after a sigh that was not part of a real argument but definitely occurred at a moment of tension, he had asked her how she could work inside other people's mouths. She had sighed again, but worse and seemed ready to explode, then left the house. For three days, or actually three nights; she was only there during the day to work. Never really said where she went and he never asked. Seemed to be a dangerous question.

Do it, Theo! Dale fucking Sveum. Right from under Cherington's nose. Yes! And then Lucchino makes the announcement that they will extend the search. Not Cherington, Lucchino. Then Cherington issues a weak agreement. Sveum doesn't know how lucky he is. No one is expected to succeed in Chicago. Everyone is supposed to succeed in Boston.

Chat today with Dierkes. I like him, takes tons of questions and admits he is more of a conduit for information than a really knowledgeable guy, although he is getting there. Give him something to do while he fumes about Stuart. He will have to pay more attention to transferring work rather than just approving it. But, hell, the company was not exactly bust and most of them were small claims. Well all but three. From now on, best to check the final amount at least, big ones to be read, small ones to be approved. Probably what they do when they check up on him, look mostly at the big ones. Bet they don't check every damn thing Bert does. Or Michele.

Rizzo says he has laid ground work for a trade and there is lots of interest. Meaning nothing in the pipeline. Rizzo would want the Yankees to throw in Teixeira if he was offered Sabathia for Balester straight up. Best go the free agent route. Not the injured ones, Mike, someone who still has his legs.

God, Zainab was a wreck. Someone should talk to her. You would think one of the women. Not Michele, one of the real women. Not that he had anything against dykes; it was just that she was, well, such a dyke. Not exactly Zainab's scene. But Zainab needed help and everyone was ignoring it. He could not bear to look at her anymore.

Marianne was in bed by the time he got home. She could be like that when she was annoyed. Not that she had anything to be annoyed about as far as he knew. He hadn't mentioned Stuart's little outburst.

The more he thought about what Stuart said, the angrier he got. How long had he worked for them? So one or two bad claims had got through? Big deal. Could happen to anyone. Of course, Stuart's point was that it was not happening to anyone but him. Maybe they were checking up on all of them. Real Big Brother bullshit that. Like a police state.

*

Marianne was in her office by the time he was down for breakfast. So something was up. He may need to talk to her this weekend. Apologies for whatever. He seemed to think she was visiting Barney this weekend. Or was it Cheryl? One of the kids. Maybe he was going too. He couldn't remember. Cheryl wasn't so bad. Or she hadn't been before she got pregnant. But Arnie was all DIY and politics. What a combination. And republican politics at that. Not tea party or any of that shit. Just cut taxes and fuck the poor sort of stuff. How could Cheryl marry a Republican? Mind you, he had. But Marianne had her reasonable side when she wasn't with other dentists. Or Arnie. Or Barney. God, where did he come from? He looked like Peter, so he had to be his, but Christ. Maybe it was just Marianne's doing. Mind you, even she found Barney and Bobbie difficult. What sort of fucking name was that for a woman? Not that Bobbie wanted to be a woman? Not in those clothes. She wanted to be a sweet little girl. One who lynched rapists, murderers, and people of color. Mind you, she would not know that there was a difference. Any color other than blue-eyed blond. He often wondered how Barney passed. He had dark hair. Not much. But what there was, was dark.

Hey, even Law was okay today. Never mentioned Master and Margarita once, although Master Chef popped up. Vaguely supportive of the Nats, reasonable about Espinosa and almost encouraging about Harper. He would like Harper. Another bighead. At least he didn't talk about the new players' agreement. Clinton said all that ever needed saying about player agreements.

Sveum did it, went with Theo and the Cubs. Good move, sunshine. Now the Sox owners were meeting Valentine. Probably forgot they had hired a GM. Assholes. Come on Jays. Even Baltimore is smarter than the Red Sox. Except Angelos, of course.

What a mistake. Should never have bought Zainab a coffee. It was just he was going out for one himself after Law was finished and he knew she liked milky, sugary slop, so he just brought one back and put it on her desk. And then, at quitting time, she grabbed his arm and started crying and saying thank you before she rushed out. Made him feel bad. Still, he forwarded her a few claims. Not as many as he had planned, maybe ten or so. Maybe fifteen.

He went home fairly early. Thought he might eat with Marianne but she was just washing her dishes when he got home, so he fixed himself a sandwich and went into the den and got on the computer. God knows why, he had read everything at work. It just seemed the place to be. Marianne looked unhappy. Not like Zainab, but still. Sort of spoiled the evening.

*

Poor old Cherington. Not that he was old and not that he ever felt sorry for anyone in the Red Sox organization. Bunch of smug creeps. Reports were right on the button this morning. Valentine would mean the owners had flexed their flabby middle-aged muscles and established that Cherington is only getting paid to express his loyalty and faith. Assholes. And, meanwhile, back at the closed meetings, they announce they have a CBA agreed but we are not going to tell you. Na, na, ni, naya. Selig should be shot. What a prick. Probably still hoping to fold the Expos. He deserves to go to a special hell full of Canadian teams with the Canadian dollar worth a fucking quarter.

*

So, he was not going to visit the pregnant Cheryl with Marianne this weekend. Maybe better I go on my own and have sort of woman to woman talk, she said. Something must be up. Christ knows he didn't need a mano a mano talk with Arnie. What ya think Pete, pressboard or plywood? He hated being called Pete. He hated DIY. For that matter, he pretty much hated Arnie. Come to think of it, Cheryl was a pain in the ass now that she was pregnant. Too much like her mother. At least Marianne only voted for sane Republicans. God knows what Cheryl voted for, but that DIY idiot would support Satan if he promised to cut taxes half a per cent. He was lucky to be excluded but still felt a bit insulted. And he still loved Burlington. Marianne didn't say if she was going for the weekend or the day. Probably the whole weekend. That is what they usually did when they both went. Funny thing to go just before Thanksgiving. Maybe not. Cheryl and Arnie usually went to his family somewhere in Maine. Fucking Maine. Probably wrestle bears and shit like that. He'd met the family at the wedding and had no intention of ever meeting them again. Three of them hardly fit in the SUV they were so big. Big and dumb. Arnie had it in the DNA.

*

Work was a drag. No chats, nothing really going down. Hard to settle to anything. Slipped Michele a few claims more for the sheer pleasure of doing it than anything. Found himself approving several written claims without reading them again. Small ones and he did glance through them. Company had to think a bit. Spending too much time on small claims was inefficient use of his time. Shit, BA was doing Cubs prospects. Cub's prospects were grim, Sink and Sveum. Zainab give him a few smiles. Trying. Poor girl. What a mess. Have to be careful there, she might want to talk. What were the women doing for god's sake? By the time he got home, Marianne had left. Usually they went Saturday morning. No big deal, he had eaten.

3. Thanksgiving Week

He was up late Saturday. Well, why not. Not that he would have done anything with Marianne had she been there, but still, it was very quiet without her. Difficult to believe that you could miss someone you hardly spoke to, but there it was. Bad timing as well. Baseball news all on the totally uninteresting agreement with the players. He might go to The Junction but the idea of hearing anyone having an intense conversation about the Pats and the Chiefs was just laughable. Kansas fucking City for Christ sake. What next? Maybe a big game with Cleveland was coming up. Idiots.

Weather permitting he might catch a bus to Copley and have a wander on the Common. Maybe a late breakfast at the Paramount. He wondered what Marianne and Cheryl were up to. Marianne had said nothing. In fact, she had hardly said anything to him in weeks now that he thought about it. He had thought of offering to go along but he had a feeling that would have been unwelcome. And there was Arnie. Arnie would be as relieved as he was that he had stayed behind. He liked Burlington, though. Always had. Four hour drive with lunch in Hartford on the way. Well, not this time. Wonder why she left Friday. God, he would have had even more time with Arnie. Discuss building a tree house for the kid. That was another thing. All the talk about the first grandchild. Gets a bit boring. He decided on the Common, the Paramount for an early lunch and the afternoon and early evening with a newspaper and a few beers, ending in The Junction. Not exciting, but the day passed.

Sundays were bad enough without being alone. Marianne would have gone to church, of course. How could an intelligent adult believe all that shit? Mind you, the Expos were almost brought back from the dead. That was really reincarnation. Coming back as the Nats. Buddhist claptrap, not Christian claptrap. He'd go to church if he thought it would help Rizzo find a center fielder. Marianne said that as she worked in the community it was important to support the local church. Like as if it made much difference when their mouths were open and she was drilling. Never mind god, give me a needle. Still, he usually enjoyed The Globe and a coffee on Sunday morning before she got back. Thing was, it wasn't as pleasant with her in Vermont as it was with her in church. Cafardo would be worth a read.

Miller did a nice little hatchet job on the Red Sox. Perfect sense. Either the whole organization is without a clue, or the big boys are regretting Cherington already and have decided the best way to deal with him is undermine him completely. Nice guys. Either complete fools or complete bastards. Probably both now that he thought about it. Sort of getting ready to fire Cherington already. Maybe make him quit. You could almost feel sorry for him. Read the Herald and it seems like if the Sox hire Lamont, Cherington is in charge, hire Valentine and he is just an office boy. Well, we'll see.

God, what a dull day. Pats play Monday night, so can't even go to a bar and ignore the game. And the Bruins are on a winning streak, god help us. The Bruins are worse than the Pats. Might walk around Marine Park and Pleasure Bay. Pleasure. Oh yeah. Kill some time then maybe drop in at The Junction just to listen to a bit of chatter, like he wasn't alone on the earth. Nothing from Marianne, not even a text. He could text her, of course. How are you doing, how's Cheryl? I am bored to buggery. A bit selfish to go off for the whole weekend. No message. Maybe he should call to see if she was going to be home for dinner. Stupid idea, there was nothing for her to cook. So she would be back later. Another meal in a bar. He loved eating in bars and grills on week nights, even lunch on Saturday. But all weekend. With no baseball. It beat talking to Arnie he reminded himself, but he could have had a wander in Burlington, maybe while Arnie fixed his mower or something. Some of his old haunts, maybe Winooski and Centennial Field. With the fucking Oakland A's now, Burlington couldn't be further from fucking Oakland. Still there had been some great games. Kids play with so much emotion. Saw Orlando Cabrera there several times. There was a guy with a heart.

Thanksgiving week. God. All the GM's eating turkey. Dull week ahead after the very dull weekend. And a four day weekend coming up devoted to eating and football. At least no one bothered to give thanks. Better to be at work. Maybe not. No chats either so not much to do at work but actual work. Wonder what Marianne has in mind for Thanksgiving? Please keep Barney and Bobbie out of my life. Even if he would give thanks for that. Maybe Marianne would have done enough of this mother bullshit this weekend and they could skip Barney for a few months. Or years.

*

Come on, Mike. Take them a turkey. Take them presents for the kids. Does Buerhle have any kids? Must have, every writer says he is a nice guy. Nice guys have kids. Probably loves them. Or says he does. Can't be a nice guy if you don't love your kids. If they get Buerhle they can manage without a center fielder. Just play Lombardozzi in the infield. Get all those ground balls. Maybe sign a Cuban and wait for 2013. Or that Japanese guy supposed to be a pure hitter. Does that mean he would strike out less than BJ Upton? What a laugh. Nats have so many K's in the lineup and they are looking at Upton, maybe go for a full 27 in a game. Unless it goes to extras. Mark Buerhle. Hot damn. Come on Mike.

Marianne was really strange this morning. Bad enough having had the weekend on his own but now this. A spa weekend with Dyllis. Now that Sid was dead, they hardly ever saw Dyllis. Well, he didn't. Sid had been a decent guy. Hated the Red Sox. Not an Expo fan. Or Nationals. But at least not a Red Sox fan. Probably hated them as much as he did. Well, he hated the Yankees more than anything, but a Twins fan would. Peter liked the Twins and Sid liked the Nationals. That is, they did when they allowed themselves to cross dress. Sid called it that when they talked about who they liked in the other league. Good guy, Sid. Pity he died. Mind you, playing squash with all that weight was not a smart thing to do. Supposed to have been real good when he was young. Played for Boston College. Or U Mass. Or someone. Some University. God, when did he die? Year the Yankees beat the Twins in the playoffs. Hardly narrows it down. Sid hated the Yankees. Hardly blame him.

*

What the fuck was this spa weekend all about. Just like that. That's why she went to Burlington last weekend she said. He never liked Thanksgiving and never wanted to see the kids and Dyllis was on her own and he wouldn't go to church and, and. Basically, she wasn't having Thanksgiving with him and she would like to talk to him tomorrow night, not tonight because she was going over to talk to Dyllis about their plans, but tomorrow she was free in the evening. Well, thank you for that Marianne. Maybe between seven and seven fifteen? Or I could come to your office, perhaps?

God work could drag. Zainab looked a little better. Stuart looked a little worse. Michele looked a little gayer. How could a butch bitch like that be called gay? Probably never smiled in her gay life. Who were they kidding, stealing a perfectly good word and applying it indiscriminately to people like Michele? Bert looked like he always looked. Asshole. Just as he was leaving, Zainab came over to him and put her hand on his arm and said she was sorry, burst into tears and fled. Not just sorry. So sorry. What the hell. Another night to kill, what with Marianne planning the spa weekend and all. Shit. He would go to Jake's for dinner. Good beer and always crowded. Sit near the door and half watch the television. Trouble with Jake's was the offensive Red Sox shit all over, but the schnitzel was all right.

*

Another day, another yawn. Cherington was obviously holding out against Valentine. Might as well resign now, son. Reject Valentine and the disaster is your fault, accept Valentine and he will have you fired for getting the wrong overpaid superstars for him to win with. Don't worry; Duquette was training in the art of acquiescence over with Showalter. They can bring him back next.

Marianne hardly spoke this morning. Not aggressive or anything, almost wistful. Said she hadn't heard him come in last night. Just as well as last night was really early this morning. Well, she was doing her spa thing, why not?

Zainab would not look at him. Something up. Stuart wanted to see him before he left. Something up. No chats as the world got ready to give thanks. Come on

Mike, make it work and we can all give thanks. There was no evidence, of course, that god had anything but malice in his mind for the Nats, and so even if they did get Buerhle, he would do a Jason Marquis. Poor old Marquis, never injured until he pulled on a Nats' shirt.

No wonder Zainab was so upset last week. No wonder she was sorry. Bitch had no loyalty to her colleagues. Why didn't she speak to him? God, he could lose his job because of that foreign bitch. That was the trouble. Company had no loyalty to good Americans. Hired these foreigners and then used them against the old employees. Sort of like scabs. Monitored her work for a few days and found he had been forwarding some of his assignments. So what, she had the time and he was always behind. Did they want the work done, or what? Dumb bastards. But that was management for you. All the wrong decisions for all the wrong reasons. He needed a drink.

*

That was a very bad move last night. Marianne was obviously very upset that he had forgotten their scheduled talk. Like as if an appointment to talk with your wife should be necessary. Still, he could feel the tension, especially when she said that she couldn't see what difference it made, so forget it. You didn't have to be a psychiatrist to work that one out. And now he had to face Stuart again. At least he would make that meeting.

Zainab was waiting for him with a coffee when he entered the office. He could have poured it over her. But she was all apologies. Said he was the only one who was ever kind and how guilty she felt when he brought her coffee last week. Claimed that she had spoken to Stuart about overwork and he had set one of the systems Rottweilers onto it and found out that some of it was coming from him. Stuart claimed almost forty per cent, but who could believe Stuart. Stuart was out to get him. The axe could fall today. Needless to say, Stuart put the meeting off until late so he would have lots of time to worry.

Thank god for Dierkes. Bit of a nothing chat but it passed the time. And he survived the Stuart thing with a letter of warning. Two letters of warning. Stuart point blank refused to make it one letter with two points. Said it just wasn't strong enough. Nice and subtle. Good thing was that Zainab came to see him as he was leaving. Said she would take four or five claims a day from him if he was really busy because Stuart had told her that she should check and the computer guy showed her how to do it, but if she didn't complain, it should be fine. Nice to know she had the decency to feel bad. He thought she would probably take six or seven a day and keep her mouth shut. So he now had a system. Up to eight electronic claims a day to Zainab, very careful only to pass paper claims to Bert and Michele when he was alone in the office, and read all the larger claims he processed himself. Really, it could work well. If he was organized, he may end up doing less than ever.

No sense going home; might as well drop in at The Junction.

*

Thanksgiving wasn't so bad. Went over the arbitration offers. Only good thing was the Nats would not lose a draft pick if they sign Buerhle. Or Oswalt. But they would for Wilson so let him go to the Yankees. Or the Red Sox with Valentine and Cherington to nurture his career.

He did sort of a pub crawl for lunch and didn't get home until it was too late to try to cook the dinner Marianne had left him. Sure, I'm off to the spa, so cook this on your own you sad ass. Might as well have left a frozen dinner from Safeway. God, he felt awful. He should have talked to her last night. Or was it Tuesday? Yeah, Tuesday. Mind you, lot of pressure at work just now, working on his new system. Marianne had to realize that he had a life too, and a job. She may make more than him. She may make more than five times what he makes. But his job was important to him. He needed his career as well.

Friday morning he woke up late. Thank god. Less time to kill. He felt awful. Not just the drink, although that helped; but he also felt lonely. Why not call a friend. Now, just who would that be? Marianne had friends. Marianne had some friends who had husbands, some of whom he actually liked. No Nats fans, of course, but all right. But he had no friends. He hardly knew the name of some of the people he shared the office with. Shared the barn with, there must have been twenty of them in there. And Stuart with his little glass cage and secretary sitting outside. He wished he had said more to Stuart. Like maybe fuck off. Even in The Junction he had no friends. No real friends. Fucking Red Sox fans.

He thought maybe he would try Marianne's cell. Made him feel sort of desperate. Maybe not. Maybe.

By the end of the day he had tried Marianne four times without a reply. He texted that he hoped everything was fine and that he was fine. He went over some old stuff on the computer. Phillies were interested in Soler. Come on Mike. Get Soler and maybe the Japanese guy as well, Aoki. At least it was a pretty short name. He could remember it even if it was Japanese. He cooked the meal Marianne had left. Really good. Nice of her. Should have eaten it on Thanksgiving.

*

Saturday started badly and got worse. Just nothing. Too many teams interested in Buerhle to suit him, no center fielders popping out. Lousy Thanksgiving. At least the Red Sox remain in disarray. Poor old Cherington. Might as well bite the bullet and accept Valentine. Going to lose your job one way or the other.

Nothing from Marianne. A bit selfish. He had enough to worry about at work. Next week should be exciting and here he was having to worry about his job and his wife. There should be lots of rumors and even one or two big signings. Couple of Japanese players may be posted. And he had to watch Stuart and keep his head down. All he needed was Stuart sneaking up behind him while he was on a chat. It had happened a few times already.

And Marianne. No avoiding that little chat now. He hadn't really avoided it last week. Well, he had, but only because he forgot. Freud would have something to see about that sort of forgetting. But Freud was a prick.

Black Friday had come and gone. Thank god. What a non-event. Got more publicity than Thanksgiving. Step right up folks and get your Black Friday greeting cards. Stupid country. Shopping is more important than any tradition. Want to make a million, open the stores on Christmas day, give people something to do after the ogre of opening useless presents. Not that Christmas was such a great idea. Worse than Thanksgiving for baseball news.

*

Sunday was the perfect ending to a four day weekend. Up late, felt awful, beer for lunch, beer in the afternoon, beer for dinner. Marianne should have stayed. Should have been here. Should have called. At least texted. Maybe he could mention a few things when they had their little talk. She was a bit quick to criticize him while zipping off to health class with her grieving friend.

He went to bed early. Didn't hear Marianne come in. She didn't even consider waking him.

4. The Best Of Times

This was supposed to be one of the most exciting weeks of the year. Winter meetings a week away and rumors would abound. Work would be a pleasure as long as no one was looking over his shoulder. Fucking Stuart. Just like him to make some remark about his duties just when something big was coming over the wire or a Nats question was being answered. It was just the worst week to have to take his duties seriously. Zainab may be sincere in her offer to continue doing some of his claims, but was she reliable? She had already caused problems by complaining. She would need to be watched closely. Bert and Michele always needed to be watched as they would quite cheerfully cause him problems. What terrible colleagues they were. Get a man fired. He would love to get something on them, but that was unlikely. They were too boring to have a passion.

And now Marianne. Hardly spoke this morning. Yes, it had been very pleasant. Yes, they needed to talk. Maybe one night this week. She had a big week because she had missed so much last week, please excuse her; she was off to the office. Thanks. Not even a 'How did you manage?' I managed badly is how I managed. While you were in the spa with your friend.

There were at least a few things to read. Cherington and Lamont versus Valentine and Lucchino. Everyone wanting Buerhle. No chats today but Schoenfield was up for tomorrow. And Goessling with a live thing on the Nats if Stuart would just bury himself in his office. Live meant headphones. Maybe not. Not this week. Fucking company was so suspicious that a man couldn't even get on with his life anymore.

Marianne was a worry. He thought she might have felt a little guilty. Or sheepish. Or something. Cool as cool. Like she didn't care. Which she probably didn't. It was a worry. As if he didn't have enough on his plate with Stuart and Zainab. And Bert and Michele. And Buerhle. Come on Rizzo.

*

He got home to an empty house. Marianne must have gone out. Maybe to the movies or something. Was Nutcracker on? Was there a Monday performance? She loved the ballet. He couldn't see it, really. Come to think of it, he had only been once. Before they were married. At a University of Vermont thing. Still it was almost midnight when he heard her come in. He pretended to be asleep but when she didn't come into the bedroom, he stopped pretending. Then he fell asleep. That was one of the good things about drinking too much, you could usually sleep. Waking up was a problem, of course.

*

What on earth was Rizzo thinking? Marrero is injured so he chases Fielder so he has someone who plods around first base like a hippo? Marrero probably can't wait to be a free agent. Pulls a muscle and now Rizzo is chasing Fielder. Boras must own the guy. Get in the game Mike. Fielder can't pitch. He can't field. He can hit and should be allowed to go to Seattle to be a fat Designated Eater. Christ. How do these guys get their jobs?

He brought Zainab a cup of coffee. And sent her six claims. Might as well see if she's sincere. She smiled when he gave her the coffee, but the claims arrived a bit later. What the hell, she seems reasonable. Probably going to be fine. He would stay a bit later tonight, make it look like he is busy and use the opportunity to shift some paper work. To Bert. God he hated Bert.

Marianne had said 'Not tonight' so she was probably going to be out again. It was getting him down. Costing a lot in meals, as well. And beer. Lucky she was a good dentist or they could never afford it. He used to feel a bit guilty because she earned so much more but, if she couldn't be bothered cooking, why shouldn't he go out and have some fun. Except he wasn't having any fun. But he had to eat.

Marriage was a funny thing. He usually didn't give it much thought, but with all the silly things Marianne was up to lately, he was going to have to talk to her. She was the one who wanted to 'talk things through' all the time. This thing women had about opening up issues. Always made everyone feel worse. Maybe that was what made them feel better: feeling worse. Why listing his faults was such a positive experience for her was hard to tell. He never retaliated. What use? In any relationship, both parties thought the other was at fault. He was interested in baseball. All she could think about was ballet and opera. She read a lot, of course, probably because she was bored. And she liked the theater. She always moaned about not going on holiday. Europe and places like that. Christ. He didn't like the idea, but he was going to have to stick up for himself this time. She was just getting a bit too whatever.

*

Marianne certainly was acting strange. Just when things were heating up with rumors, she has to start all this. At least she said she would be in tonight, but at breakfast it was as if they were strangers. He even had to make his own coffee.

She just sort of mentioned she would be in tonight as she left for the office. Not an I'll do dinner or maybe we can talk. Well, they would talk. He had taken just about enough.

Cherington had obviously decided to get fired because Valentine couldn't win the series with the crap team he provided rather than getting fired because the manager he hired couldn't win the series. Either way, it would have been his fault, so he capitulated and hired Valentine. Or the Red Sox hired Valentine. Cherington probably had less say than fucking Zainab. They would be all sweetness until Valentine decided Cherington should have got another starter and a better closer and maybe replaced Big Papi. Sure he should have Bobby, and the honorable Larry. Pair of turds. Mind you, it serves Cherington right for working for the Red Sox.

Dierkes at least chatted. Boring really. Same old rumors going round and round. Where the hell were Stark and Crasnick these days? Stuart had snuck up behind him while he was looking at the chat but he had quickly flipped to a claim. Just in time. Stuart mumbled something which was supposed to be pleasant. Creep. As if he wasn't checking up.

He did a bit more work than usual what with Stuart creeping about and all, so he left early. Give him time for a few at the Teatro before going home. Meant he was home a bit late so dinner was wrecked. Or Marianne thought so. Why she waited was beyond him. If it was ready, why not eat and just leave his rather than blame him for everything. Meant their little talk got off to a bad start. She was surprisingly aggressive, he thought. In fact, sort of scary. Separate bedrooms would work fine, made it easier, really, but telling him to piss off when he tried to make a point about her going off and never being around at meals and such was pretty tough. Then she just told him he had better shut up and listen, she would explain what she wanted, then he could decide whether he wanted to stay or not. Separate bedrooms. Agree to having some meals together and then getting there on time. Not stinking of beer. Christ, he had only had a few. She would pay the household expenses as usual but he would contribute two grand a month into her account. That should get rid of the smell of beer. He wouldn't be able to buy a small draft most nights. When he started to speak she had told him to shut up, he could take it or piss off. Easy, isn't it? She was scary. Then she said they could try it for maybe six months and if things remained this bad, he would have to leave.

Well, it made sense. She had bought the house and her office was part of it, but still it all sounded a bit final. He needed time. Not that he was frightened of her bullying, but she was in such an awful mood, talking would have been futile. And how could he afford to leave? She didn't offer any sort of compensation. He would see a lawyer maybe, but for now, best to just give it a day or two. He didn't even argue about Christmas, but dinner with Dyllis and that wretched Puerto Rican couple was an awful thought. But it could hardly be worse than Thanksgiving.

He really did not need all this just before the winter meetings. This week was interesting but next week should be truly exciting. Marianne would settle down by then.

Marianne was civil at breakfast. Made the coffee at least. Asked how he slept. The sleeping apart could work well as it saved the pretending to be asleep or the waiting until the other one was asleep. He would move some of his things out to the spare room tonight; let her know in a subtle way that she could have the bedroom. They agreed to eat together. Then she told him he would have to cook as she had a 6:30 this evening. So she was still doing this power trip thing.

*

Too much on his mind to really enjoy work. Managed to sneak a few things to Bert. So much was electronic these days. He would have to find an alternative to Zainab. Since Stuart had spoken to him he had not been given many large claims to deal with, which was good news. Couldn't slip too many through unread; but a few. A few each day. Law got him through the afternoon but it was pretty boring.

God, Keith Law could be a pain. All wrapped up in his latest article arguing about birthdays and such. At least he had three Nats on his top fifty. Mind you, Strasburg at seven. Asshole. And then a few questions about cooking. How was the duck, Keith? Just fine, I'm such a brilliant cook, what else could it have been? Jesus. And Stuart sneaking about didn't help. It just wasn't that interesting, but it beat work.

Dinner was shit.

*

Now Zainab was being funny. Just that little 'I'm busy too' shit was unnecessary. They had an agreement and now she was dropping hints that maybe she might not keep up her side. Trouble with foreigners was they lacked American values. As far as he was concerned, your word was as good as a contract. Nothing much to read about so he processed several claims but he resented having to pick up the slack for Zainab.

He was surprised in the evening. Maybe sleeping apart permanently was not such a good idea. Marianne had looked good to him at dinner. He had sort of forgotten. Damn fine legs and she was still slim and, well, just he had sort of forgotten. But she went her own way and he went his and she would be out tomorrow and, oh yes, had he remembered the monthly transfer to her account. Bitch.

*

Come on, Mike. Wilson before Buerhle, you must be joking. Still, Rizzo was no fool. Must be a smoke screen and the newspaper fools bought it. Things were getting tense now with the general managers all gathering for the feeding frenzy in Dallas. He had all of Saturday to worry about pitching. Marianne had a few Saturday morning appointments and then was going out for the afternoon and evening. It was getting to him. Yesterday he had arranged a monthly transfer but it would leave him very little. He should have got her to settle for less. If she was out all the time, he needed money to be out. And now there was this Wilson thing. Who needs CJ Wilson? It's Buerhle they need.

At last the winter meetings were starting. Not that much would happen on Sunday. Everyone arrive and make a sacrifice to Scott Boras and then get drunk. Still, it was worth keeping Dierkes up all day. Cafardo was an idiot, went through every team and all he could suggest for the Nationals was Coco fucking Crisp. Thanks for showing your interest Nick.

Jesus, Reyes went to Florida, oops, to Miami. Great stuff. They have wisely spent on a washed up closer and a hospital regular at short. Maybe no money left for Buerhle. Thought Beinfest was a lot smarter than that. Must be Loria and his asshole son-in-law playing at being Larry Lucchino down there. Great news, babies. Next on the list? Manny? Maybe play third when Hanley has a tantrum over being pushed out of position. Sure Hanley, maybe Jose could catch so you could bobble your way through another season at shortstop. That's the Marlins and the Mets out of it. Now if The Phillies could self-destruct.

*

Monday was a killer at work, what with all the rumors and Stuart hovering like a buzzard. And he was a bit wary of Zainab. He needed her to do her share of his claims but she had been a bit funny. He had no time to worry about office politics. Not with the meetings going. Maybe he should court Zainab a bit. Buy her a few more coffees, ask about the family. He knew she had kids. Well, he thought he knew. Wonder what they were like. She wore ordinary clothes so she was trying to be a real American. Didn't even keep the head scarf on all of the time. Not likely to be accepted with a name like that. Her last name was Rappaport which was sort of a strange name for an Arab. He thought she was an Arab. Must be. They had it tough. No fun being an Arab in Iraq or anything but not much better in America. Land of the free. Oh yeah, free to kick the shit out of Arabs. Not that he had ever heard about anyone kicking the shit out of Zainab but he had heard some things being said. He tried to be pleasant, especially as she did so many of his claims. Even once she found out she was doing his work she continued. Just balked at doing so many. Not really that unreasonable. Just not convenient for him just now. Not during the winter meetings.

Women hardly tried to understand things like the winter meetings. Look at Marianne. Married to him for over twenty years and made no attempt to take an interest. Bet she didn't even know about the meetings. Maybe if she knew, she wouldn't be so unsympathetic just now. Demanding money and all this share the cooking shit and weekends with Dyllis. She should grow up a bit and realize marriage is a partnership and at key times you have to compromise a bit. Like during the winter meetings. At least she was cooking tonight. He would do his part. Straight home, maybe bring some wine. Mind you, she had the money and it was her meal, she should bring the wine.

He checked the computer on his way to bed. Ten years for Pujols? Are the Marlins mad? The really ominous thing is that the Cardinals could let him go. Just that quiet little twit about St Louis shopping Lohse. To pursue Buerhle? Must be. Thinking how to spend the money they save if Pujols goes to Miami. Everyone knows Buerhle wants St Louis, now maybe they want him. Christ. And he was worried about Wilson. Maybe Wilson was as good as it would get. And are they talking six years? Can't be. Rizzo isn't stupid. There was Jayson Werth, of course. Mike, you have time, 2013 is our year. Let Wilson go. Let Buerhle go. Christ, let Bernadina play center if you must, but don't waste all your pennies on a relief pitcher like Wilson for six fucking years.

*

Second day of the meetings and Peter was feeling a bit better. Lot of talk about making do with Lannan and Detwiler, maybe Peacock. Maybe even Milone. If Rizzo can't get Buerhle, why not? No one else out there. Umpteen million for Jackson! No way. And now they were talking up Werth in center. Made sense as well. Keep telling yourself it is not about 2012, Mike, 2013 is the year. Mind you, a lot of silly talk still around and Rizzo is probably spreading the word that he can manage with what he has got for the simple reason that he has no intention of managing with what he has got. Even some talk of Nori Aoki.

He would love to be in the room when Pujols announces he is going back to St Louis. Just to see the smug smiles wiped off the faces of Loria and Samson. Come on Albert. Keep them on the hook and dangle them for the press. God, he hated those two bastards. Took the fucking baseballs from the practice ground, for Christ's sake. Pair of real pricks. Love to catch their press conference if Buerhle goes to the Nats and Pujols returns to the Cards. And now Hanley saying he wants to play shortstop just like Jose. Loria couldn't run a brothel in the fucking Vatican.

It was going to be a great week. The best of times. Of course there were still a few problems. What with Marianne and all. Said she would go out for the whole day on Sunday, straight from church. Church again. What was with this god shit? He had suggested maybe they could go out to dinner on Saturday but she said she would be a bit tired, she thought, maybe they could just eat in and watch a film. Like what. She liked fucking Black Swan and he liked Hombre. Maybe compromise and watch Dances with Wolves. Except it was shit. They agreed on that. Whatever happened after Bull Durham? And Silverado. Costner was good once upon a time.

*

He had enjoyed having a coffee with Zainab. Surprised him. He made that comment about English. How Americans were always inventing words to sound smart and it made them sound ignorant. Like Rizzo saying he wanted an impactful player. Sure, Mike, and a prideful one for Christ sake. Maybe you can message the other teams that you need an impactful player who is prideful. Anyhow, when he blurted out that impactful wasn't a word, Zainab smiled and said, well, don't tell Shakespeare.

Turns out her husband is an English professor from fucking Oxford working at Northeastern. Mad on language, the pair of them. British, the pair of them. He had looked funny and she said her grandparents were from Pakistan. She had met her husband at university. Fucking Oxford. Explained her accent. She said English was the most dynamic of all modern languages and Americans were leading the way. And technology, what with texting and archiving and googling and such. Real bright woman. Fucking British, she was. From Oxford.

*

Jesus, now they were saying Pujols really might go to Miami. What, is he nuts? Fucking Loria. How was he supposed to sleep? Especially after he forgot he was cooking dinner. Marianne hated Chinese food, but what could he do? At least he slept well. It was easier on his own when Marianne was being unreasonable.

Today is the day the Nats should sign Buerhle. Once Rizzo says things like he is comfortable with the situation, you could expect things to go well. Once Buerhle is in the fold, we can worry about center field. Hell, Werth makes enough, let him play there. It was a day to keep his eye on MLB Rumors but Stuart was all over the office. It was as if he knew the Nats were on to something big and he wanted him to miss it. He wanted to be on line when Buerhle agreed. And when Pujols goes back to the Cards. Suck it up Jeff, have a look at Prince, he's the one in the hotel dining room.

The day dragged on and on because he could not get to the computer. Well, not to the right websites. He managed three claims all day, if you counted the one he didn't read. Didn't forward anything to Zainab. She had brought him a book this morning. Not that he would ever read it. Said it was about the development of English worldwide. Nice of her but he usually stuck to detective stories when there was nothing on baseball to read. He might look through it tonight in the office. He planned to stay a bit late to catch up on transactions.

It was the worst of times. All right, the Marlins didn't get Pujols. Because they went after fucking Buerhle. Typical Loria move that. Taking Buerhle away from them at the last minute. Bastard. Bastard. Bastard. Him and fucking Samson. First they get all that money from taxpayers, and then they poach the Nats pitcher. If there was a god, they would finish sixth in the east. Bastards. At least they didn't get Pujols. But now they were after Wilson. Why not Darvish. Easy come, easy go when it's not your money. So fucking offensive when the economy is crumbling. Fucking Rizzo should have given Buerhle four years. No pitcher, no center fielder. What's he think, the Rule 5 Draft? Wake up, Mike. And who the fuck is Brett Carroll?

Dinner was ruined when he got in. Mind you, he wasn't hungry. In fact he was sick a couple of times. And he left the book in the Bistro. Or The Junction. No use trying to explain things to Marianne when she was in this sort of mood. Anyhow, she was in bed when he got in. He dumped his dinner in the bin. She could wash the dishes in the morning.

He hardly slept, worrying about everything that was going on. No bench, no pitcher, no center fielder.

5. Hard Times

He felt no better in the morning. There was no denying the hurt. He had expected something big from the meetings and nothing. Fucking Loria. And Rizzo. If he could go seven for Werth, he could have done four for Buerhle. Maybe Buerhle preferred Miami to Washington. Greedy bastard. It was the no tax thing. Deserves to get mugged. Then there was center field. Sure, Werth could play there but Harper can't be ready for right. They need a year from someone and not Bernadina. And the bench. All the talk of getting more power and they are talking to Willie Harris and Mark DeRosa. Big power guys. Not like the versatile subs Riggleman likes.

Marianne was a shit at breakfast. Not so much at breakfast as not at breakfast. She would be out tonight, out Saturday, out Sunday. Where the hell does she go? He sure as hell wasn't going to ask her but this was getting serious. He noticed the plate from last night wasn't washed. She must have been up an hour before him, as well. Stayed just long enough to make sure he saw that she was upset and announce that he had a weekend to himself. He hated it. All he would do was worry. Christ, please don't let them go for Jackson.

The day dragged at work. The Rule 5 Draft was no big deal but it beat claims. Except Stuart seemed to be around all the time. Mostly behind him. He checked in at lunch time. Christ, the Angels have gone mad. Trying to make Loria look cheap and Werth's contract look like a bargain. I mean, Albert's probably mid-thirties already. Ten fucking years. Chew on that, Jeff. Have to raise taxes. But Wilson is the man. What a quote. The Marlins offered more money and there are less taxes, but you end up being an Angel. Christ, Rizzo should have offered him the stadium or something. Just to hear him say that about the Marlins while wearing a Nats uniform must be worth Pujols money.

Now all the talk was about Darvish. Rizzo playing cute. Of course he would bid. Come in second, just like with Chapman. Prove you are an aggressive loser. Good for the fans to know you are trying. Mind you, the last thing they need is a Japanese pitcher. They're all flops. Another test for poor Cherington. Valentine wants him but Cherington knows what happens to Japanese arms. What did they get from Dice-K for a hundred mill? Slow games and a hospital bill. Cherington should call up Rizzo. Come in third, a dollar or two behind Mike.

Told Zainab that he was loving the book. Tried to engage her a bit so she might drop the name or something. Maybe he could replace it. Really, the best ticket was to repeat last night's round of bars. Only three. They may have the book. Or it may be on some bus. Sure as hell wouldn't be stolen. He stayed late to pass around a few claims. Couldn't give a shit right now, more to worry about than fucking claims. A few to Bert, a few to Michele. Tried a few on the new guy, what was his name? Randy? What sort of fucking name was that? Seemed keen, ready to prove himself, so he gave him a few electronic claims as well. What with Zainab being a bit of a problem. Took it easier on Zainab. In case he couldn't replace the book.

He hated being sick when he got home. Marianne would suspect he was drinking too much. And she could probably smell it. He had made the bathroom, just not the toilet. At least he had found the book. He could clean it in the morning. He lay in bed trying to sleep. Must have been after 2 a.m. when he heard Marianne come in. Heard her swear, must have smelled the vomit. Then he drifted off to sleep.

*

He heard Marianne get up in the morning but decided to stay in bed until she left for the office. He felt horrible and was not in the mood to discuss vomit. When he did get up, Zainab's book was in the bin. Marianne had no respect for the belongings of others. He would have to clean it up on the weekend. He would have the time.

The meetings being over there was very little to do at work unless you counted his job as something to do but without the stimulus of baseball news, he found it hard to get enthusiastic about anything. He had expected something from the meetings. Now they were mentioning Darvish, or some writers were. Well, study your history, Mike, because others will. The projected bid will be sixty million plus, maybe seventy-five. That means that if he really is that good, someone will try to blow the bidding away at eighty-five. So, stick in a sixty-five if you want to look like you are trying, eighty-five if you want to play for real and be prepared to pay another seventy-five for a six year contract. Do you really have that much money? Stick with Detwiler. Try Peacock when Wang goes down. Remember 2013.
Nice move trading Balester. He needed a new start and might still make it. What a disappointment he has been, poor kid. MASN suggested Torii Hunter might be available. Well, I guess. Nice friendly contract. Who would have thought the Angels might be looking at salary dumps? Maybe Vernon Wells is our next center fielder.

He thought a lot about Marianne. He knew there was trouble brewing and, despite her attitude, he still loved her. He bought a couple of steaks and went home early. Asked if she might like to eat in after all. He was feeling expansive. Even had a bottle of Beaujolais Nouveau. A couple of weeks late. Over-rated but he thought it had some romance to it. She just looked at him as if he were crazy.

I told you I was going out. Like he was dumb. This was an attempt to mend fences.

What about tomorrow?

Look, I'm tied up all week-end. Have one steak tonight and one tomorrow. Sure, that sounds just great.

Thank god for Ken Burns or he would have had a horrible evening. But he could cook steak and he loved the Civil War. Well, loved the DVD, the war itself was a bit harsh of course. It would just about save his weekend if he rationed the episodes. Then maybe do the baseball one. Again. Then Jazz. Even World War II was all right.

Saturday he didn't go out at all. He had the steak ready for dinner, so why bother? He checked in with the news, of course. Cherington had a choice. He could lose his job because he signs Darvish and he's useless or he can lose his job for not signing Darvish and Valentine blames him for the Red Sox continued decline. Tell you what, Ben, telephone your old friend Theo and see what he has to say about Japanese pitchers. Maybe Valentine will argue that Darvish is Iranian. Theo probably determined to make a splash. Think Prince. Big boy, big splash. The reporters have yet to rumble these GMs. What does Dipoto care about ten years from now? While Pujols is batting ninth as designated hitter with five homeruns and two thousand strikeouts in 2022, he'll be long gone. Angels probably have a decent season or two before the famine. Look at Colorado, Arizona, Seattle. Spend now, pay later. Mind you, Werth for seven was not totally brilliant. But Rizzo will go before he does. Apparently Werth got a no-trade clause. Look at the contract. It's a no-trade clause all on its own. Mind you, that Greek guy up in Toronto traded Wells. Should have been made exec of the decade for that. Where did he go? Oh yes, the Angels. In training for albatross time when they wear out Wilson and Pujols gets his cane. Still, word is Anthopoulos is in on Fielder and Darvish. Fielder for seven in the American League might not be a bad contract. His Dad could still hit when he looked like Jackie Gleason. Like Dimitri Young, probably still hit if you could drag him to the plate. Slimmed down and looking for work, we are told. Maybe him and Manny could platoon, one at the buffet, one at the plate. Or one at the plate and one at the other plate. Crazy thing is I'd still back Manny or Young to get a hit. Wouldn't hire them unless they would take a one game at a time contract.

Bowden had a thing about these social disasters. The all demented outfield of Dukes, Milledge and, Pena with Dimitri at first. It was just about the time he made his only attempt at sending a comment. To Ladson. About some Nats fans complaining they didn't like constant references to the heritage. Compared to the Expos, for Christ sake. The Expos. Fanning was a genius. Mauch and Williams too. And they had Dawson, Raines, Wallach; all those slobs. Not like the paragons Bowden was bringing in. Mind you, Bowden himself is a jerk. Selig is such a prick. Minyana hired to trade away a World Series contender, then Bowden comes along and hires out of the psychiatric unit. Lee, Sizemore, and Phillips for two months of Colon when we were already out of it. Then the Mets give Minyana a job. Assholes. You don't need Bernie Madoff to fuck up if you've got Omar. Funny now they went for Alderson instead of Bowden. Careful Mets, he might actually know what he's doing.

*

He woke up when Marianne came in. Looked at the clock. Christ. He tried to go back to sleep but couldn't.

In the morning he got up as soon as he heard her. Casually asked if she had a good time. Come in late? I was asleep. Not that late. Then she gathered her things, said she would go off straight from church and not to expect her until latish tonight. Where are you off to? Out. And the door slammed. And he was worried.

Peter and Marianne had been together a long time. Some good and some bad. Well maybe some mediocre and some bad. It had, in all honesty, never been a great match. Just her lack of interest in his interests was an impediment. She never went to a game. Not since the Lake Monsters. And that was pure romance. Something about Vermont in August and September. Summer becoming autumn. That was wonderful really, much more than mediocre. Of course it was before they were married. If it wasn't for the Lake Monsters, he would never have become an Expo fan, never taken her to Montreal. Jarry fucking Park. Jesus, those were the days. But now it was beyond growing weary of each other because now she was lying outright. Three in the morning cannot be described as not that late. Maybe he should confront her. Trouble is, having let it go at the time; now it might look a bit odd. But three in the morning. Marianne wasn't out until three with her bridge club. Had to be a man. Christ.

He spent the day worrying, unable to settle to anything. Finally decided to tidy the house completely. Even vacuumed. The put some Sauvignon Blanc to cool and planned how he would approach it. Just thought we should have some time together, put some wine to cool, sort of make it special. See so little of each other. Really miss it. Our talks. What talks, for Christ sake? Maybe he could really miss the companionship. Or the closeness. Shit. He just missed her and he was scared.

At midnight he went to sleep. Being awake the previous night had tired him Marianne had not come in.

*

In the morning he was a bit short with her. Expected you a bit earlier, must have been after midnight. Was it that late? I didn't realize. See you tonight. Maybe dinner? You cook. Sure, you must want a rest from your domestic duties. She looked at him, smiled a very tired looking smile, and left for the office. He left for his.

It was a long day at the office. Stuart was busy with meetings which gave him a little freedom but as there was little happening, it meant nothing. Tender or non-tendering marginal players was not exactly compelling. Sort of hoped Gorzelanny would be tendered, if Davey wants swingmen Gorzelanny and Stammen would seem a reasonable pair for the 'pen, one left, one right, both decidedly mediocre. Big deal. Remember 2013. Increasingly obvious that Rizzo is having trouble making moves. Well, well. Tell the world you are definitely going to buy a used car and every used car salesman on the street is going to put the price up. Angels probably asking for Ramos and Espinosa for Vernon Wells. Maybe the Nats could pay half of Espinosa's salary.

Left early. Stopped for some veal cutlets. Bought a really expensive Chardonnay. What on earth did Marianne see in Chardonnay? What's wrong with light and crisp? No matter, he was in a generous mood. More terrified than generous. But they had a very pleasant evening together. Didn't mention the weekend. Didn't asked what she meant by coming in at those hours. Even agreed to go to Nutcracker on Friday night. Shit. But she agreed to eat at Jake's first. Maybe be able to take Nutcracker with a schnitzel and some beer inside him.

They had breakfast together on Tuesday. Just like the old days. Talked a bit. Discussed Christmas. He remained neutral. No sense ruining the atmosphere. Was Dyllis really that bad? Well, yes.

Things were slowing down at work. No fewer claims, just everyone was in a Christmas mood. Vaguely stunned and not very happy. Sort of trying to wish it away while pretending to look forward to it. Fucking Christians were the worst. Moaning about commercialism. Like America lacked commercialism the rest of the year. Give Christmas back to Christ. Why not give the solstice back to the pagans? Might be cheaper and more interesting. Mind you, a bit cold for dancing round the pagan tree on the Common this morning, or whatever pagans did. Whatever they did probably beat eating fucking turkey. With fucking Dyllis. And those Puerto Ricans.

Non-tender day was a bore. No one good available. Joe Saunders? Sure, then dump Lannan. Who'd spot the difference? All the talk was about Darvish. Just what they need, another young pitcher who needs a mentor. Bring back Livo. May not show them how to pitch but he should amuse them. Rather lose with Livo than Saunders. That's for sure. At least you'd lose quickly. God, he was fun to watch.

*

Another pleasant evening, another pleasant breakfast. Marianne seems to have learned her lesson. About time. This menopause shit doesn't suit a woman her age. Get on with your life. He wondered about trying to get back into her bed. Maybe not yet. Give it a few days.

Talked a bit with Zainab at work. Who'd of thought? Anglican. Calls it Church of England. Probably because of her husband. Not a name that would sell well in Boston. Or Lexington. Says she loves Christmas but not all the presents. Her husband cooks because he loves turkey but she is not confident cooking it. Curried turkey doesn't work she laughed. Couldn't be worse than the dry muck everyone else ate.

Glad when Darvish signs with whoever and Rizzo can get back on the center field problem. If you want to go Asian, Mike, try Aoki. Maybe Aoki and Darvish both. They could bond with the two Japanese pitchers Baltimore signed. Way to go, Dan, big players in the international market. Guy throws maybe an 85 mile an hour fastball. Should be a star in the AL East. Jesus, what a jerk. Thank god for Rizzo.

Marianne out. Left a note. Big deal, he forgot to buy dinner anyhow. How long had it been since he ate peanut butter? He used to like it, but it needed fresh bread. He fell asleep before she came home. Again.

Marianne was all sweetness and light at breakfast. Promised she would cook tonight. Didn't mention last night and neither did he. Why bother? She wants to play games, she can play games. He would decide later if he might just forget to come home tonight.

*

Bored at work. What's new? Too much Darvish and not enough real action. With Stuart being calmer he had caught a lot of Schoenfield yesterday and there were a few Nats questions. Snuck in an earplug today for Beltway Baseball and then got Dierkes chat as well. Hard to believe the Werth in center shit. Wake up, he's got to get through seven years on these knees, he ain't going to center. And then there was the worry about where to play Rendon. The oft to be injured replacement for the often injured face of the franchise. The real question is whether they need a solid veteran to play the hundred games or so when both the superstar third basemen are injured. Amusing to suggest that the Nats might have trouble fitting all their big hitters into the line-up once Harper hit the big city. But the misplaced optimism sure beat all the pessimism of previous years, so why knock it?

Zainab gave him a Christmas card today. No one had ever given him a card at work before. And, as far as he could see, she only gave out one or two. Nice. Try to remember to clean up that book for her.

He decided to go home on time and play nicely with Marianne. Catch the results of the Darvish sweepstakes before bed maybe. Maybe not. Still found it hard to believe that the Yankees and Red Sox were out of it. Sort of dumb ass moves the big money makes all the time.

Know what? Marianne is a good cook and still looks good. First erection he had for years. Other than the odd moment on a porn site. Why not? He wasn't dead yet.
Checked the computer before bed. Nothing on Darvish.

*

Not too bad on the computer today. Law still an asshole with his cookery shit. Nats hardly got a mention, of course, but he did say Michael Taylor was an interesting prospect. Probably because he read Callis who had him as one of his ten prospects to watch who hadn't had a mention in the organizational reports. Baseball America can have some obscure shit in it but at least they knew what they were doing and none of them seemed to be out to show how witty he is or what a great cook he is or that he read a book while flunking out of Harvard. Stuart was off his case. No hovering, so he was able to read the chat as it transpired. He actually preferred to read it later without the pauses except if he read it as it happened it meant he couldn't work. Never occurred to him to send in a question. Not to Law. Maybe Crasnick, he was always polite.

God, they should get this Darvish thing done. Looked like Toronto. Always some greedy bastard wants the new toy and is willing to spend all his owner's pennies just to get. Or in Florida, all the taxpayers pennies. Loria and Samson should be shot. Right after Selig. Would have thought Anthopoulos over in

Toronto was smarter. Could probably have had Jackson and Wilson for about the same money. But of course, they aren't the new Japanese super toy.

God, Christmas was coming. Rizzo should do something, for Christ sake. The week was boring enough when all the rumors went cold for Christmas but if there wasn't even one new player to think about or one deal in the fire there was only dry turkey and another fucking sweater from Marianne. She loved those big heavy sweaters in grey and dark brown. He never wore the fucking things. She should learn. Mind you, she never wore the perfume he bought as far as he could tell, but he couldn't think of anything else. She had enough money to buy anything she wanted anyway. He hated Christmas. He hated New Year more. Maybe when 2013 hit and Harper was ready and maybe Peacock or one of the youngsters. And if Rizzo stops pissing about and gets someone to play center. Must remember to pick up dinner. Maybe buy the perfume at the same time. Someplace where they gift wrap it. Most places did. He'd do burgers. He did good burgers and Marianne always said you could never get them as good in a restaurant.

*

Friday was Jake's and Nutcracker. Maybe Rizzo would do something. Last day of the week, Mike, get going because Christmas is coming and the kids want you at home. Or grandkids, or whatever the fuck you've got at home. Sure as hell isn't a center fielder. He chose a jacket and tie Marianne liked. Arranged to meet at Jake's over a very civil breakfast. Maybe the crisis was over. Maybe he would offer to Christmas shop with her on the weekend. Get real. They would both hate it. Maybe they could try, mind you.

Friday was a surprising success. Nothing much at work but he actually worked hard to clear some claims. Reminded himself that once he was the best. No mistakes and faster than any of them. That was before Michele, of course, but he wasn't sure she didn't make a few mistakes. He used to get all the big ones. Then they promoted Stuart. Well, fuck them. But working efficiently today was almost satisfying. Trouble was; he hated the company now.

Not much happening in baseball. No last minute rush there. Would have thought the teams would like to have the big issues settled for Christmas. Boras won't let Fielder sign until April, maybe March 31. He'll go to the Tigers. Like his dad. Like Bonds and his dad. Except Prince doesn't talk to his dad. And Bonds doesn't talk to anyone. Griffey seemed to like his dad. Rather have Prince for eight than Pujols for ten; twenty if you count the hanging about after you've been booed off the park years. Prince should go to the AL if he wants a long contract. Just like his dad, three hundred pounds of power hitter but not an asset in the field. Or on the base paths. Maybe only hits all those homers to avoid the running.

Marianne looked pretty good when she arrived at Jake's. Sat so she faced all that Red Sox shit and he faced the back. And she seemed to enjoy it. And she loved Nutcracker. How can she love the same damn thing every year? He couldn't even watch Shane that often. Well maybe Shane, but not many others. He offered to Christmas shop with her on Saturday but she said she was finished. Cheryl's was sent off and Barney and Bobbie would pick up their gifts at dinner on Wednesday. Dinner? Surely you can't have forgotten? Of course not. Anyhow she suggested they go into town in the morning, have a walk around the common, then a coffee at the Paramount. He could then do his shopping and she would go home and cook dinner. Wow. Sounded real hopeful.

Checked the net before breakfast. Kilgore says Nats didn't bid on Darvish. Good old Rizzo. Hope he bid 2.5 for Aoki, though. That's worth a gamble. All they seem to be doing right now is building a crap team in Syracuse. Morosi says they all want to finish the big stuff by Christmas. Well, Mike, I hope you got your turkey because you've accomplished fuck all for the Nats. Except not bid on Darvish. That was smart.

He really enjoyed the morning. Marianne even took his hand in the park. Just for a minute. But it was a nice minute. After she left he bought her a tablecloth and napkins from Anthropology. She loved that shop. Then he went to Barnes and Noble on the way to the bus to try to buy a replacement for Zainab's book. Found it and also bought her some fool thing about the bible and English: Begat. Same writer. She might like it. He would maybe make a joke about Church of English or something, her being Anglican and all. Picked up Wolf Hall for Marianne as a little extra because she kept mentioning it.

She'd done a lovely dinner. Nice to have fish after Jake's last night. Candles and everything. Afterwards, when she went to bed, he stood up but she shook her head sort of sadly. Then she kissed her fingers and rubbed them against his cheek. He thought he may have seen a tear. Oh well, time to check the computer before bed.

Shit, Aoki's gone. Not that he was supposed to have the arm for center but surely Rizzo has to do something sometime. Bad PR to announce that you will definitely sign a pitcher and trade for a center fielder and then not even sign a bench player before Christmas. Makes you look like you can't get it done.

Signing draft picks is no big deal, no one competing. Call Jocketty, he seems to know how to swing a deal.

*

Sunday was Sunday. They didn't have breakfast together because it would have been embarrassing after what happened last night, him wanting to go to bed with her and Marianne having an emotional minute. He was not sure if it was good or bad news. Probably bad, most news these days was bad news. Or no news, like with the Nats. Marianne decorated the house for Christmas in the afternoon. He felt sort of useful, which was nice, mostly fetching and carrying. She had made mince tarts and they had coffee and mince tarts in the afternoon when they had finished and she just sort of touched his hand at one point. He felt really warm and affectionate and was careful not to suggest anything. Just played it cool. But he was more confused than cool.

*

Monday morning he took six of Marianne's mince tarts to Zainab. Hell, she said she was English, so she should like mince tarts. Pies? He thought Marianne would be annoyed that he asked her for them but she was pleased. Flattered. Said it was a wonderful idea and be sure to wish Zainab's family all the best for Christmas.

He gave Zainab the new book, just said he lost the other one, didn't mention the vomit or anything; and the little present, and the mince tarts. Zainab was pleased and said how kind they were and that they all loved mince pies. Pies? Oh, tarts. Bit small for pies. Then she turned away quickly. He thought he noticed a tear. Christ, everyone was crying. Christmas was a drag in a way. But there were nice things about it. He worked really hard, just like the old days when he was the best. He would leave baseball to the evening. Nothing would happen so going back and forth to the internet just frustrated him. Stuart came over late in the afternoon. Asked if he was feeling better. Better? Yeah, you went through a bad patch but you look a lot happier now. It shows in your work. Typical of Stuart. All that mattered was the work. But Stuart had brought over two cups of coffee and chatted for five minutes. Asked about the family and Christmas.

He wondered a bit about the family himself. He hadn't contacted Cheryl or Barney in weeks. Months maybe. Barney was coming to dinner this week Marianne had said. Wonderful. Cheryl was not so bad. Arnie was a tolerable pain in the ass. Barney was just a washout and Bobbie was a waste of space, worse than Barney. Marianne had seen Cheryl and sent presents to her and Arnie. He was pretty sure he had not seen here since she got pregnant. He certainly hadn't talked to her on the telephone. He hated the telephone. Worst thing ever invented. Except maybe the microphone. Or the cell phone. Follows you around. Pity email came after the telephone because they would never have needed telephones. He had a cell phone, of course, everyone had one these days. I wonder where it is. Must be at home. Somewhere.

Rizzo signed Mike Cameron. Wow, must be trying to fill out his Disabled List. Now that Syracuse and the DL are set, Mike, you might want to think about center field. Unless you plan to send Cameron out there in a wheel chair. Slow was one thing, but this off season was getting him down. Shit, if the team is shit, you should at least be able to enjoy the off season. At least Bowden spent his time signing players. Absolute crap but it was not as noticeable that they were all crap in December as it became in April. Best deal he made was getting Jose Rijo. Got them both fired.

Anthopoulos lost out on Darvish. Should have seen it coming when he heard he was also second on Latos. Better give him a Mike Rizzo doll. Always second. Christ, what a place to send an Iranian. They kill American presidents down there, never mind Iranian pitchers. And that park is no place for him to pitch. Texas seemed to be smart with their strong teams and decent pitching to fit their park. It's a hitters' park so get Fielder. Let Darvish go to Toronto. They'd have loved him there. Canadians don't care about terrorism. Hard enough to pitch in Arlington without having to wear a bullet proof vest. Poor bastard.

And now Rizzo is planning to be second in the Geo Gonzalez sweepstakes. Selig should make it so only him and Anthopoulos can bid. One of them might get lucky. If they get him it will cost AJ Cole, Peacock, Norris and some other lucky bastard who will get to go to Oakland. Then maybe San Jose. San Jose's meant to be a pleasant enough place. If they go. Better to pull a Loria. Lie and cheat and steal money from taxpayers and then sign all the free agents who might agree to come. Maybe Rizzo could sign all the free agents developed in Tampa Bay. Sort of use Tampa Bay as a farm team. God, remember when every year the Yankees would go to Kansas City with a shopping basket and a trailer full of rejects. Those were the days. You get Norm Siebern, we get Roger Maris. Oh yeah, and marvelous Marv. But trading with Oakland? Forget it Mike. Nobody deals with Billy Beane and wins. Or so they say. For someone so smart he sure as hell produces shit teams. Watch how Tampa does it, Billy, and I'll bet you do not even know the GM's name over there. He builds. You grab headlines. I think you were a better player than manager. Which makes you crap. All promise and no production. Playing your silly games. Oh sure, the deal is almost done, the Nats are about to give me Strasburg, Harper, Cole and Norris for Gonzalez so you better step up if you want him. Rizzo is reluctant enough to trade prospects without having to deal with you. Tell your friend Kenny over at Fox that it was a nice try and thanks for spreading the rumor, but Mike won't play. Ask Friedman if he could do a workshop for you. That's his name, by the way, the guy in Tampa.

But god it's slow. Signing the reserve team for Syracuse and it made the Nats news. Oh, yeah, and maybe Greg Dobbs. Wow. What a difference maker he would be. They keep saying the bench was crap last year. Bullshit. The bench was great but they were all on the field as regulars. When Morse went to first, Nix was a regular. Hairston at third did well. And Ankiel became a regular only because Morgan was traded and Bernadina couldn't cut it. Nix, Ankiel and Hairston with Pudge or Flores is not a bad bench. Unfortunately the DL was much better. But don't blame the bench. Except that once the bench players were regulars, the second bench took over. And Cora, Bixler and Stairs couldn't make a strong bench in AAA. Still, Dobbs would be okay. With Cameron and Lombardozzi. I don't go for sending him to the minors. Let him learn versatility and play in the Bigs. He'll learn more and learn faster if he has the smarts. Jamie Carroll except he is a switch hitter. Anyhow, Desmond could still go if Rizzo gets inspired about center field.

Trouble with Nats fans is they were never trained by Jim Fanning. He knew how to build and how to be patient. And Expo fans were tuned into the long haul. Lot of talk now about if, if, if. Fuck if, think when. And when is 2013 at the earliest. Harper isn't going to hit fifty as a rookie next year. Strasburg may struggle more than they think. And if he is great and they make the World Series, he will have done his 161.2 innings or whatever. Think of the Nats as cheese that needs to ripen. Not wine, wine needs years. The Nats need fourteen lousy months.

In Montreal waiting for the kids was a lot of the fun. Most of the fun. Raines and Dawson and Wallach. The Big Cat. Guys like that. Now the Nats fans want Prince. Well, a few of them. Like a boil in the bag superstar. Just dump him in water and he hydrates and you got a star. No farm team, no waiting. Be patient. In 2013 you can have Morse at first, who's not so bad, and then Werth can play left. So, Mike, take your time. Get a center fielder in the next eighteen months and all will be well. Sign Oswalt if you are feeling antsy, but don't mortgage the farm for Gio. Hell, you know what happens to pitchers in DC; ask Marquis, ask Strasburg, ask Zimmermann. Hell, ask Chad Cordero.

Bowden should have been shot for the way he handled that guy. Real fine team player blows his arm. It can happen. Especially in DC. And the boy wonder has to announce that he would non-tender before the poor bastard even leaves the hospital. Thanks for everything Chad, sorry the career is over. Hey, best of luck in Mexico or wherever crocks like you end up. We gotta move on. Baseball is a business. Gotta look after my boys; Dimitri and Elijah, and Lastings. You know; all the good junior woodchucks. Trash like you can go fuck yourself. Real class act, Little Jimmie.

Anthopoulos must be either the stupidest GM in baseball, or the smartest. If he wanted Darvish, he was stupid because anyone could have told him to beat the Dice-K bid if he wanted Yu. Maybe he wanted to look like he wanted him. Make Mr. Rodgers happy up in the arctic without having to negotiate a bad contract. Mind you Daniels wasn't too smart, beating the Dice-K bid by a buck fifty. The smart bid, if you wanted him, was fifty-five. If you wanted to look keen in front of the grown-ups, fifty even. The Yankees with twenty just look like dicks. Which they are. But rich dicks. What did they think they were registering? The new, frugal and responsible Yankees. Sure thing, Brian, except you'd a gone to seventy plus if you really wanted him. So why not just not bid. Like Mike.

*

Shit. Marianne reminded him about Barney and Bobbie tomorrow. But tomorrow was the Christmas party at work. They weren't big deals. Not anymore. But they were pretty good. Some of the young secretaries get pretty loaded. Saw one of them actually getting off with an actuary last year. What are the chances of that? The parties were all separate these days. Claims no longer able to mix socially with underwriting. Made sense when you remember what the parties were like ten years ago. Of course, the actuaries could go around and screw anyone. Some of the managers cruised as well. He tended to take it easy. Keep his eyes open. Sneak a few paper claims onto unsuspecting desks maybe. Still he liked to go. And he didn't much like Barney and Bobbie. Maybe if he only stayed for an hour. He said nothing to Marianne at dinner because they were getting on so well. Tomorrow he would just telephone to say he would be an hour late. Still be there before Barney because he would have to wait for Bobbie and Bobbie was always late.

*

Wednesday was a disaster. A complete disaster. Maybe not complete. He passed over a dozen claims on to Michele and Bert and seven electronic ones to Zainab. And Stuart was hardly in the office all day. So work went well. Having passed so much of his work on, he felt justified in reading the Nicholson-Smith chat in the afternoon. At least he can handle his software. Just when Schoenfield seemed to be improving you get a fiasco like Tuesday. Takes lots of interesting questions, just doesn't answer them. Great to watch the questions pile up like that. So rewarding. Not that Nicholson-Smith had much to say on the Nationals. Not much to say. Billy Beane is using them and Gonzalez is going to Toronto.

Poor old Toronto. Apparently they didn't bid all that much for Darvish. Poor old Texas. They did. But Anthopoulos will go full bore for Gonzalez now and he has the players. A momentum builds, loses out on Ayatollah Darvish and Latos so he is facing strike three. Rizzo is only on strike two. Mind you, he has what Beane wants, half a dozen kids who will never reach their potential like Norris and Hood and Perez. Just don't give up too many who might, like Cole. Pity Purke and Meyers aren't tradable. Perfect for Beane, those two. Guy's a jerk but trading prospects always leaves the fear that they may just turn out okay. Beane is obviously in house clearing mode. He does that. Trades anyone who might bring at least two prospects. Figures if one of the several dozen he picks up pans out, he will claim to be a genius. Funny thing is, people believe him. What with Brad Pitt playing him, he'll likely get an extension. Still it would be a shame if Rizzo was the guy who gives up the good prospect. Rizzo wouldn't give up Detwiler for Bourne but now he is stuck with a pitcher without options that he has to play or trade, so if Wang is fit and they get Gonzalez, what do you do with Detwiler. Put him on the DL with all the others? We'll see, but if Rizzo must make the trade he should try to keep Peacock rather than Detwiler just for the option years. Bad move. Bet Detwiler has the better chance of making it.

Peter still preferred keeping the prospects. He knew damn well most flopped, but when one didn't, especially if the development was a bit slow, it was great to watch. He was more interested in Marrero, Norris, Peacock and Detwiler than Strasburg and Harper. Liked Zimmermann, though. And Lombardozzi. Another Jamie Carroll, that one. Not that Rizzo should trade Desmond just to prove it. He and Espinosa also worked right through the system. He liked that. He had no feeling for Werth or Marquis or that lot. Christ. Paul La Doca, how could you pull for him? He had strong feelings for some of Bowden's dross. Just not good feelings. Watching the kids develop was what was interesting. Winning the World Series was pretty much a long shot even if you were the Red Sox, which the Red Sox happily proved with gratifying frequency. Smart club, though, fired the only guy who ever managed to do it.

He stayed around for the first half hour of the party. Great buffet and lots to drink. That must have been what Stuart was doing all day. Wasted on him as Marianne was doing a special dinner for Barney and Bobbie. He sipped a glass of wine and was just about to leave. No need even to telephone. But he saw Zainab, sitting on her own. She looked glum. Worse than glum. Don't much like Christmas or just not a party girl?

Wow. She burst into tears. Really sobbing. He couldn't just walk away so he stopped to talk for a bit. Stopped to listen for a bit.

She hated Boston. Hated America. Hated claims. Missed her family. Her husband loved Boston. Loved teaching. Didn't miss his family. In fact was relieved to get away from his family and more relieved to get away from hers. Told her to stay out tonight and have fun at the party. How? She didn't drink and found them vulgar and stupid. All that pretending it was okay to do all that sexual teasing because you had a drink. What a bunch of vulgar fools. And here she was, sipping mineral water and watching it. Two degrees, one from Oxford on a scholarship and this was all she could manage in America. Land of opportunity if you were white enough and she wasn't. Her father had worked as a bus conductor in England because of his color and she was doing the equivalent. She hated America and hated working here and hated the party. Wow. He began to really like and admire Zainab. Maybe he should stop sending her claims.

He couldn't just leave her there so he asked her if she wanted to go out for something simple to eat and a drink. She didn't drink at all, but a coffee and maybe a sandwich if he really didn't mind. So he heard a lot more about her and her family. All that education wasted. Imagine a doctor collecting bus tickets. And her mother cleaning offices with her Physics degree. Funny old world. Peter had a degree. Minimum passing grades in sociology and media studies. He felt a bit ashamed. He had treated university a bit like the claims department. A necessary evil. In fact the woman who actually hired him had also been to Vermont. Loved it. Well, so did he, but mostly because of the Lake Monsters. And the Expos. Shit, Jarry Park. Le Grand Rouge.

By the time he remembered Barney and Bobbie, it was quite late. Too late to phone. Maybe take a taxi. Shit no, so late the extra ten minutes meant nothing and it was so expensive. Now that he was sort of on an allowance. He got home just as they were pouring coffee. He got as far as asking to be allowed to explain before he was told to save it. Barney was a rude bastard. Then Bobbie said she heard that it was the Christmas party at work, was that right? Bitch. Smiling, horrible bitch. He got as far as saying it was a bit more complicated than that when Barney told him not to bother. Rude bastard. And Bobbie asked if his job was always so complicated. Bitch. So he left. Had a drink at The

Junction. Let himself in quietly and went to his room. Wonder if Marianne told them they were in separate rooms now?

Checked the computer before he went to bed. God, still a fuss about Gonzalez. Don't do it, Mike, try Detwiler. Signing DeRosa now. Well, that should make the difference. Him and Cameron on the bench should strike fear into the hearts of one and all. At least all Nats fans.

He heard Barney and Bobbie leave. Didn't bother to say good-bye. Typical of those two. No manners at all. Everything would be his fault, of course. No chance to explain. He snuck back to the dining room. Mostly cleared away and the kitchen was empty. He had hoped that Marianne might have given him a chance to explain once they were gone but she must have gone straight to bed. Those two were exhausting. At least Bobbie seemed sober. That was a change. He would try to get up a bit early. Maybe squeeze some oranges and do coffee and toast ready for Marianne and then tell her about poor Zainab. Marianne had a good heart. She would still be angry but she would at least understand. Yes, he would do that. Check the computer before bed. Nah, nothing. Beane is playing games.

*

He got up early and prepared breakfast ready for Marianne. She walked into the kitchen, looked at breakfast, looked at him, drank the juice, poured some coffee into a plastic cup, picked up some toast and walked out. Not a word. He called after her. Maybe I could explain. She turned and looked again. Not a pleasant look.

Why bother?

A good question. Who really cared anymore?

There were a lot of tired people with hangovers at work. He felt a little out of place. Took refuge in his work which was pretty strange for him. He had a lot to worry about, what with the Gio Gonzalez thing flying about. Still felt Beane was playing games and he would go to Toronto. Or Boston. Boston sort of deserved him, a lefty who walks a lot of batters and perhaps has problems with controlling his emotions, perfect for Fenway. Maybe likes chicken and beer. Let it go, Mike.

Zainab seemed better today. Brought a coffee over and thanked him for last night. No problem, Zainab, just wrecked what was left of my marriage and further estranged my son. Nothing to concern us here at work. She told him he was the only one in the office who seemed to think she was a real person so thanks for listening to her moan. Funny, he felt he was not a real person anymore. Just sort of shuffling through life hoping maybe Marianne would notice that he was trying. Zainab gave him a book. Said it was a little present for Christmas. Something about spelling. He was quite a good speller. Funny choice.

God, Law was a pain today. True, it is a quiet time but all that shit about cooking and restaurants. I mean, who cares about which Italian restaurants are crap in Phoenix. Most of the ones in the North End were crap as well; he didn't need to add to his list. And the Hall of Fame. He had his own views about the Hall of Fame. Firstly, who cared? Secondly, if you want us to care, base the Hall on real icons, not just the ten thousand or so players who were popular with the writers at the time. I mean, Jim Rice? Now if it was just Mays and Ruth and maybe Christy Mathewson. One or two more. Jackie Robinson maybe. Hank Aaron. But now they discussed ad nauseam who weren't that exciting when they were active and we are supposed to get excited because they are eligible for the Hall of Fame.

It was really depressing today. After lunch all the hangovers began to fade so everyone wanted to talk about how drunk they were last night. Mostly so it gave them an excuse for their stupid behavior. Obviously one or two things went sadly wrong. Bert was loud and Michele was sullen. Something had happened there. And Stuart kept far away from it all. Good move that. He just kept his head down. Surprising how much work you could get through if you were bored with Keith Law and didn't want to even look at your colleagues. Even Zainab. Nice woman and all, but too much emotional baggage just now. He would try to be nice to her but he really didn't give a shit about her family in Staines. Where the fuck was Staines?

He had his own problems with family. If he was honest, and he knew he seldom was. At least not to himself. But if he was, he would have to consider what Sigmund Freud might have said about his arriving home last night as dinner ended. Truth was he did avoid Barney at the best of times and he couldn't stand Bobbie. Sure, he was being nice to Zainab, but that was not exactly his style. He avoided being nice. Led to complications. For that matter, why did he go to the party in the first place? He hated his colleagues. More or less. Except Zainab. He would have to avoid her for awhile.

He decided to pick up some fresh trout and a salad for dinner tonight. Left a message on Marianne's answer machine. I'll cook, see you at about seven. Even bought some flowers. Just supermarket shit, but still. He'd phone Barney tonight. Make up a story about Zainab. Well, it was true enough but maybe he should exaggerate it a bit.

He got home to a note.

Out tonight, maybe see you in the morning.

What the hell was that? She must have got his message, she could have contacted him. Must find that cell phone. He grilled the trout. Stank. Why did he always forget to turn the fan on when he cooked trout? Poured a glass of wine. Dressed the salad. No reason not to enjoy the food. Decided to maybe wait a day or two to call Barney. No rush. Let the dust settle. Still, he would try to explain it to Marianne tonight. If she was okay with it, she would talk to Barney. Could still be fine. In a way. Turned the computer on. Jesus H Christ. Rizzo did it. Four players for the base on balls king of the world. Cole, for Christ sake. Everyone knew Peacock and Norris would go if the thing came off, but Cole as well. Seemed an awful lot. Thing is, Beane usually missed the boat on his prospects, trying to be too clever, but this looked serious. And Milone. Now Milone was his sort of prospect. Likely never make it but he just loved these guys who really work and almost get there with less ability than so many other prospects. Milone, JD Martin, Chico, even Lannan. Always compared to Glavine or Maddux. As if? Still, he loved guys like that.

Mike, now what do you do when Wang breaks down or Strasburg reaches his limit and there is no one? No Peacock or Milone waiting in Syracuse. Detwiler is out of options, remember? Stammen? Gorzelanny? Christ, Maya? And then there is center field. I keep telling you, 2013. And there is still center field.

71

Someone has to catch the ones that get out of the infield. Morse in left, Werth in center and a rookie in right is just the ticket for a young staff. I'll give you a game plan. Young, impressionable pitchers need good defense because if they see the team bleeding runs they tend to cry. Older ones eat fried chicken and drink beer, but the youngsters will burst into tears. So now that you have the kiddie korps pitching, you better get a center fielder.

Shit. The fish. It stank enough before he burned it to a crisp. Fucking Rizzo and his dumbass trades. Now what? Maybe a burger up the road. Drop in at The Junction.

*

He returned late. Marianne was in bed. He thought. She was home, there was her coat. Shit, fish still lying on the counter. Grill pan still sitting there. Should have put the flowers in water. Where were they? He found them when he tipped the charred fish into the rubbish bin.

The next morning he set out for work a bit late. Had to wait for Marianne to go to her office. Really couldn't face her. The grill pan was still soaking when he got up. Have to see to it tonight, no time now. God things were a mess.

Once upon a time, when the company still tried to maintain some fiction of being a caring company, today would have been a half day. Friday. Christmas Eve tomorrow, come on. But the official position of management was that people were as likely to have accidents or crises on Christmas Eve as any other day, so some people had to work and it was unfair to give the others extra time. So everyone worked right up until five and then there was an emergency service out in the boonies. Sure, sure, no way they could work anything out without bonus pay or anything. Best thing was to make everyone completely disgusted and pissed off. If he heard Stuart say that there was nothing he could do and it wasn't his fault one more time, he would strangle him. Needless to say, the staff responded by doing nothing. Not in a happy way. They sat sullenly and talked about what a crap place this was to work. Even Zainab came over with a coffee and remarked on how awful it was. God, Michele wasn't even working. Nor Bert. What a lovely start to Christmas.

Peter was happy enough to be in work, doing nothing. Tomorrow and Christmas and Monday were holidays and he would be at home with Marianne. And Marianne was not very happy. He knew she had a right to be angry but he felt that if he could only talk to her she might understand. A bit. I mean, Zainab was pretty upset and lonely and it was not as if it was another woman sort of thing, although, of course, she was another woman, it was just that she looked so vulnerable and upset. Surely Marianne would understand. If he could just talk to her. Barney wouldn't understand because Barney wouldn't want to. And Bobbie had never understood a damn thing in her entire life as far as he could see. But Marianne might try. If he could only talk with her.

When was the last time he had talked with her? I mean, really talked. Years. Christ, decades, it seemed. She was so busy with her work. Why anyone would like digging around in other people's mouths was beyond him. It was a disgusting job, really. Stinking breath, rotting teeth, pain, fear. Who would be a dentist? But Marianne took pride in her work, for some reason. They couldn't talk about it anymore. The last time she had said that she could hardly ask someone who had no interest in his work at all, no interest on anything except a fucking useless baseball team, to understand her commitment. Understand that

73

she could bring better health to thousands of people. Sure by digging around in their stinking mouths with their stinking breath and gouging around in their stinking cavities.

Still, Marianne was a kind person, and interesting. They sometimes used to exchange favorite books and then discuss them. Wow, how long ago was that? And they used to go to films and even plays. And the ballet when he had to. Well, once. Not the opera. There were limits. Never baseball. Not anymore. She might think about that. He'd just been to Nutcracker. Not even when the Nats played at Fenway. So it was not all his fault that they were having problems. But they had to talk. Maybe on Boxing Day, once all the Christmas shit was behind them. Christmas was such an emotional time. And Dyllis was coming. And the Puerto Ricans.

He wished he could do some work. He was bored but, with no one else working, it seemed disloyal. Mind you, he often did no work when everyone else was hard at it, so it would have had a certain symmetry.

Not likely to be anything going on the baseball sites. Rizzo quoted as saying something was trending the right was. Trending for Christ sake. How could anyone talk like that? We are trending today, tomorrow we will be nouning and after that adjectiving. How can you run a baseball team if you can't speak fucking English. He was still pissed off about the trade. Rizzo was unprospecting the team pitcherizing Oakland and not center fielding his own team. He also had to start benching it so they could success in the new season. Asshole. Peacock and Cole. And Milone was such a story. Fuck the World Series. Fanning would have never done that.

Jesus, Mark fucking Langston. All they gave up was Randy Johnson and a few peripheral pieces. Worth if for sure. Team collapsed and Langston's wife went off to be a movie star. Probably still pumping gas in San Jose. Bitch.

He stopped at the Bistro on the way home. And at The Junction. Didn't matter, Marianne was out. No note. Nothing. Fish grill pan still sitting there. He threw it out. Buy one in the morning. Place still stank of fish and smoke. Merry Christmas.

*

As soon as he heard Marianne in the kitchen, he got out of bed and went to the kitchen. Christmas Eve, time to patch things up a bit. Not that he liked Christmas Eve. How could he, when he hated Christmas? Marianne had this thing about midnight mass. Not even a fucking catholic and she goes to mass for Christ sake. That's Christmas for you. Screws up people's thinking. Marianne was pretty good about religion but Christmas Eve was always a washout. Spoiled Christmas Eve if you couldn't get out and have a few drinks, get a bit drunk and enjoy yourself. She had always said, that he could go ahead, but he hated going out to bars on his own on Christmas. It made him feel lonely even if he had a wife at home. Well, in church. Sundays was one thing, but why screw up Christmas with church? Mind you, what difference did it make? Christmas was a pain, anyhow. And this year might just be the worst one yet. This year Christmas was on a Sunday so the church would go all out to fuck it up for all the kids. Well, for everybody. Let's not forget what Christmas is all about? Yeah, it's all about stealing pagan festivals when the grubby little pagans used to dance around in a frenzy and have one last mind-bending orgy before settling down for the winter. Break the ice for the last wash before May because tonight is the night, baby. A few twirls around the fire and bring on the boys. Now what do we have? Baby Jesus and three wise men marching across the desert in a snow storm. Blond babies in cribs in a snow bound Jerusalem or wherever. What a laugh. Wonder what W would say if he knew Jesus was an Arab. Asshole.

Peter wasn't very religious, of course. He had lost it when he was about ten. Sunday school. As far as he could tell, his parents screwed once a week. Sunday mornings. So he and his brother were sent off to Sunday school. Brought the two lovers a cup of tea first, then off they went to save the entire family from eternal fucking damnation while the parents wallowed in sex. Still, they were always in a good mood when he and Bryan came home. Except the time when Bryan was hit by the car, of course. That was awful. He never went to Sunday school after that. Wasn't much fun anymore. Bryan had always made it fun. When he was alive. Laughed about their devout parents. It was great to have an older brother. Sort of forgotten about it for awhile. Cheryl had an older brother but that must be awful. Imagine having Barney as an older brother. Imagine having Cheryl as a younger sister. Well, Cheryl had been okay when she was younger. Not Barney.

God, didn't Christmas made you think back? Tim Wallach was once traded on Christmas Eve. For Tim Barker. Who the fuck was Tim Barker? A shortstop in the 69 organization with the promise of being useless and thus costing nothing. Even then the Expos were in cheap mode. The great exodus. And then after the strike. After Selig decided he could not possibly let the World Series champions come from French Canada. Hell, they murder local politicians, kidnap British diplomats and altogether show their disgust with the ruling English. Probably Al Qaida. Or Saddam. Then Selig calls for the total destruction of the Expos so he can fold them. Hires that prick Brochu to recite yes sir, no sir three bags full sir. Then Loria. Jesus, Selig was a prick. Still here, isn't he. Still is a prick, not was a prick. Disappeared the Expos, as Rizzo might say.

He wanted to have sort of a friendly time with Marianne.

How are things going?

Fine.

Everything ready for the big day?

What big day might that be?

You know, Christmas.

Oh yes, I sometimes forget how much Christmas means to you.

Just thought if there is anything to do, I could help.

Like I would have left it to the last moment. But I can tell you what you might do. Call your son and apologize. Call your daughter while you are at it. And one more thing, while you are doing all those lovely family things. Buy me a present that isn't a bottle of fucking cheap stinking toilet water. Try real perfume for a change. And one more thing, but that was it, she was out. Crying. Too bad, he really wanted to talk.

He checked the computer. What could happen? Especially it being a weekend. Maybe check out The Junction. What a Christmas Eve.

When Marianne came home she came into the living room. Said she was sorry for getting so upset. Did he telephone the children? Well, no. She looked crushed. I thought I'd wait until maybe five, sure to catch them. It's five thirty. Oh, wow, better get to it. By the way, maybe I could go to mass with you. No, thanks, you are trying, I suppose, but I am meeting friends. Dyllis and someone. You go ahead and make your calls. Maybe church tomorrow? No, not really.

So he called Cheryl and got Arnie. Short and sweet. She's not that well, can you call back later? Then Barney and he got Bobbie. Short and sweet. He's just stepped out, can you call back? No, not tonight, we're going out. Maybe tomorrow. Bobbie already sounded drunk and the evening hadn't started. Christmas in bed with a sick hangover. Nice.

Marianne went out. Nothing. Checked the computer. Nothing. Wrap his presents? Oh no, they were wrapped for him when he bought them. Try The Junction. Christ, Christmas Eve. No one to talk to. Who cared that there was talk about the Nats signing Fielder on Christmas Eve. Or that Rizzo may trade Lannan for a bat. That would be typical. Guy had been the best pitcher last four years, so dump him, maybe throw in Espinosa and Ramos. Mind you, if Peter ran the Nats the rotation would be Stammen, Martin, Lannan, Milone, Chico. And Vidro at second.

So Boras may be dealing with the Lerners and hoping to surprise Rizzo with Fielder. Nice for LaRoche, that. Too late for Christmas so maybe a Valentine. Or, knowing Boras, Mothers' Day. Forget it and get a center fielder. Crisp would do for a year and then look at it. See if Morse goes to first. All those young pitchers deserve a good fielding team and Fielder at first, Morse in left, and Werth in center would be bad news, Change the name to the Washington Bad News Bears. Get Walter Matthau to manage. Of course, he's dead. They sign Fielder and use Werth in center, Johnson could be dead as well. And Rizzo.

Just because they are better, doesn't make them good. Remember 2013 you assholes. Trouble with managers, get a sniff of the playoffs and they sell the farm. Look at Cleveland last year. Fucking Minyana with the Expos. Not that they had a sniff that year, not really. Only in Minyana's imagination. Asshole.

Christ he was drunk. Time for home. Christmas is coming, god help him.

*

He woke up late. Marianne was already off to church when he went into the kitchen. No coffee in the pot. Shit. Instant would have to do. Have some decent later with Marianne. Assuming they did some sort of breakfast together. Usually he could smell the Christmas bread rising by now. German stuff, really nice. Maybe Marianne didn't bother. Still, if she wasn't prepared to make the effort, Christmas was bound to be disappointing. He went to the bathroom and vomited. That was better. Better brush his teeth. Maybe after the coffee. God, he hated instant.

Marianne was obviously in no hurry to be home for Christmas as it was after midday when she finally walked in. He smiled and wished her Merry Christmas but got little response. He could sense bad day all over this one but, despite her negative attitude, he persisted and brought out her presents. Not now, I have to get going on the dinner, maybe in an hour or so. He played about with the computer for a bit. Nothing doing. No one likely to sign Prince Fielder today, although Boras is such a greedy shit, he would be up for a deal if it meant an extra fifty bucks. Prepare a whole new booklet showing that while Babe Ruth was a decent hitter, Prince eats more at dinner. Bet the Babe could out drink him.

They opened their presents a little later. Marianne was even more upset. How was he supposed to know he had missed the toilet with a bit of his vomit? At least he was home. Where was she? She seemed a bit surprised with the table cloth. And the book, probably because she got the same book from Cheryl and Arnie. Trust them. Pretty unimaginative present, at least he had given it only as a secondary present. She had bought him a sweater, as usual. He hated it, as usual. But he put it on and vowed to keep it on even though he was far too hot. One of them had to try to make Christmas pleasant. She told him to try not to be sick on it. Totally unnecessary to be like that.

Dyllis came over mid-afternoon. Supposedly to help, but the quiet voices made it obvious that it was mostly to gossip. Likely to moan about him. Dyllis was very supportive on that score. Well, let them go, he went out for a walk. Maybe The Junction was open. Maybe something was open. Other than a fucking church. They couldn't even leave you alone at Christmas.

By the time he got home, everyone was there so Marianne was angry all over again. Unless she'd never stopped being angry. So he wasn't there to greet them. They were her friends, not his. And Dyllis's. At least he had not hit his new sweater when he had been sick. Dyllis had obviously picked up a man. God knows when that could have happened. Poor bastard. Frank something or other.

All smiles and good will. He felt like making a comment about how good will was out of fashion in this house today but there was no need to upset Marianne further. Christ, she looked furious. What a way to spend Christmas.

Frank whoever was actually a decent guy. For a Red Sox fan. And the Patriots. Guy was certainly original in his thinking. Support all the local teams. So he was a bit boring, what could Dyllis expect at her age? And with her body. Not really that she was ugly, there was just too much of her. Marianne looked pretty good in comparison. Well, damn good really. Give her that, not too cheerful and inclined to be disapproving though she may be. She looked pretty damn good. If she could only try a bit, they could make it work. Make a nice Christmas present, that.

Turns out the Puerto Ricans weren't so much Puerto Rican as Argentinean. How was he supposed to have remembered that? Anyhow, was being Puerto Rican so bad? Once Marianne was in a mood, she could be impossible. No way was he going to risk trying to get into her bed tonight. Who cares how good she looks. Anyhow, they were not much better than Marianne, not after he asked them how they spent Christmas in Argentina. So they were born here? So was he but if someone though he was born in Poland or England or Canada, what difference? Canada would be good. Even without the Expos. National Health scheme. The Blue Jays were all right, even without Darvish. At least they weren't the Red Sox.

Frank whatever his name was decent really. Dyllis had struck lucky. Kept the conversation going on several tense occasions. He recognized that Marianne was in a horrible mood and went out of his way to be nice to her. Complimented the food, the decorations, helped carrying food and dishes in and out. He was just an all round decent guy. The Argentineans did very little but look disapproving and angry, and even Dyllis was subdued. Considering how nice her new squeeze was. She hardly spoke to him and when Frank helped take dishes through, she just sat. So the four of them glared at each other while Marianne cleared up. Lucky she had Frank to help.

After dinner, when people were thankfully heading home, there was tension in the air. He could feel that. Marianne was still in a funny mood, although she was nice enough to everyone. Well, everyone except him. Dyllis was totally embarrassed by something and pranced about saying silly things. The Argentineans ignored him but said thank you to Marianne. About seven times. Kissed her on most of the seven. Only Frank seemed normal. And him, of course, he was hardly going to let all the stupidity spoil his Christmas. It was already shit, so he could not have cared less. When they had gone. Finally. Why does it take people twenty minutes to shut a fucking door? When they had gone, Marianne turned to him and said she would see him in the morning. Just like that. He said that he thought it had been a wonderful dinner. She told him to go fuck himself. She was definitely going through a funny spell. No way he was trying her bedroom. Not tonight.

He went into the kitchen to get a last beer. Maybe a second to last beer. It was a mess. What were they doing in there when they were cleaning up? And who did Marianne think was going to do it? Him? They sure as hell weren't his friends. Frank whatever was the only one who even spoke to him. It was not that late but he went to bed. Thought about maybe Rizzo signing Cespedes. Maybe better than Coco Crisp.

*

He awoke to breaking dishes. A real crash. He thought he should maybe go into the kitchen. But, then again. Maybe give it another hour; it was early so he could pretend to be asleep. He listened but heard nothing. Silence. She should be cleaning up the mess. She must have dropped some dishes, so what was she doing? He got up and had a quick look in the kitchen. Marianne was sitting on the floor with broken dishes and leftover food everywhere, now he heard something. She was sobbing. The sort when it seemed hard to breath. Maybe she felt badly for wrecking his Christmas. He tiptoed into the entrance hall, grabbed his coat and went out. She would feel better once she had cleaned up. Because Christmas was on a Sunday, Monday was a holiday, but at least the bars were open.

Late that afternoon, when he got home, the kitchen was cleaned up and Marianne was sitting quietly in the living room. Trying to be conciliatory, he commented on the fact the kitchen looked much better. She looked at him. She was pale now, but not tearful. Maybe they could talk. She should apologize and then maybe they could go from there. Try to achieve some sort of accommodation. He was still hoping to maybe get some sex in before going back to work tomorrow. After all, it was Christmas.

But it wasn't to be. She looked at him. Sighed. Looked at him again.

Look, you had better sit down.

He sat down beside her. She got up and sat across the room.

I know you have probably been expecting this, but let's get it out in the open because if it's going to happen, it might as well happen as quickly as possible. No sense waiting six months.

What?

I want you out of here as soon as possible.

What the fuck?

I'm leaving you. Or, you're leaving me as it's my house.

What the fuck?

Frank's moving in as soon as you go and I want him here now.

What the fuck?

Today would be good. I have rented you a one bedroom furnished place on Pacific. You can get something else as soon as you want; they only require a month's notice. I want you as far away as possible.

What the fuck?

While you were out, I packed some suitcases for you; you can come back for your other things if you want to arrange it, but only when Frank is here.

What the fuck?

I want your keys.

What the fuck?

Look, I know it won't be easy so I have arranged a small allowance for you. Frank has a good job, so we can afford it.

We can afford it? We? So this is what they were doing in the kitchen when they should have been washing dishes. And nice guy Frank. Parasite. Home wrecker. Not that it started just like that. Something was up before yesterday. That was certain. Still. He asked what Dyllis thought about her taking Frank from her.

What are you talking about?

Then it struck him. Frank had never been with Dyllis. The nights out. The spa maybe. Shit, he had been a fool. While he was at home, trying to make the best of a troubled marriage, Marianne was out with Frank. Having an affair right under his nose. No dignity. No thought about his feelings. God she was hard. But what could he do now. He asked about the allowance. And the rent. Not bad and six months paid in advance. Well, he wouldn't offer to pay that back. Frankie boy gets the girl, they could pay a little. And when he got there, it was a nice place. Telephone connected. Maybe a deposit there as well. And the fridge was stocked. Except for beer. And Wi-Fi. Fuck it, he'd show them. He didn't need her. She had looked good at Christmas. Except when she was crying. At least she had shown some remorse.

*

Work was difficult on Tuesday. He didn't really feel like talking much and everyone was asking if everyone else had a good Christmas. And everyone had, except him. And Zainab. He did speak to her. Told her he had a miserable Christmas. She said she really hated Christmas and New Year. Always found them sad. Made her homesick now. Or missing the family sick. She said she would bet half the people who said that they had had a great Christmas, had been unhappy too. He said that he didn't know she was a gambler and, to save her soul, he would not take the bet. And they laughed. His first laugh of Christmas. Maybe his first laugh of December. Which would soon be over, thank god. Jesus, New Year. New Year's Eve. He hated it enough without sitting in a basement apartment contemplating his broken marriage. He missed Marianne already. It would help if there was some baseball activity. Someone should do something. If you could trade Tim Raines between Christmas and New Year, you could trade anyone. Certainly Peter Bourjos. Now that would cheer him up.

Tim Raines. Now there was a player. Maybe did a little cocaine on the side, but there was nothing to suggest that it enhanced his ability. Maybe helped him to forget there was a game going on once in awhile. Still, the guy could play. Loved him. Better than Dawson, any day. Ivan Calderon? There hasn't been a White Sox born to match Raines.

He did some shopping on the way home. No beer, no bar, no bleating. Home to cook. He was just fine. Frank was a bastard. Pretended to be so nice. Might have guessed. Red Sox fan. Liked football.

*

By Wednesday the office had settled down. The whole week would be pretty slow, mind you, as everyone prepared themselves emotionally to get drunk on New Year's Eve. And Monday would be another holiday. Hardly much for him to look forward to but he had arranged to go over to the house on Friday evening and collect some of his things. Her house. Their house. Frank was such a scumbag with his pretence at Christmas. Actually said that if they got Fielder, the Nats would be strong contenders. Maybe go all the way. Asshole. Rizzo kept saying he didn't want Fielder but the newspapers now were going on about Boras dealing with the owners. Lerner pull a Lucchino on Rizzo. That would be nice for Mike. There's this guy I don't want, costs more than an entire team and has a limited shelf life because of his unlimited dinner plate. And then they buy him and limit his budget for the next ten years and he will still need a center fielder and have no position for Mike Morse because Werth and Harper will be at the corners. Unless they trade Harper, of course, maybe fetch a decent reliever, you never know. Once the owners take over you get an Oriole's fuck-up and who needs it. Maybe he should start supporting the Cubs or something. Shit, it was not as if Frank was an expert. What does he know about Prince and Boras? Or baseball for that matter? Mind you, he called the Bailey move that went down today. But who didn't? So now Cherington is a boy wonder. Mind you, Beane didn't fleece him like he fleeced Rizzo. Peacock and Cole. And Milone was such a story.

He would spend some time making his apartment more comfortable. More his. Marianne could throw him out but he would make it decent. So it was a nice place to maybe sit and read the blogs and have some music or something. Maybe bring a friend over. Who? Fuck it.

There was little enough to do but work at work. With the off season having a slow week and being thrown out of his own home, work was almost a refuge. At least he could speak to people, even if it was about insurance and claims and shit. In a bar he would tend to spend too much time thinking about Marianne. And that bastard, Frank. Probably planned it for months, the pair of them. Marianne sure looked good. A bit upset, but she was still attractive. She should be upset after what she did to him. Her and Frank.

Zainab didn't seem much happier than he did. She must have had a bad Christmas as well. Can't imagine her getting loaded at New Year. He brought her a cup of coffee. Smiled and just moved on. He had his own troubles. But she came over just to say thank you and to thank him again for the present. I mean, it's just a book. But she said she loved his writing. Didn't Peter. Oh sure, great writer. One of the finest of his time. Only he writes about shit no one could possibly find interesting except maybe Zainab. And her husband. Christ, what was he doing while she got so depressed? Must be an insensitive jerk if he can't see what she is going through.

At least work provided something to take his mind off his troubles. God help him if claims were the highlight of his life. Maybe just for a few weeks until he got settled. Maybe until the season started. Or spring training. He took a few claims off Zainab because she was distressed and was not functioning well. Might of taken a few back from Bert and Michele if they weren't such assholes. Stuart stopped to exchange a word or two. Say what you like about Stuart, he noticed when you worked hard and made a point of being generous in his praise. Trouble was, it also meant he noticed how little he was doing normally. Better be careful.

Stopped on the way home and picked up some eggs and salad. No drink. His flat screen was set up now and he would watch a DVD. Shit, they were all still at the house. Fucking Frank probably watching Ken Burns tonight. Never mind. He'd have all his own things on the weekend.

*

Another day, another boring day of claims. Working hard for a couple of days was about his limit. Nothing doing with the Nats except a lot of talk about Werth playing center. He was also beginning to realize the limitations of living alone. Once the towels and sheets are in the cupboard and the shirts are hung up, what the hell do you do? He liked cooking but not just for himself. Sitting over a few beers at home was hardly satisfying. Going out for a drink was slightly better, but he tended to think too much about Marianne. He realized that most of his friends were their friends, his and Marianne's. Really, Marianne's friends. There were a few casual friends he had from the bars, but no one to spend time with. And he had nothing but time. So he worked through another day. Still, stick with the plan. Cook for himself and no bars. Not this week. Picked up a book on the way home.

His dinner was rubbish. Another grill. Another salad. Big Deal. Terrible book. Hero was just a tiny bit stronger than Superman. Couldn't fly, mind you. Just totally invulnerable. Killed off his brother in this book so he had no relatives, no friends, no attachments. No baggage, no clean underwear, no toothbrush, no deodorant. Dug swimming pools by hand to keep fit. Wow. Absolutely irresistible to woman as most stinking oafs are, of course. Rather do claims than read that rubbish.

89

Hope Rizzo is reading Olney, suggests Marlon Byrd. Why not, one cheap year and the guy knows the ropes. Problem solved for twelve months. Has to be better than Cameron and Bernadina. I still sort of like Bernadina but he seems to have burnt his last Nats bridge.

He hated sleeping in the new place. Even knowing he was alone he still woke up half-listening for the noise of Marianne in the kitchen. He hated getting up and making coffee by himself, knowing that he would not see anyone until he was on his way to work. Fucking Frank. Wished he could remember his last name, not that he could remember ever knowing it. Seemed likely that he was introduced as someone with two names inasmuch as he was about to move into his bed. Well, he hadn't been in his bed for awhile now. Made more sense when you realized Frank was around. Wonder when they started. Must ask this weekend. Maybe not. When exactly did you two meet and when did you start screwing and when did you decide to kick me out of the house? Sounded like self-pity. Better to just ignore it. Like if they hadn't thought of booting him out, he might have gone on his own anyhow. Fat chance. Fucking Frank.

Marianne had at least been generous with his allowance. Or settlement or whatever you called her guilt money. Awful to think he needed to take it. You would think he would get a decent salary himself after all these years. Well, it wasn't so bad, but with the allowance he could really do well. Even if he started to pay rent himself. He might get a better place after the six months were up. Not yet, shame to waste the rent. He liked the area and had lived there a long time, so maybe he would stay. He didn't need more than one bedroom and a place to sit and a kitchen. Not likely to be throwing dinner parties. Maybe too close to Marianne. Not that she was likely to wander by or drop in The Junction anytime soon.

*

New Year's Eve would be better this year. He normally hated it but this year he would watch a film and ignore the occasion. Trouble was, another three day weekend coming up. Still, he would pick up his stuff and sort out the apartment. Marianne had kept the car, of course. It was in her name and all. And she had bought it. But maybe he could borrow it to move some things. Shit, borrow his own car. Even though it was hers, they had always treated it as theirs.

Nothing much with the Nats. Rizzo still bleating about LaRoche at first while everyone else says they get Fielder. Boras announces that he doesn't deal with GMs anymore, just owners. Christ, what GM would swallow that? Trouble is, they know they are one bad decision away from the hiring line so they swallow what the big brains like Angelos tell them to swallow. But they get themselves in tangles. Pitch Wang and lose Detwiler then Wang gets hurt and there is no Peacock or Milone. Sign Fielder and have no place for Morse unless you put Werth in center where his aging legs fade before his contract does. Of course, Rizzo knows the odds of him being in DC when Jayson starts stumbling in the outfield are slim to none. Some poor bastard will be hired to dump Werth and Fielder, maybe Zimmerman and build afresh around Cole and Norris and Peacock. Oops, they're over on the coast. In San Jose. Maybe Rizzo could sort out claims, give him a shot at GM.

Law not chatting today. Well, he is, but over in Houston. Nice place for the prick. Crap team and crap organization. Hope the restaurants are crap as well. Maybe ESPN can hire someone who is more interested in baseball than cooking. Thing is, if he doesn't get the job there will be three years of him shitting on Houston as a crap franchise. Which it is, of course, but hardly likely to be worse because they saw through Keith Law. Maybe they just invited him over to cook for them. Probably can't even do that. Like baseball, he is mostly mouth. Or mostly keyboard. This is earth calling Houston, come on guys; give the rest of us a break.

He stopped at the Bistro on the way home. Then The Junction. Never managed dinner. Nor breakfast the next morning. How could you puke that much if there was nothing in your stomach? He got to work late. Stuart gave him a look. Fuck you Stuart. Zainab gave him a look. At least she had some compassion. Christ, claims and more claims. Family here lost everything Christmas Day. Tough shit. Should have watched the fire. Careless bastards. Fuck them all, he needed coffee.

Marianne had told him not to come around tonight, could he come in the morning, maybe ten. As if it made any difference to him. He had three days of nothing while she and Frank wallowed in love and celebrated the thought of being together in 2012. In his house. With his car. And his wife. And he had a basement apartment around the corner. At least they were paying for it. For six months. He wondered if she had told Cheryl and Barney. Must have done. Of course, the trip to Burlington on her own and then the dinner before Christmas. At least he didn't have to talk to them. See them trying to be sympathetic while silently cheering their mother on. Weren't kids supposed to resent it when their parents found new partners? Even if it was replacing a dead partner. But his bloody children probably helped her find Frank. Maybe registered her with e-Harmony or something. Or Bobbie. She was capable of that sort of shit. Real computer nerd, that one. Spent more time on e-Bay than she did on the bottle, and that was something.

Maybe Rizzo should check out e-Bay for a center fielder. Wish this Marlon Byrd thing would gain some steam. Wish this Jayson Werth thing would lose some steam. Look Mike, last year you spent way too much money for a decent player and let your managers move him up and down the line up like a yoyo. So he had a stinking year and took even more flak than he should have. So now you go to Davey and tell him, the guy is comfortable in right and he likes to bat sixth. Maybe he has a decent year and I look a bit less stupid. Why not give him a break. And me. I'll buy you a beer if he hits .280. Even let him bat second. One or the other, mind, not both. Course Davey could tell him, sure get me a leadoff hitter, we bat Desmond second and Werth can hit sixth just like you say. Even play right if you find me a center fielder. Say, there's an idea, what about a center fielder who can bat leadoff. Shit, why did we never think of that? Oh, you did. But decided it was more important to dump all our A prospects on Billy Beane and then maybe dump Detwiler as well. Great thinking, Mike. No wonder they fired the boy wonder. Oops, he quit didn't he?

He couldn't take it. Snuck out for a few beers at lunch. Felt better. For maybe thirty minutes then had to go and puke again. Maybe should have eaten something with the beer. Maybe should have eaten something instead of the beer. He could not work. Stuart kept looking at him but, shit, who was working? Fucking New Year's Eve. Almost. He managed to slip a couple of claims onto Bert's desk. Not really necessary as he had done a lot himself earlier in the week but he just hated Bert so much. And Michele. Pair of creeps. Anyway, good to keep up the routine otherwise they would notice a decline in their work load. Maybe get suspicious. Just like them. Always worrying about what other people might be doing. Suspicious bastards. He would sneak a few to Michele later. And a few electronic ones to Zainab. After all, she had agreed.

He left work early, couldn't stand it. Stopped for a few drinks on the way home. Then a few more in The Junction. Got into an argument with some jerk who claimed hockey was the greatest spectator sport. All that speed and precision. Just the pace at which they performed was fantastic. Just the fighting he meant. He had been to the old Garden. Watched the fans. Or listened to them. Baying for blood. He walked home. Something was really wrong. Sick again. And again. Then at home he was sick. Good thing Marianne didn't see this. God, ten o'clock tomorrow morning. Should pass by then. Should have something to eat.

*

In the morning he was a little better. Not much, but he managed a piece of toast with his coffee. Still in there. Thank god. He was late getting to the house. Marianne was obviously annoyed but Frank was all smiles. Sure, he had the house, the car, the woman, the furniture. Not likely to be miserable. It was almost noon and they were going out but Frank said he would give him a hand and they could get everything in the car in no time. That's right, the quicker they got rid of him the better. Frank had already put some things in the car. In fact, just about everything he wanted and a lot more. Some CDs he would never have bothered with and most of the DVDs. Trying to buy him off with trinkets. Worked with the Indians. For a while.

Marianne asked if they could have a word in private. Here it comes. What does she want?

Look, Peter, I have spoken to Cheryl and Barney but they really need to hear from you. Oh sure, must be really worried about old dad. Haven't spoken to the bastard in years but they are now overwhelmed with worry and concern.

And Peter, I've thought about the car. Frank and I don't need two cars. So I signed ours over to you. Insurance is paid up until October. I changed the address when I put it in your name. I know there is no parking place with your apartment but you could always park it here until you apply for a parking permit. Shit, don't do this to me, I don't want generosity, I need you to be awful.

And, oh Peter, I am just so sorry in so many ways. You can't plan for these things. They happen. You and I were so far apart and I was so lonely until I found Frank but I know you must be hurting. I hate the thought of you alone. Sure you do. And poor old Frank, must be killing him too.

So, New Year's Eve. In the back of his mind he thought he would spend the day arranging the things he brought back from the house. It took less than an hour. Hang up a few shirts, dump the shoes in the bottom of the closet. Arrange the CDs and DVDs and then what. He still had most of the afternoon to kill and then New Year's Eve. Even when he was with Marianne he hated it so what would it be like alone. Maybe no worse. It couldn't be much worse. At least there was no one to keep looking at him, accusing him of spoiling the evening. Like spoiling a child's funeral, spoiling New Year's Eve. I mean, could his misery really make it any worse?

He went out and bought some food. Essentials like salt, sugar and beer. A bottle of whiskey. Some wine. A few more things. He would last until Tuesday.

Christ, tonight and two more full days. One of them a Sunday. When a holiday falls on a Sunday, is it twice as dead? Not much chance of Rizzo getting a center fielder today. MLBRUMORS was still rumoring away despite the holiday. Nice to know there were other people who didn't have a life. Even Rosenthal was pretty quiet. No bad thing. Bit of a smug bastard. Mister Scoop. That meant the guy they dropped rumors to when they want the price to up. Nationals pushing for Gonzalez. All they need to do is include Cole and Norris instead of Nieto and Smoker. At least he isn't a cook.

If New Year's Eve was a sad time. Bars on New Year's Eve must be as sad as places get. He managed until 11:30 before heading home. Watched an oater with Gregory Peck. Great actor. About a bad guy who was sick of the whole scene. A lot of the best westerns were about the last days of the west. Best ones were all in the fifties and sixties. Real directors, not like Scorsese, direct all the big scenes. Lots of bells and whistles but no real directing. Watch Jack Palance move the coffee pot sometime, you pretentious jerk. Or drink water. Mind you, they used actors back then. Not super pricks, think their name is bigger than the business. Either have to watch Meryl Streep thinking she's so damn hot that she could play Abraham Lincoln if she wanted, or Tom Cruise who thinks that if he is nice to the crew and smiles, no one will notice he can't act. Church of Scientology for Christ sake. As if the ordinary church wasn't perverted enough they invent these weird religions for the stars.

Checked the computer before going to bed. Had to hand it to Kenny Williams, no day is sacred if you can make a really bad trade. Looks like he picked up two pitchers who will certainly never cause him any problems. No chance either of them will give up a hit in the Bigs. Surely he could do better than that. Should have tried Rizzo, he has places on his DL. Mind you, Williams must have something going for himself, I mean, what a place to make a salary dump. San Diego. What are they thinking? A very big outfield for a very poor fielder who is far too expensive. Not exactly a Padre's sort of move.

New Year's Day was warm. Eerily warm. Winter is supposed to be cold. Clear and cold was best but snow could be wonderful as well. But this. Might as well be October. That bit in the Buffalo Soldier about the snow storm had really got to him. Real winter. Marvelous stuff. A bit over the top what with bridges going and all, but just the onset of a real snow storm was marvelous. Here if it snowed, it generally melted within a week. Or went all wet and tired. Nothing worse than tired snow. Except maybe rainy wind.

Wonderful. A whole day of nothing ahead of him. He would go for a long walk. Once round the common, watch the swimming on the skating rink. He loved watching pickup hockey there. No fighting. Only once did he see a fight break out. Stupid kids. Trying to be Zdeno Chara. What an ambition that was. At least in Montreal they had loved the real hockey players, not the thugs. Mind you they had loved John Ferguson. Shit. Rocket Richard, Jean Beliveau, Guy Lafleur and John Ferguson. Wasn't even French like the real hockey players. Mind you, Bobby Orr could play and he wasn't French. How could a city that had seen Bobby Orr play, like thugs? Stupid game. Wrecked by fans. Wrecked by money and selling fights. Watch hockey highlights and you might never see a goal. Just the fights.

Of course, money was ruining baseball too. Maybe already ruined baseball too. Read about the old days and you read about players who loved the game. Guys from the streets. Still lived in the streets. Played pick-up games with the kids on the way to the park. Owners were always shits of course. They blame the players for being greedy. Like a pig moaning about the table manners of a sleek cat. His father used to talk about the rich as having both feet in the trough. Never thought much about his parents anymore. He wouldn't would he? Assholes. The highlight of their lives was meatloaf on Friday night. Not Meatloaf. Meatloaf. The fucking one with real fatty mince dripping in it. He loved Meatloaf. Coach Loaf, real star that guy. The acoustic motorcycle. Giving his team copies of Bat out of Hell. That video with Cher. Still the best ever.

At least he could get a drink if he looked, Sunday or no Sunday. What a fucking stupid day to have New Years. By the time he had finished walking, he was in Cambridge. How did that happen? Sure as hell wasn't walking home. But it took a long time to get home. He was hung over before he got there. Needed a little sleep, except by the time he woke up it was very dark and past midnight. Which meant that instead of having to kill a long day, he had to kill a long night. Watched another DVD. Drank some beer. Remembered he hadn't checked the computer. Nothing. Not even Ken Williams was working today. Olney said the Nats would be in the top ten teams in baseball if they signed Fielder. You could see why these guys got jobs writing. I mean, what analysis, what insight. And if the Yankees traded for Halliday and Lee, they might challenge for a wild card spot. Way to go Buster. He went to bed. Fell asleep as the sun rose. At least Monday would be shorter.

Peter slept until noon. No need for breakfast, maybe find a bar that does coffee and something to eat. The weekend was almost over he told himself. Have relaxing day. Short walk, then maybe home for a DVD. Who knows, 2012 may prove to be a good year. Hard to imagine. What with Frank and all. Neither kid talking to him, not really. Don't even speak to him to say that they are not talking to them. Marianne pretends to be upset. Sure, just left you for another man but I really feel badly. Don't know why I did it. Oh yeah, now I remember. It's because he is sober, younger, richer, better looking, more sympathetic, more interesting and even the kids prefer him. But other than that, this is real hard for me, sweetie. Much harder on you, of course, because the chance that you could ever meet someone else who might have you are about the same as finding life on another planet next week. He looked at himself in the mirror. Shit. Better take that walk and stick to coffee.

He found a bar that was open. They did coffee, but he had walked for almost an hour so felt that one beer wouldn't hurt. He was probably right but by the time he left he had finished a few more than one. More like ten. He dragged himself home, losing his way several times, so it took two hours. Home, that was a laugh. How would he ever think of this dump as home? Well, I suppose it's home if you have no other place to go. Other than work. And bars.

At least he didn't have to cook himself any food. That was one good thing about being sick. He had never minded cooking when he was with Marianne. Simple stuff, of course, but he sort of enjoyed it. But now. Well, now was now and it was awful. Fucking Frank. It was not late and he had only been up since noon, so he was not ready to go to bed. He was more than ready, of course, if he thought he might sleep, but that was never going to happen. He checked the computer; of course, see what Mike was up to.

This Fielder thing would just not go away. While it was likely just Boras feeding the media little tidbits of information suggesting that the Nats were on the verge of coughing up several hundred million so Theo, or whoever, might make a good offer, it was still worrying. Listen Mike, signing Fielder would be stupid. With no center fielder and Strasburg on a short lease, next year is not the year, so you keep LaRoche who will turn errors into outs rather than the reverse. And you will have a bit of money left over to sign Zimmerman to a long term contract. And Zimmermann. And Harper. And Strasburg unless you trade him to Billy Beane. You will save enough on food bills alone to sign Morse to a few years. And Rendon won't replace Zimmerman except on the DL. Look at his record, no better than Zimmerman so forget this Rendon being cheaper than Zimmerman bullshit. So is Eric Chavez. Think. Think. Repeat after me, 2013 will be just fine with Morse at first and Zimmerman at third and a fucking center fielder in fucking center field. Surely a bright guy like you can see Prince would struggle in center. Get Crisp or Byrd and see what happens a year from now. Scott will forgive you. Well, maybe not, let's see what Fielder gets. Five years at 15 mill and Rizzo might get a spanking from Scott. Not that it is likely to happen. Boras cannot possibly be as smart as he thinks he is but he is smart enough to know that, with thirty GMs out there, show a little patience and one of them will prove he is an idiot. Look at Dipoto. Still be paying Albert gazillions when he's in a Zimmer frame. Personal services my arse, you can't personally serve at that age, you get personally served. Jerry, bring me some herb tea and when is my enema scheduled? Yes the nurse with the short dark hair would be fine. What, she quit. Must be from the National League. No respect for the DH. Peter went to bed, but he was a worried man.

6. New Year, New Man

Peter woke up late. Luckily his stomach was still upset and he had no desire to eat breakfast. Even so, after showering, he had no chance of getting to work on time. Or even close to being on time. He searched for a clean shirt. There were several, but they were all creased from the move. He really had to get an iron and an ironing board today on the way home. He found a tie but it had a stain and his suit was crumpled. Maybe he should just phone in sick and get his life organized. But what would he do all day? Worry about Prince Fielder? He had just spent three miserable days on his own and now he was thinking of taking a sickie. To be on his own. He set off for work, arriving over an hour late. Stuart watched him go to his desk. Bert asked him if he had enjoyed New Year and everyone laughed. Muffled laughs, but laughs. Stuart came over. Asked if he was alright. Sure thing Stu, wife ran off with a shit, kids don't talk to me, living in a fucking cellar. I'm terrific, just terrific. He smiled and declined to comment.

Zainab came over with coffee. Suggested they go for lunch together. Maybe in an hour or so. He should try to get some work done. People were noticing and Bert had made a few remarks. At lunch, she said little at first. Just smiled at him and said that it was nice to have lunch with someone. He had never noticed, but she said that she always ate alone. Usually brought her own. He actually enjoyed lunch. Enjoyed being with Zainab and enjoyed the food. Just Au Bon Pain usual stuff, but he hadn't eaten anything that wasn't ruined or a burger in a bar for days. He had a coffee afterwards, she declined. But she started talking then. Very quietly and almost apologizing as she spoke.

You really must try, Peter. People are noticing you. You seem so distracted and not to care. I don't mind doing some of your claims if you are in a mess, but be careful, Bert and Michele were talking. They are watching for you. They were even talking about setting traps. Stuart isn't so bad. He may even be your friend, protecting you when he can. But when you come in like, well, like today, it must be difficult. You were late and you look sick and your clothes are messy which makes it worse. Just please be careful. He could feel himself getting angry. Not with Zainab, of course, but with the others in the office. Especially Michele and Bert. That comment Bert made. When they walked back, he let Zainab go up alone. Waited for ten minutes more before returning. He watched them. Bert and Michele. And Stuart. And all three were watching him right back. But maybe Zainab was right, maybe Stuart was more concerned than annoyed.

The afternoon went slowly. Tried to work but it was very slow. Thinking about what was said. Nothing in the Schoenfield chat to distract him, either. All steroids and Hall of Fame. Nothing on Fielder. Needless to say, no center fielder. Coco Crisp went back to Oakland. Could have been had, Mike, could have been had. Maybe he likes San Jose. Coco, forget it, team moves to San Jose and you get to stay in Oakland. Billy's building for the big move. Already got a pitching staff from the Nats. Power hitting catcher. Won't be room for you Coco. Two years and a buyout ain't bad for a fading star. Small star, but he had moments. And he would have handled center nicely for us for two years.

Just before he left Zainab came over and suggested he transfer a dozen claims to her. Patted him on the arm. Said she was feeling much better and she could easily handle it until he got himself together. It was almost as if she knew about Marianne. And Frank.

He was able to carry an iron and a board home, then went out for some eggs and salad. Then remembered and went back out for hangers. Simple meal and three hours ironing and tidying his clothes. Watched the Jazz DVD. Kept telling himself that Frank and Bert and Michele were laughing at him, but he would make it. The job was not that bad. He used to be one of the best. And he would take more interest in things. Telephone the kids, maybe. Watch a little hockey. Try to be polite about the Red Sox. Even the Patriots. Not the Celts, there was a limit. He would maybe go to The Junction once in the week and once on the weekend. Cut back. Maybe join the library again. Do a course. Well, not yet. He could hardly sleep as the plans raced around in his head. He had plenty of money if he lived in this apartment. He could go out when he wanted, but maybe he should try movies, even a play or something.

*

He was up in time for some breakfast. Orange juice, coffee and toast. Juice was from a carton, but it said fresh orange juice. Hey, why not drive to Burlington this weekend, maybe drop in on Cheryl. Maybe phone her first. No, give it a few weeks.

He was at his desk early. Set some goals. Clear the paper claims by the weekend, and, with a little help from Zainab, electronic claims would be up to date even sooner. And stay on top of it. Zainab walked by. Smiled at him, sort of gave a hand signal to say that she noticed that he looked better. Right, get on with it. Dierkes had a chat later, didn't want to miss it. He didn't have the background of the big name reporters and really he just filtered other people's news, but he answered questions. On baseball. Didn't seem as interested in

Halls of Fame or cooking or crap literature. ESPN could learn from people like him, keep it simple. The Baseball Prospectus guys and Baseball America were marvelous, of course; stuck to their game plan without being clever about anything but baseball. But Dierkes and Nicholson-Smith were learning.

Worked hard all morning clearing paper claims. Spoke to Zainab and she agreed to take on a few electronic ones. He was making good progress. Even in the afternoon he worked quite hard on the electronic ones while skipping backwards and forwards to the chat. Nothing special. He found himself shrugging and going back to his claims. That was weird. He looked at his backlog and it was more like a hill than a mountain. A few days like this and it would be a fucking valley. He would have to drop by Bert and Michele. See if they needed some help. On a more serious note, it would be good if he didn't have to bother Zainab anymore. Trouble is, when he does get behind, she is the surest way out.

As he was leaving Stuart spoke to him briefly. Just said he was glad to see him looking better. Said he appreciated that he had made the effort yesterday even though he had obviously been ill. So maybe Zainab was right about Stuart. Stopped to buy food on the way home. Another wash tonight, maybe finish off the ironing. Hoped to have time for a little of Burns' Jazz DVD. Christ, he was becoming domesticated.

There was a note from Marianne in his post box. It contained a parking permit so he could pick up the car anytime and park it right here on Pacific. Just a short note saying she hoped he was doing okay. And maybe he should phone the kids. Shit, he knew he should. Maybe on the weekend.

Checked the computer before he went to bed. God, you had to hand it to Theo. Zambrano gone. Mind you, Chris Volstad is no prize and I'll bet the Cubs pay both salaries. Still. What next? Soriano? Not supposed to be any salary dump trades in baseball. Have to be approved by Bud. That asshole. Approve anything except saving the Expos. Mind you, Zambrano was more of a personality dump. God, when Bowden was around they could have made a dozen personality dumps. Bringing in Estrada when he already had Lo Duca to cause all the trouble anybody could need. Two catchers both with negative personalities; played about eight games between them. What a brain that man had. Makes Rizzo's dump of live arms look like a move of positive genius. Two poisonous catchers, no pitchers, and a dysfunctional outfield. Bring in a rookie manager. Christ, then thought we should be seen as wild card material. Along with Pittsburgh and Kansas City. Not all Bowden's fault; look who hired him, the Expo Terminator, himself. Minyana and then Bowden. Thanks Bud. At least the Nationals never had to go to Puerto Rico to play their so-called home games. He checked the computer once more before bed. Nothing. He needed something to think about in bed other than the fact he should phone his children but Rizzo had no compassion.

*

By the end work on Thursday Peter was in a very strange mood. He had more or less cleared his backlog and was actually beginning to feel a certain amount of pride in his ability to do his job. Maybe not as fast as Michele, but every bit as good as Bert. Zainab was faster, but Zainab was special. He had asked her to join him for lunch and offered to try to make up for all the work he had passed to her. She had laughed. Basically, she found the work boring and almost regretted his intention to do all his own work in the future. As she said, there

105

was no hope for promotion, she just did the work so might as well keep busy. To a large extent she was seen as a brilliant temporary employee because technically her husband was on leave from his British university. She talked freely with him. She had gone through a bad patch at Christmas, not for the first time she had had a spell of severe homesickness. It was better now. She would still go back to England if it was her choice, but she knew her husband would oppose it. She laughed. A good Pakistani wife doesn't stand up to her husband.

He was less open with her but he did admit that his problems stemmed from trouble at home. Went as far as to say that his kids were becoming strangers to him. They had always turned to Marianne. Thought it would upset Zainab if he told her just how alienated they were. Left out the fact that he really disliked Barney, hated Bobbie and Arnie, and could only take Cheryl in small doses. Then Zainab said a funny thing. As she grew older she realized that her children were becoming her best friends. It went beyond love; they were the ones she enjoyed most. They could talk and laugh together. Christ, imagine talking and laughing with Cheryl or Barney. Or that bitch Bobbie. Mind you, Marianne did. And she had Frank.

After lunch he went through the baseball news. Kilgore was great on Fielder. Pointed out that the Nats already had one albatross contract and it was likely to become a choice between Fielder and Zimmerman in the long run if you factor in the contracts that were going to start coming through with the kids. Olney wrote a decent piece about the possible fearsome batting lineup they would have with Fielder, neglecting to say that it would include an outfield with a rookie, a right fielder in center and a very ordinary left fielder; a left side of the infield that couldn't throw and a first baseman who couldn't catch even if he could get to the bag in time. This with young starters and a young closer plus two starters who pitch to contact. Think Mike. If you won't listen to me, look at what Bowden says. Says it's a must to sign Fielder. Now there's your key. If Bowden thinks it's a good idea you can write it off as insane. Splashy Bowden and his headlines. Forget it. Wait and see what Rendon and Harper do. Sign Zimmerman now, he might move to first for Christ sake. Your job is to build a system which produces regular contenders, not go all out for a year or two and have to watch the good young players walk because of an overpaid right fielder who wore out his legs in center and an overpaid first baseman who wore out his welcome at the dinner table. And you move on to Baltimore or something. Phone Frank Wren. Ask him about it.

All this crap with Fielder. No wonder he couldn't sleep.

*

On Friday he made a new resolution. Work steadily and check the baseball only at the end of the day. Maybe at lunch. Especially as there were hardly any chats right now. Today he would stop letting Prince Fielder spoil his life. And Rizzo. He should have suspected Rizzo when it became obvious that he got along with Boras. God, it would be good if Boras got stuck with a few of his free agents. Prince taking a year at 15 mill plus incentives from Pittsburgh. Jackson going to Houston maybe for two mill over five. Then Boras could say he got him a five year deal. Just forty-eight mill short of his promise. So, to prove his resolve he didn't check the baseball all day. Went out for a simple dinner and then to a movie.

*

Tinker Tailor Soldier Spy was damn good. He went ready to criticize but there were no car chases, no explosions, no lurid sex scenes. It was a real film. No attempt to jump around so you didn't know what was going on. Maybe he should write Scorsese about it. He hated directors who jumped all over the place to pretend they were clever. No, he really liked the film. Maybe take a Le Carre book out of the library. He had read one or two way back and enjoyed them. After the film he stopped for a coffee, and then went home. To check the baseball.

Nothing much, the Zambrano deal went down, big win for the Cubs, that one. They also got Anthony Rizzo. Theo was good; no question about that. He still wondered if maybe he might give up Byrd for a reliever. Even a reliever and Bernadina. Hell, Bernadina needs a change and is not exactly a management favorite. Chuck in a reliever and see what happens.

*

Saturday Peter got up and went out for coffee and a croissant. Read the Globe. A lot of talk about the election, of course. Primary season starting. Waste of millions. Considering what we spend on getting elected it is hardly surprising that there is no money left over for health care. Obama now saying that we can't fight wars all over the world. Wonder if he ever heard of James Monroe? Probably doesn't realize that wars are necessary for all our rich ex-officials in the armaments industries. He looks a bit naïve, poor bastard. All this working together and consensus shit is at least out the window.

Obama was bound to win the election, of course, despite his ratings. Not like the Republicans to piss about destroying each other like this. Farting around trying to find someone even less popular than Obama. They were doing well if that was their goal. Christ, what a bunch of assholes. Maybe Rizzo could be president. Then the Nationals could find a GM who understood this center field thing.

He walked to the South Boston Library and found Tinker, Tailor, Soldier Spy. Also picked up The Girl with the Dragon Tattoo. Might see that tonight. Getting a lot of publicity but likely to be all crash bang. Someone in the office said the Swedish version was much better.

He went back to his apartment with his books where he lay on the sofa and read several pages before falling asleep. When he woke up it was mid-afternoon. Great. At this rate the weekend would soon be over. Shit, then it would be back to work. That was the trouble when you were on your own. You looked forward to the weekend and not having to work but then realized that you were looking forward to at least being with other people even if it meant being at work. He could go to a bar, of course, but it was hardly being with anyone. All they talked about was the football playoffs. Be glad when the Superbowl is behind us. And the March Madness horseshit.

He could never understand why they allowed the NCAA to run their fucking tournament just as the season started. Basketball was a game designed for freaks that promoted obnoxious superstars. College shit wasn't as bad as the NBA, of course. I mean, Kobe Bryant, LeBron James? At least Shaq had a sense of humor. Couldn't get a game on a sandlot now unless you were maybe 7 foot and 300 pounds. He sometimes watched pickup games for a few minutes. No denying the kids could play but they were mostly working on their egos even at that level. Watch the superstars and learn how to be an asshole.

He must try to telephone the kids. Maybe tomorrow. Maybe they would make a bigger effort now that Marianne had left him. Hell, he had the car now; he could drive over to see Barney. Even Cheryl. He liked Burlington. Liked Vermont. Maybe get snowed in, he loved snow. Real white snow, deep. Not like the shit in Boston. Yeah, must phone the kids. Tomorrow. Right now he would check the baseball online then go to that movie. He used to like going to films. With Marianne. Fucking Frank.

*

He was not as impressed with The Girl with the Dragon Tattoo as he was with Tinker Tailor. Somehow it seemed to be an American film made about Sweden, whereas Tinker Tailor was a British film made about Britain. This was probably largely because that exactly what they were. Anyhow, why would James Bond want to go to Sweden? He was more of a Caribbean spy. Warm beaches and hot women. The world should get over James Bond and start making real films again. Like High Noon. Mind you, he liked Tinker Tailor. Well, he enjoyed the Tattoo shit as well. He would try the book. If it was worth it, he might even buy the Swedish DVDs. Do the sub-title thing. He hated dubbing but sub-titles were not so bad. Once, when he went to see Yojimba for about the hundredth time, it had been dubbed. Dubbed. Shit. Might as well get a stand in for Charlie Chaplin. How could you grunt like that in English, for Christ sake? And they were friends of Marianne's too, so he couldn't walk out of their house like he could a theater. Awful evening. Vol au fucking Vents. Who the fuck eats Vol au Vents in the real world. And Chardonnay. Gum up your mouth with both of them. Yojimbo was a beer and chips movie. Any fool could see hat. And when he tried to talk to Marianne on the way home she just got angry. Silent more than angry. Let Frank deal with the vol au vents. Asshole.

Nothing much on baseball. A bit on whether The Rock should make the Hall. He wished he could get excited about that. Great player but the Hall was a farce. Soon be putting Boras in for wrecking the game. He'd get Lerner's vote. If he had a vote. And maybe Rizzo's. Maybe Mike sees that really he should be making the decisions. It's a baseball team not the Scott and Ted show. Just a note before you go to bed, Mike, ever ask yourself if Zimmerman is a Boras freak. Maybe that's why he is selling Fielder to Ted. Maybe he feels all the new media money should go to him and his friends and Zimmerman has the nerve to have another agent so no new contract for Ryan. Think about it Mike. Let Lerner design your team and you become the new Baltimore and Prince gets forty dingers and forty-five RBI's. Great season. Least valuable player who ever won the Triple Crown? Shit, time for bed.

*

Wow, spent the whole Sunday with his books. It was actually very pleasant. In a way. About six he decided to try to telephone the kids. That sort of spoiled it. Bobbie answered, said Barney was out, she would give him the message. What message he thought. Your father telephoned because your mother, who ran off with an asshole, said it would be a good idea even though I still think you've turned into a creep and married a bigger creep. So he just said to tell Barney he called. That all? Yeah, just a caring father, you got a problem with that you drunken little parasite. They weren't even married. Thank god. Barney was a creep but he wouldn't want him to marry Bobbie. Even he didn't deserve that. Said they just weren't ready. When would anyone be ready to marry Bobbie?

Mind you, who would marry Barney? Well, Bobbie, probably. Blood sucker. He tried Cheryl. No answer. Maybe during the week. He went back to Le Carre. Wonderful book. Just like the movie.

Terrible article in the Post. Sign Fielder as a black icon and sell more caps. Trouble is; there is a point there. So many great black players and none in Washington. Not like the Expos. Well, what difference, hardly any blacks in Washington anyway. Full of African Americans. Christ, he hated that. Centuries of shit and all we talk about is what to call people who aren't blond and blue-eyed. Zainab says that in England some cities are so mixed that they look like the United Nations. Not able to discuss color because there are too many different colors to count. Can you imagine Boston not being white? Or European American? That would shake them up on Beacon Hill. They'd wonder where all the maids came from. Think the economy must be picking up. All these blacks, everyone must have maids and gardeners. And chauffeurs.

Tomorrow starts another week. Once Darvish signs it will mean Fielder has to either go to Seattle and play for a crap team or Boras will tell Ted to pony up or he'll take Harper away from him. And then Zimmerman will go. And Morse. And the Nats will have Werth manfully stumbling around center on his ancient legs and Fielder at the buffet hoping they bring the DH into the National League.

He did not let his worries about Rizzo's obvious incompetence to interfere with his new approach to work. He was approaching the point where he might be like Zainab, a bit bored and looking for a few extra claims. In fact, like most insurance offices, they were actually staffed for busy times like January, but once the month was over, they would actually be over-staffed. He knew that from past experience. In summer he could only hope the Nats would remain interesting into August or even September just to relieve the boredom. He had hardly passed much work to Bert and Michele in the summer. Well, until last summer.

Expecting the Nats to be interesting in the summer was a bit optimistic. They were usually out of the pennant race fairly early in April. It was almost a point of principle to lose twenty in April, including nine each to Florida and Philadelphia. Atlanta must hate the Nationals. They actually played decent baseball against the Braves, just rolled over for the two teams he hated most in the world. After the Red Sox. And Yankees.

Had lunch with Zainab, or she had coffee while he ate a sandwich. She tended to bring something from home. They talk about the movies he had seen. She had seen the Swedish version of all three films about the Girl with the Dragon Tattoo, said she couldn't be bothered with the Hollywood version. She would lend him the DVDs. He made a remark about Hollywood rubbish and mentioned Scorsese but she defended him. Told him a story that she had heard on the radio in England. Apparently some young student who went on to work for the BBC met him and happened to be carrying a folder so he told Scorsese he had written his thesis on his films and would he mind just looking thought it, handing him the folder with about 100 pages in it. Thought Scorsese might be embarrassed or rude or just plain angry. But he was wrong. Right there Scorsese took out his glasses and asked to see it. Real nice guy. Humble, polite, gentle. All the things Peter wouldn't have expected. Shit. Another myth destroyed. He hated that. Part of the reason he had hated Scorsese was that he received so much praise so he assumed he was arrogant, and now this. He told Zainab about his disappointment. She had burst out laughing and said that might be the best thing she heard all year. Then she smiled and asked him if he was feeling better. Put her hand on his arm. He said yes. But it wasn't really true.

He couldn't kid himself. He may be feeling a little better because the work was caught up, but when he thought about it, the reason he caught up so quickly was simply because it was such trivial work in the first place. No wonder Bert and Michele seemed so quick. They probably found it challenging. The most exciting part of their trivial days. Sadly, it was also the most exciting part of his. Now. Fucking Frank. Maybe he would try the kids again tonight. No, maybe tomorrow.

*

Baseball news was all Hall of Fame. Good for Barry Larkin, but really, Hall of Fame? Sure based on the players who regularly got in, but was he really up there with Honus Wagner and Ripken. Baseball needed more heroes than Matthewson, Ruth and Wagner, of course, and had to honor the best players if only for the fans. Maybe they should have a real Hall of Fame and a Hall of Pretty Damn Good. The Rock would make that one. Easy. And El Presidente. What a pitcher.

So the Hall is decided, back to signing players. Kilgore is great, nice thing about Lannan. Hope he sent a copy to Rizzo. Comes about two hundred mill cheaper than Prince and eats less, Mike, give it some thought. Then maybe you could get a bench player or two and, oh yeah, did you know you needed a center fielder? Not that two hundred mill gets you much anymore, maybe four or five years of Albert and a Zimmer frame for the last years of the contract.

Finished Tinker Tailor and moved on to The Girl with the Dragon Tattoo. Reading wasn't so bad. Have to drop in the library on the way home from work tomorrow, maybe finish the trilogy. Maybe more Le Carre.

*

When he got to work he asked Zainab for coffee just so he could ask her if she liked Le Carre's books. She had read quite a few. The whole Smiley series. She said he was one of her favorites and talked about the British Man-Booker prize for which he never even seem to get a nomination. She said it was almost as if they preferred to search around for more obscure writers but two years ago it had been awarded for a wonderful book by Mickey Mantle or something. He pretended to be interested but literature was not high on his list of likes. Good stories maybe, but not real books. They would be boring. He was glad she liked Tinker Tailor, though.

Stuart talked to him. Said there were going to be a few changes in the office. He was talking to everyone. Nothing too worrying, he said, but some re-organization. Said he was likely moving to group insurance himself. That was a bit of a surprise, Stuart had been here for some time and Peter was sort of used to him. So it did make him a bit nervous. He could see that there was a lot of talking going on as Stuart spoke to individuals and small groups. He tried to speak to Zainab, but she just shrugged. Said it could hardly affect her.

He was bored enough to follow the Schoenfield chat in the afternoon. Too much PEDs and Hall of Fame shit. Poor old Tim Raines, but he would get in eventually. Peter found the Hall of Fame boring but still pulled for Raines. Maybe his all time favorite. Him and El Presidente.

God, a two year extension for Selig. Whatever happened to the concept of a commissioner who protected the interests of the game? Not the interests of the owners bank accounts. Slow the game down for commercials, play the World Series late at night to exclude the kids, move a franchise as soon as it struggles; close it down if we can. Why not have a four team league: Red Sox, Yankees, Dodgers and his fucking Brewers. Then he would get into meaningful revenue sharing. The sooner government killed the monopoly, the better. Maybe throw Bud in prison for a decade or so. So he got buggered the way he buggered the Expos. Prick.

*

Tell you what; Fanning would have never gone after Fielder. Too much dignity to chase around after Boras. Anyway, he would have kept the kids and maybe signed Crisp and then extended his good players. Or worked out that one alternative to Fielder would have been Darvish, a strong bench, an improved pen, a center fielder, umpteen extensions and still have maybe 100 mill to play with. Maybe more if you think of the money saved on the buffet. Still, the Fielder talk was cooling a bit. Meant nothing until a contract was announced. Boras is such a devious bastard. Everyone says he is brilliant but no one examines the obvious alternative theory. He is a fucking moron but still considerably smarter than the assholes he deals with.

He stopped in a bar on the way home. Couldn't remember where. Then The Junction. Did he eat? Maybe. Message through the door. You really must call Cheryl. I have tried to reach you all night. Do you ever turn your cell phone on?

From Marianne. Wonder what's up with Cheryl. Maybe call tomorrow. Too late tonight.

*

Peter was awake very early. Lay there confused. He regretted last night, but really, what was he supposed to do? Work, come home. Read. Maybe watch a DVD. When he applied himself at work, it was easy enough and he took real pride in his ability to clear his backlog and be right on top of things. But the satisfaction faded and he realized just what a trivial job it was. Oh sure, families relying on him. Company policy to deal with it quickly. What did he really care? On an intellectual level, not much. On an emotional level, not at all. And the work itself took all the intelligence of a high school dropout. So, he was left with a tedious job, an empty home life and very few interests.

He didn't even enjoy drinking. He went into bars out of boredom and stayed because of inertia. He hated the sort of people who hung around in bars. Like him. He was beginning to have reservations about the Nationals, for Christ sake. Rizzo did nothing. No center fielder. No bench. Just talk about spending money so they could be one of the big boys. Like the Red Sox. Who the fuck wanted to be like the fucking Red Sox. Well, the Chicago Cubs, it would seem, but there you go. Another big market, small minds, crap team sort of situation. He rolled over in the bed. Felt sick. Got up. Lay down. Got up and puked in the toilet. Lay down. Rolled over. Christ, he was late.

When he got to work there was a buzz in the office about the supposed changes. Big re-organization. Oh, sure. Insurance was like that. Radical stuff. Move the claimant signature from the left to the right of the claims form, maybe. Some of the worst minds in the universe were attracted to insurance. Apparently the latest massive change involved transferring Stuart out of his role as a supervisor to new challenges in group insurance. Group underwriting. Poor old Stuart. What a way to describe a lateral shift. Or a demotion. They use to call the Group Insurance General Office, Grope Central because it was full of young women most of whom were married within a year of their arrival. Working in group insurance could make anything and anybody look good. If it got you out. He envied them their escape.

Claims was to be divided into small, manageable teams of four or five, each with a team leader who would work right along with his or her team. No full time supervisor. Real boss would be up the famous corridor of smart suits. General Insurance Central and Charlie whatever in the big office looking out. Over them. Seems Stuart was rumbled. Supervising bored adults as a full time job must be as useless as jobs get. So now claims would come down in neat little batches with each team being asked to take its share. In other words, there would be a nice little competitive atmosphere in which each team would hate the other teams and hate anyone in their own team that did not cut the mustard. Everyone was, of course, wondering who the team leaders would be. Bert was strutting, so he obviously felt he was one of the chosen. Michele was silent, so she was hoping. Zainab was indifferent. She knew damn well she would not be considered. Maybe if she changed her name to Marjorie. There was really only one less likely candidate, of course, and that was him.

Please god; don't put in a team led by Bert or Michele. Trouble with god is that, although he did not exist, he somehow contrived to be malignant. That was remarkable. Maybe a miracle. Another miracle and does he get to be a saint? Saint God, the Malignant.

And what did the Nationals do to alleviate god's divine intervention to make him even more miserable? Step up their pursuit of the world's biggest vegetarian. Now the talk was that Boras had screwed up. Madson settled for one year, Jackson facing the fact that he is not left-handed and Fielder lacking suitors. Great to see Boras take a few hits. Jackson signs with Houston for a year and Prince goes to Japan, maybe. Or Korea. Korea, that would be good. South Korea, mind you. Nothing against Prince. Just not a fit in Washington. Rice and fish might sort out the weight thing. Won't happen, of course. Owners are meeting today probably devote several hours in trying to bale Scott out.

Some awful articles about all that Selig has done for baseball. Makes you go weak at the knees. God, things were slow. Headline news; Cespedes is going to play in the Dominican Republic for a week. Wow. Loria and Samson want him. Well, good luck. We'll settle for Soler. Dierkes chat was boring. The office was all boring talk about the re-organization. The claims were beginning to mount up again. Shit. Zainab came over, had two books to lend him. One by Hilary Mantel called Wolf Hall. Not Mickey, apparently. Wasn't that the book he bought Marianne for Christmas? Isn't that the book everybody gave Marianne at Christmas? Zainab says it was one of the few prize winners that deserved a prize. And a Le Carre about gardening. Not really, but it amused her when he asked if it was. He liked Zainab. Hoped the re-organization didn't hurt her. No one was saying, but the plan must be to cut back. New, lean approach. Shit. Should make all the difference to premiums if they could fire two people from claims. Give them that competitive edge. Some asshole somewhere in a private office thinking up new and better ways to screw the employees.

By the time he got home it was too late to phone Cheryl. The note was still sitting on the table with the remains of the breakfast he hadn't eaten. Too late to eat. God, where those books. He hoped he had left them in the office. Zainab was so thoughtful.

*

Mornings were awful. Days were pretty bad too, of course, but mornings were particularly awful. Maybe it was not just the headache and the puking; maybe it was knowing that it would be followed by another day in the office. Obsessive re-organization blues. They should get a life. Mind you, no one had less of a life than him. Maybe he should get involved in all the gossip. Take his mind off Rizzo doing nothing.

At least he got to the office on time. No way he was going to get much done, but at least he was there. And so were Zainab's books. Right on the desk. He went straight over, told her he had an appointment after work so he left them until today. Stuart came over. Asked to see him in his office. His cubicle. Glass partitions that didn't even go to the ceiling. Now demoted to new challenges. Poor bastard.

Could be worse. Stuart had explained that his desire for independence had led them to believe he would not really be interested in team leadership. In other words, his record for doing squat and arriving hung over made it a certainty that he was never considered. They had mistaken his contempt for independence. Still, Stuart had been pleasant. Said there was a new guy coming in from underwriting to be one of the supervisors. Young guy, on the way up but he felt Peter might prefer working with him than having one of his present colleagues promoted over him. Actually, that was not true. Much as he hated Bert and Michele, and probably anyone else who was made a team leader, the potential for hating some new young hotshot was pretty great. So what? What difference? Maybe Zainab would be in his team.

Shit, Law was back. Discussed cooking and his own humility and family values and why he would not answer questions on prospects or why he did not get the job in Houston. Turns out that all that kept him from turning the Astros into champions was the great love of his readers and his family. Sweet. Such a sweet sentimental guy. Boring as shit today. At least he has no time for the Hall.

Got through exactly zero claims today. Tied the record. Must try to do better or he would be back to the old days and that was worse. Remembered his books. Bought dinner and cooked it. No wine even. Settled in and read The Girl with the Dragon Tattoo. Not sure he was enjoying it but still couldn't put it down. Damndest thing. Must be better than it seems.

Woke with a start. He was still on the couch; the finished book was on the floor beside him. Six o'clock. No headache. Maybe reading was better than beer. Seems unlikely, but, what the hell, it worked last night. It was Friday again. He would attack the other two Dragon Tattoo books this weekend. He would clear the new backlog at work today. He would phone Cheryl tonight. Maybe Barney. Maybe leave Barney until Sunday. Maybe there was some orange juice in the fridge.

*

When he got to work, he quickly checked his email. I hope you have contacted Cheryl. Well, he had tried. Best not to upset Marianne. He didn't want the hassle. Sure, did it after your note. Must remember to do it tonight. Not really a lie, that. He had more or less contacted her. Just not got through.

The new guy was in today. Just to be introduced around the office by Stuart. You could see Stuart was embarrassed. Just a kid. Call me Chet. Chet, for Christ's sake. Yeah, sure thing Chet and you can call me Petey. Asshole. Must be almost old enough to shave. Looked about eighteen. Blond and blue-eyed. Of course. Hair was receding, poor bastard. Smiled at Peter and said he had heard a lot about him. I'll bet, he was, after all, a great hero in the office. The Albert Pujols of claims. I have heard about you. I'll bet you say that to all the boys. Jesus, don't let him be my team leader.

But it wasn't to be. Or was to be. Stuart spoke to him shortly after lunch. Thought I'd put you in Chet's team. Might be the best thing, new start and all that. God, he'd been here since god was a boy. New start. Horseshit. No one else would have him. He knew what went through their minds. Michele and Bert and people like that. Well, he would be fine with the blond whiz kid from underwriting. He was starting in February. Typical insurance company shit, couldn't start in the middle of the month, how on earth would we do the accounting for that? Yes, of course just divide the days, but there are weekends and remember January 2nd was a holiday and; oh my, oh my. The only jerks bigger than insurance jerks were accounting jerks and accountants in insurance? Well.

There was nothing to do but work. Seven Nats filed for arbitration. Count them, Mike. While you're pissing about pretending not to be trying to sign Fielder, your team is getting antsy. Just because you win your arbitration cases doesn't make it smart to push it. Maybe, just maybe, guys like Lannan and Zimmermann might like to feel wanted. Like maybe it was important to offer them a decent contract before it came to this. Ever hear of extension. They work like this. You fucking well forget thirteen year contracts to fat hitters who can't field for shit, and concentrate on the decent players you have under contract right now. Called management, as opposed to panic buying. Or not buying if Boras gets him a penny more in Texas. Come on Yu, you'd love Japan. Texas is the perfect fit for Fielder, practically the same size. No place for a vegetarian, Prince. Maybe try Seattle. West coast. Into bean sprouts and other shit like that out there. It's treason to be a vegetarian in Texas.

Arbitration was about as bad as baseball stories got. Jesus Flores asks for 715 000 but is offered 695 000. Everyone knows they'll argue until the night before then settle for 706 000. Just over half way, great victory for Jesus. Meanwhile Boras is asking 200 mill for Fielder and the Lerners are saying maybe do it for 199 and a bit and maybe a ride in our private jet and dinner at the restaurant of his choice if he wins the MVP. Enough to make you a communist. Maybe not. Maybe Jesus can get by on 700 000 and change.

Stayed half an hour late just to clear the backlog. Not all of it, just the electronic backlog. Paper backlog was peanuts. Easily cope on Monday. Won't stop for a drink. Steak and salad and then Stieg. Maybe a glass of wine. Maybe a bottle.

Checked the computer. Another email from Marianne. Please get in touch. Poor Cheryl. Must telephone tomorrow. His cell was off. Again. He had been enjoying the book and had not thought too much about calling Marianne. Oh, well. Too late now. Maybe just check the baseball before bed.

Christ all fucking mighty. Cherington is dead in the water. Cashman's a cruel bastard. All winter articles about how he was being conservative. No big deals. Now this. Well, that's his rotation sorted out. He gets Pineda and Kuroda. Cherington gets Padilla and Aaron Cook. Way to go Ben. Bobby will have something to say about this. Maybe at your leaving party. Maybe Jack Zduriencik can take over because he sure as hell won't have a job next year. Pitcher like Pineda for a would be Prince Fielder. Stomach and a bat. DH in the making. If he hits. Christ, Prince isn't going to Seattle. Who's left? Go home, Yu, you'd hate Texas. Fucking shit-hole.

In the morning he decided to finish his book before phoning Cheryl. Left the cell off. Another message from Marianne. Ring me. Maybe after Cheryl. Shame to mess up his reading now that he was beginning to enjoy it. It was not as if the family gave a shit about him. This book was not as good as the first but it had the same effect. Hard to put down. Frenzied pace that makes you want to read it at a frenzied pace. Peter thought it might not stand up to a close textual analysis. Peter knew he certainly wouldn't stand up to close textual analysis.

When he finally put the book down it was past noon, so he went out to get something to eat. Stopped in at The Junction. It was a comfortable place to spend an afternoon. Even with football on the television. Forty-niners seemed to be in control when he left. Big deal. He used to like Joe Montana but those days were long gone.

It was a nice day so he took the long way home. He was planning to attack the third Dragon Tattoo book later. He would have dinner at home; he had had enough to drink. Tried Cheryl's number when he got in but there was no answer. Marianne kept telling him to telephone but nobody ever answered. Not his fault.

He read for a few hours before he cooked dinner. Same frenzied pace. Becoming tiresome after two full books. Maybe he should have read something in between but despite beginning to find the pace annoying, he also found it hard to stop reading. Even when Stieg went into list note mode, he found himself pushing on. He finally noticed he was hungry and stopped to heat some soup and cut some bread. While he was waiting he made another try to get through to Cheryl. Arnie answered and he asked to speak to Cheryl.

Is that you Peter?

Yes, how are you Arnie, great to talk to you. I was hoping to speak to Cheryl. Is she there? If she's already in bed, don't worry, I can call tomorrow.

Fuck off, Peter. And Arnie banged the phone down.

Shit, what was he supposed to make of that. Rude bastard. Fuck it. He checked the computer. Red Sox still madly pursing superstar Padilla. Rizzo still doing sweet nothing. Still talk about Fielder. And more talk. At least Texas was getting mentioned again. Maybe Daniels will feel it necessary to counter Pujols and Wilson with Fielder and Darvish. Great if Boras takes a hit, but doubtful. As the price goes down, more teams get interested and once they start thinking about having a monster in the line-up, they bid higher again. Boras doesn't have to be smart this time. Maybe with Jackson but Fielder can hit and the GMs will fall into his honey trap. Just don't let it be Rizzo. Hey Mike, ever think of signing Oswalt on the cheap and flipping Wang? And did I ever mention center field?

He cleaned the soup off the stove where it had boiled over. Fuck it, have a cheese sandwich and a glass of red. He took his book and retired to the couch. Finished it at three and decided to stay there.

*

He awoke to the sound of his telephone. Shit, must have left it on after his call to Arnie. He waited for it to stop then checked to find he had missed Marianne. At least this time he had the phone on, so she couldn't complain it was always turned off. Maybe call after coffee. But there was no coffee. He had to go out. So he stopped for coffee. Globe and then coffee and a pastry. Some nice little coffee shops around. Read Cafardo. Like he thought, price going down on Oswalt. Wake up Mike. Cafardo didn't give Cherington a bad time over the jump the Yankees had got on him. Honeymoon still on, Ben, lucky you. He liked Cafardo. Stuck to baseball. No recipes. Like Kilgore.

When he got home he saw his cell. Still on. Three more missed calls. Better phone Marianne. Make it clear he tried to talk to Cheryl last night. Arnie was just a jerk. He tried her cell but it was off, so he tried the house. Frank answered and he asked for Marianne.

That you, Peter? How are you? I tried to get in touch. You know, maybe we should try to meet up today. Marianne's with Cheryl. She'll stay until she is out of hospital now. I feel so badly. I'm so sorry. I'm sure everything will turn out.

Peter did not know what to say. He could hardly admit that he didn't know Cheryl was in hospital because he had already told Marianne he had phoned. Neglecting to say that there had been no connection. He stalled by agreeing to meet Frank for coffee in an hour. Fucking Frank. What was he thinking?

It was an informative hour with Frank. Rich bastard. The only reason they were living where they were was because of Marianne's practice. But he hated to sell the house in Beacon Hill, he had so many memories. Poor sentimental bastard. All those memories, all that money. And Marianne. No wonder he could pretend to be nice to Peter. Nice in a condescending way, of course. Peter must be so upset but hopefully Cheryl would be fine. Shame she lost the baby. Shame she will never be able to have another. Good old Frank was full of sympathy. He had two grown up children and three grandchildren. Light of his life. Presumably after Marianne. So he has the whole deal and decides: why not take Peter's wife to complete my happiness? How nice for him. Fucking Frank. Selfish bastard. Met Marianne at the ballet. She was on her own and so was he. Wife died, you see. Who could fucking well blame her, you shithead?

So there you have it, rich and handsome Frank, thriving lawyer and all round saint, decides to rescue Marianne from life with a boring insurance adjustor. Sweet. Was Peter supposed to be grateful he got the car? They still had two cars plus two houses. And two very lucrative jobs. Oh yeah, and three grandchildren and now Cheryl can't have any. God knows Barney shouldn't. Not with that bitch Bobbie. Poor Cheryl. Should maybe try to call again. Or even call Marianne. First he needed a drink.

Got home late. He should have eaten something. Stomach was awful. Maybe he should learn from this. Eat something before you drink yourself into a stupor.

Too late to telephone anyone. Turned on the computer. Maybe an email. Started, stopped, started again. Tried to express how he was sorry. Stopped. Mentioned coffee with Frank. Stopped. Tried to explain how he had not realized how serious it was. Stopped. Erased the lot and just asked if everything was fine. Over to baseball.

Chuckled to himself. So Mike was making sure Gio was going to be there forever to remind us the Nats once had a pitcher called Brad Peacock. And Cole and Milone. And Norris could be good. So Rizzo had to make people think Gonzalez is so good that we give him this huge contract. While we wait for Fielder to go to Texas and do nothing about center field. Please, Prince, you'd love Texas. Six arbitration cases and the one we settle amicably is the one guy who has yet to do us any bloody good. What about Clippard? Zimmermann? Oh, shit, why bother?

And Cherington is talking to Oswalt. I'll bet he is. Never mind, Ben, you still look good on Vincente. Poor bastard. Cashman eating him alive.

*

He arrived late in the morning. Monday morning. Bad start to the week. He was still determined to clear the backlog. But, of course, when he got to the office it was closed. Public holiday. Another long weekend. Was there no end of the damn things? He was almost grateful that he had not realized. Killing Monday would probably be easy enough but facing a long weekend on Friday would have depressed him. Wandered across the Common. It was a lovely day. It cleared his head so he headed over to the Paramount for a late breakfast. Feeling better, he decided to be a bit domesticated, do a wash, maybe iron a few things.

Boring but better than claims. Better than doing nothing. Maybe start one of Zainab's books. Or maybe one of the ones he got for Christmas. Actually the only one he got for Christmas. Except he got three copies. About a shortstop who was sort of like Chip Hilton, only short. Chip Hilton was tall. God, how long ago was that? Chip fucking Hilton. Before he went into maid mode he opened the computer. Message from Marianne. Said that of course things aren't bloody well fine. What's upset her? That was so like her. He gets in touch, emails, tries to phone, spends time with her asshole lover and she thinks she is the one who should express irritation. Fuck it.

Arbitration Monday. Surely even Rizzo could rustle up a little action today. Other than his new favorite, there were still five to go. Zinmmermann was as important as Gio, for Christ's sake. What was the man thinking? His new hero really is so important and guys like Zimmermann get pushed aside. Not to mention Zimmerman who gets to wait outside his office while he talks to Boras about feeding Fielder. Just a moment, Ryan, I'll see what Scott has to say. Says why should we pay you the big bucks when we have guys like Werth around needing money? Sorry.

He thought of trying Marianne's cell. Why bother? She was bonding with Cheryl. She'd enjoy being the caring mother. The pair of them probably sitting there talking about what an uncaring father he is. While Marianne sends nasty emails and Arnie hangs up on him. Sure, he's a real bastard. Probably caused the miscarriage in the first place. Maybe the Iraq War as well. Arnie would likely turn up at the hospital with coffee and a bunch of flowers. Probably Starbuck's coffee. Fucking Philistine.

*

The book was called The Art of Fielding. Too close to Art of Fielder to suit him. As if Fielder was an artist. Of course, he hardly pretended to be. He was a hitter who ate a lot. Unless you listened to Boras. Then he was sort of a Lou Gehrig guy with more power. Hardly need Espinosa; Prince would cover the whole right side. Marvelous player. Just like Chip Hilton, only shorter. Of course, Clair Bee was a basketball coach, bound to write them tall. Maybe Boras should write fiction. Maybe Boras should admit that what he writes is fiction.

Tried one of Zainab's books. Fuck the washing. Fell asleep, thank god, passed the afternoon. Checked the computer. Fucking Rizzo. Struck a deal with Jesus Flores. Jesus, what a prick. Gorzelanny will be next. Get the big ones sorted, Mike, the little ones like Zimmermann and Morse will look after themselves. Clair fucking Bee couldn't have written someone as stupid as Rizzo.

There was no food in the house so he went out to get drunk. No pretence. He was pissed off at Marianne. Pissed off at Cheryl. Pissed off at Arnie. Pissed off at Rizzo. And fucking Barney and Bobbie. Sounded like the Bobbsey twins those two. Bobbie and Barney Bobbsey get drunk. Great title for a book. Better than The Art of Fielder. Maybe he shouldn't be so pissed off at Cheryl. What with the miscarriage. Not her fault.

*

God, he felt awful in the morning. Late again. Well, not really, again, yesterday could hardly count. And now Stuart was looking at him. So he was a bit late. He could make up those two hours easy. Shit, why couldn't he just get on with his life? People always watching or criticizing. Like Stuart. And Marianne. And fucking Arnie. Probably Frank as well, only he hid it with all that condescending bullshit about hoping things were sorting themselves out for him. Sure, nothing like living in a basement, being alone and drunk and having a shit job to help you get your life into perspective. Thanks for asking, Frank. You asshole.

He started well, lasted about an hour and was bored to the point of suicide. What a job. Do nothing and it was awful. Work hard and it was awful. And Rizzo doing nothing about center field, nothing about the good solid guys he had eligible for arbitration, and spends his time offering whatever may be left of his budget to a guy that already cost him his best prospects. Trying to save face, that's all. Dumb bastard. And still chasing Prince. Wasn't for Cherington and Zduriencik, Rizzo would be the dumbest guy in baseball. Hanging around waiting for Boras to tell him if he has been chosen. Again. Tell you what Mike; let Scott run the team, you go back to scouting. He went for coffee. Took an hour. Stuart was watching when he returned. Came over to say he was trying but Peter had to try too. What the fuck was that supposed to mean. Well, it was obvious really; Stuart got screwed and now was being asked to help screw those left behind. He sighed, turned to his computer. Really, he was hardly even behind. Make it up by the weekend easy.

Kilgore had a decent piece on Jordan Zimmermann in the Post. He should run the team. Tons smarter than Rizzo. Lock him up, Mike, me and Adam agree. And Ladson had a question about Zimmerman. Same answer. Lock him up, Mike. Christ, those two guys would change their name. Or at least spell them the same. Like the team did when Zimmermann first came up. Spelled his name wrong but it was no big deal because they spelled Nationals wrong as well.

Assholes. No wonder they were a crap team. Bowden days, those. Depressing. Not like now with Rizzo chasing his tail over Boras and Fielder. Pains in the ass. Point is, Rizzo should stop worrying about Boras and Fielder and start worrying about signing the real Nats. Sign them both for five, six years.

He moved over to his email account. He seldom checked it because he seldom used it and he hated email. But it beat working and the Schoenfield chat hadn't started yet. There was a message from Marianne. No apology for the last one. But it was a bit upsetting. Said that Cheryl was out of danger. Arnie had been wonderful with her and with Marianne and even though they had lost the baby, Arnie and Cheryl seemed closer than ever. Of course, she was still very weak after losing so much blood, but the doctor said she would soon be home and home was the best place for her. Arnie was back at work because Marianne was there but would take another week off when Marianne left, so she would probably be able to get back Sunday. Arnie said once Cheryl was well he would start talking up adoption if he thought it was appropriate. She had so wanted the baby.

Sounds like it was pretty bad. Christ. Frank had sort of hinted, of course. So now he was the villain again. And Arnie was Mr. Wonderful. Another week off, wow, must have been bad. And going on for over two weeks now. Pity he hadn't got through. They'd blame him for that, as well. Still, he was glad things were better. Maybe he should still call. No hurry, Cheryl was in hospital now. No sense talking to Arnie the hero. He may be a hero, but he was still a jerk.

Email spoiled his afternoon. Funny how these things get to you. He decided to concentrate on work and leave the baseball until he got home. Get a take-out meal and have a few beers with the computer.

*

By the time he was ready to go to bed he felt much better. The important thing was not to let things get you down and to concentrate on the positives. Rizzo had avoided arbitration with Clippard and Zimmermann. And Flores, of course. Left Lannan, but they were close. No problem there and Lannan was not going to get an extension. No way does Rizzo do an extension with someone who pitches to contact. And that leaves the Morse/Fielder/LaRoche maze. When he thought about it yesterday he thought they should extend Morse, but looking at it tonight his head was clearer. He felt he could see daylight. Now if only Rizzo could.

Simple really. Rizzo didn't mind being used by Boras, so nothing happens until Darvish is signed. Then Texas gets an erection and gets hot over a fat DH who they met in a restaurant this week. So they even know how much he eats and still they are interested. Good sign. If they bought the guy dinner, they have a huge financial investment already. Once Prince is safe in Texas, Scott tells Mike it is okay to get on with his other job and so he starts to think about locking up Morse because now it does not affect Boras and Fielder in Texas. Then he still looks at center field where Marlon Byrd must still be available because, great news, Theo wants Cespedes. Not realizing that he is a corner outfielder, maybe not caring. Maybe Rizzo might even get someone for the bench. He went to bed and slept better than he had for ages. Things were looking up.

*

By noon the next day he had completely cleared his desk and his computer of claims. Ready for an afternoon chat, but no one was chatting today as far as he knew. The drama centered on Darvish. Still a lot of writers thinking once the Rangers sign Darvish; they will fold their tents on Fielder but a few still thinking that once Darvish is done, they will throw their energy into Fielder negotiations. Their money as well. Well, let's hope so. Also give them an excuse not to sign Hamilton. Great player but made almost entirely of glass. Unlikely to last a season let alone a five, maybe six year contract. Still, he is a center fielder, if Prince feels strongly about playing for a team that has one; it's Texas over the Nats.

Chet dropped into the office in the afternoon. All blond smiles. Marianne would have loved those teeth. Only thing was, why didn't the son of a bitch keep them in his mouth. He was going to be a team leader, not Republican presidential candidate. Mind you, why not? I mean, he was as good as any and better than most. Bert was all over him. They had lunch together. Probably bean sprouts and herb tea. Not Michele. How about that. Maybe Michele didn't get to be a team leader. Ah, the price one pays for having a vagina.

Chet came over, suggested maybe they should have lunch together. He was hoping to meet all his team individually and then maybe all together before February. Well, gee, isn't that the greatest. Chet you're just such a manager. Such a leader. Makes your palms go a bit sweaty. Asshole. Then he said that he had already had lunch with Bert and was scheduled to meet the new girl, Rhonda, next week. New girl? Bert? Rhonda was probably in her early eighties. Why were women in desk jobs called girls? Maybe he should call himself a boy. More likely to call Chet a boy? Looked about ten. All those fucking teeth. God, and Bert was in the team. Some team. New girl, Chet the teeth, Bert and him. Hope the new girl is good. Hope the new woman is good. Why not Zainab? Sure Chet, let's do lunch.

Talked to Stuart, mentioned Bert to him and said he was surprised he wasn't a team leader. Stuart just looked at him. What? Bert? Then he said a funny thing: Peter, you watch those guys. Bert is a nasty piece of goods and I am just not sure about Chet. Smiles too much for me. You be careful. Hey, you'll like Rhonda, she's something.

By the time he got home Darvish was a Texas Ranger. Great news, we can forget the Rangers and look for a center fielder and a bat off the bench. Zuckerman didn't quite come out and say it, but his review of the off season suggested that Rizzo should maybe get off his cell phone to Boras and do some of the things he promised. Strengthen the bench and all we get is DeRosa; sign a free agent pitcher, well, not quite, one we got cost the entire farm system; trade for a center fielder, sorry the trade chips are already out on the coast. Still, if Texas can sign Fielder soon, Rizzo might be able to concentrate on his job. Make a nice change. Writers keep going on about the off season being all day every day. Bullshit. Just watch kids with their cell phones. Addiction. GMs must be like that, addicted to phoning around their friends hoping a center fielder will fall out of the sky. Like shopping online. Bet Mike's checked out eBay. Hey, never mind, he's talking extension with Zimmerman again. Guy to extend is Morse; that would end this Fielder shit.

*

Friday, last day of the week. That meant a weekend coming up, but maybe a bit hopeful. Maybe Texas would do Fielder, end all the talk. Should really make a call to Cheryl or Marianne. Or even Arnie. Still, he had the email, so he knew Cheryl was getting better and getting hold of someone would be difficult. What with them being in the hospital where they must be asked to turn off the phones. And Arnie would likely be manning the landline. Asshole.

He was totally caught up with his work and needed something to occupy him until Law came on. Talked to Zainab briefly, said he was surprised about Bert not being a team leader. Surprised? Bert? He must be the least suitable. She said she had been really pleased and flattered to be asked and was just sorry Peter wasn't in her team.

You're going to be a team leader?

Didn't you know? Michele, Alice, Chet and I.

Alice was a really quiet woman. Kept to herself at the other end of the office behind a plant. Not a real plant; plastic for Christ sake. Team leader? And three out of four were women. Zainab said that Stuart had made very strong recommendations for her and Alice. When Stuart had talked to Zainab he told her he saw it as a different sort of supervision. They would all know the job. It was hardly complicated; the company was looking for leadership by example. Zainab said that Chet seemed the odd one out and she had the feeling that Stuart was beginning to think it was a poor choice. Always grinning but not sincere. Peter winced. Nice teeth, though.

Law had little to say beyond trashing a few restaurants and reiterating that he was a good cook. He went home with a restless feeling. Tried to read the Chip Hilton thing about the shortstop who was short. Supposed to be popular but it was a little too high school miracle for Peter who turned to Le Carre. At least it was a real book, not a romance magazine story. Checked the computer before bed. Marianne emailed to say how angry she was that he had not contacted Cheryl. He emailed back, angrily, regretted, composed an apology, erased it, decided to phone, checked the time, decided to phone tomorrow, checked baseball.

Kilgore was good and Kilgore thought Nats were the favorite for Fielder. Again. Maybe it won't happen. Trouble with the Nats, other than center field, was they had six number eight hitters. Good ones, like Espinosa and Desmond, but still, bottom of the order guys. They needed a leadoff hitter and a number two. Nice little thing on Lombardozzi today but he was obviously not a hot prospect in Rizzo's eyes. Everything you read said the same damn thing, weak tools, great attitude. Mike, look at Jamey Carroll, get Lombardozzi onto your bench and then give him a try. Better chance than Desmond to become a leadoff hitter. Assume you don't turn Fielder into a center fielder batting leadoff. That might work. As well as having him come up over six hundred times with the bases empty. Better go to bed, Rizzo was really getting him down. One good thing, Fielder was no fool. He would look at the Nats, and then look at Texas and think maybe, just maybe, Texas is a better possibility. Short fence; Kinsler, Andrus and Hamilton in front of him; good pitching; good GM; good restaurants; good crowds; more good restaurants. That lulled him to sleep.

*

Friday again. Another weekend coming up. Decided it was better to phone Cheryl on the weekend. Give him something to do. Not that there was much to do at work except wait for the weekend when there would be nothing to do.

137

That was the trouble with taking the work seriously. There was nothing to it so if you worked hard you finished quickly and had nothing left to do. It was more challenging to do nothing at all and pass the work along. If he remembered correctly, that was one of the reasons he started passing work on. That and the fact that Bert and Michele pissed him off. Thought they were so clever because they could piss through work fit for a grade school dropout. At least Bert would not be a supervisor. But he would be in the same team. And Chet. What a fucking name.

There was a note from Chet. Lunch Tuesday? So he sent a note back. Great. Not that it was great, or good, or even mediocre. It was crap, Chet playing the up and coming executive. Sent over from underwriting to get some experience in claims. Then maybe group insurance before a spell as vice-president. Of what? Maybe smiling when you don't mean it. Well, it was a free lunch. No such thing as a free lunch, though. Anyway, he hardly ever ate lunch. All he really ever did at lunch was try to avoid beer.

One thing about the this part of the offseason, it was so boring that he hardly bothered sneaking looks at what was happening during the day. He would do in Spring Training again. Right now he was happy to avoid it. With Darvish safely in Texas, there was nothing but Prince Fielder speculation. Boring. Like claims. Pass the claims to Bert. Pass the fat first baseman to Texas. Pass the farm to Billy Beane. Shit, roll on five o'clock. No way he would avoid the bar tonight. If he got drunk enough, he might not wake up until it was time to go out for a drink tomorrow. Hang on; he was trying to cut back. But Rizzo could drive a good man to drink.

By the time Peter got home he was almost forgot to turn on the computer. He had started in the Bistro but forgot most of the other stops. Probably The Junction at the end. Couldn't imagine passing it by. Even in his state. So Mike signed Mike for two years. Big deal. The guy was paralyzed. Wetting himself so bad over Fielder that he can't think straight. So Morse gets two years. Just in case Prince can't find a job in Texas. Piece by Verducci says it all. Fielder is perfect for Texas once he learns to eat steers again; small park, all the amenities like leadoff hitters, DH on the days when he has an upset tummy. Man, it's perfect. But Boras is still messing around hoping they will increase the offer from 300 million to 300 million and six bits. And there's Mike with the six bits that Ted Lerner just gave him. Probably lent him. Maybe he should have a beer before bed.

*

It worked. He did not wake up until after noon. And there was enough bread for toast and enough coffee as well. Maybe it would be a better day. Sun looked like it was out. Didn't look too closely. Not yet. Give his eyes a break. Should phone Cheryl. No, better to phone on Sunday. More of a family day. Best to go out. Walk a bit. Maybe go to the Library before he had a drink. He had given up on the Chip Hilton thing and the novel Zainab had given him looked formidable.

He decided to stop for a drink on the way to the library, let the air warm up for his walk. But by the time he left the bar the sun was sinking and so he decided to go home and lie down. There was no sleeping, though, even if he was tired. How could he be tired? He had just got up. Wolf Hall was far too difficult to read. Saturday and Rizzo was having the afternoon off, again. There is the bench to think about, Mike. Still have a nice weekend with the family. Maybe watch a film together. Nice. Must remember to phone Cheryl. Maybe try Barney as well. See how Cheryl goes first.

Something must have happened because he opened his eyes and it was very dark. Checked his watch. Not too late for a drink. Should get something to eat as well. He was losing weight. Not that he had much to lose. Soon disappear. Maybe buy a new belt. Someday. Still nothing from Rizzo. Even Cherington was doing a few things. Christ, see a doctor Mike. Nothing wrong with needing some help with your mental paralysis. Lots of incompetent boobs suffer from it. By the way, you could have had Oswalt for 8 mill if Beane hadn't talked you into dumping all your promising pitchers into his lap. Now Cherington will have him no doubt. Christ, he didn't even want a drink. Anything on television? Probably the Bruins or Celtics or some such shit. How could he be an alcoholic if he didn't want a drink? Must remember to phone in the morning.

*

Sunday arrived entirely too soon. That's the trouble with falling asleep too early. He went out for coffee and a donut. Sat with The Globe. Needless to say there was nothing in Cafardo about the Nats. At least there was nothing about the Pats either. The Super Bowl was the biggest thing in sport because once it was over there was no more football to distract sports channels from baseball. Well, March Madness, but really only for a week and a bit. Fucked opening day, but after that it was clear sailing. Took the time to drink a second cup of coffee while working out the best time to call Cheryl. Tonight. This afternoon Marianne could be at the hospital. Unless Cheryl was out. But if she was, she'd be home. Yeah, best not to phone yet. It would be a long day. Had to stay out of the bars all day. Fucking football. Game for monsters on drugs. Basketball was more freaks on drugs. Once read that hockey players looked quite normal. If you saw a team waiting for a plane they all looked like people; no freaks, no monsters. Like baseball. But baseball players played baseball. Hockey players really preferred fighting. Except maybe Bobby Orr. And Gretzky and Lemieux. And all those great Montreal teams way back. Christ, you could tell Rizzo wasn't doing his job when he had to resort to thinking about hockey.

Got home and there was no food and no beer. Great Sunday ahead. Seven Eleven would have something wretched he could eat. He would try Wolf Hall again. Couldn't be worse than football.

Jesus, you didn't have to go to a bar to know the Patriots had won. So now he could look forward to two more weeks of nothing but football hysteria. Wonderful. He had brought home bread and coffee. Toast would do for tonight and the morning. Football killed his appetite.

He would try to read a few pages of Wolf Hall before calling Cheryl. He began to enjoy it. Wished he knew more about Cromwell. And Wolsey. He opened the computer. Google him. And a few more. Just to get a feel for the times. Several emails from Marianne. Last one was a bit sad. What don't you please call? Just for her sake. She's trying so hard but she is just so low right now. Arnie has been wonderful. I have to get back on Sunday but Arnie will stay off work for a few days. There is no danger, of course, it's just the depression. He should phone. Really. Just check some baseball first.

It had never occurred to him but, of course, if Selig wanted Fielder to go somewhere more fashionable, he would push through the sale of the Dodgers so they could buy him. Bud would do it because he's a malignant prick, and all he thinks about is money; he would force a good baseball decision on the Lerners. He could still be lucky. Even if Texas doesn't want him. Boras licking his greedy chops about a Dodger feeding frenzy. Probably told Rizzo to hang fire on everything until the deal is done. Look, Mike, I don't give a flying fuck about your bench, just lay off until I've got the Prince his millions then you can sign someone. Maybe Raul Ibanez will still be available. Christ, that would be the end of everyone's world. Nats were all that kept Raul's career alive. Hit below a hundred against everyone else but because of the Nats he still seemed respectable. Must have hit ninety dingers against us in the last two years.

Better phone Cheryl. Have to charge the phone first. Should have thought of that. Back to Wolf Hall.

When he woke up it was too late to phone anyone, so all he could do was roll over and go to sleep again. Shame that. At least his phone was charged. Maybe phone tomorrow night. Nice for her to get a call on a Monday night. Usually a dead night.

*

He was strangely tired on Monday despite not having done much on the weekend. Not even spent much time in the bars because of the football. And it was a slow time at work. Maybe it was always slow when he was keeping up with the work. Maybe there just wasn't all that much work. He went over to Zainab and told her how he was enjoying Wolf Hall. They discussed how the writer kept saying he without saying who he was. Like she was writing exclusively about Cromwell in a sense, everyone else was peripheral; like the king, so when in doubt, 'he' was Cromwell. Made sense. Zainab knew what she was talking about. He had been a bit confused at first, but she just thought it was a clever device.

Chet dropped by his desk to remind him about lunch tomorrow. Said he was really looking forward to it. Sure you were Chet. Big moment in your life. Handle it well and it is straight up the greasy pole. Asshole.

Nothing but nothing of interest. He was now at the stage when he raced through his work just to see how little there was. If he really tried he could finish what was regarded as a day's work in about three hours. It was beginning to dawn on him just how little he had been doing. He was actually probably much faster than even Michele. Certainly faster than Bert. Just as well with Rizzo in charge. Today's factoid was that he was probably done for the winter. Must be exhausted after sending his best prospects right across the fucking continent. Did you take them yourself in a fucking U-Haul? That why we can't get a bat. And Texas was going hard after Fielder. Thank god for Jon Daniels. Well, that should lull him to sleep. Thank god for Hilary Mantel. Shit, forgot to phone again. Maybe tomorrow.

*

He found himself choosing a decent tie and an ironed shirt for lunch. Really? For Chet, the wonder kid? He disgusted himself when he did things like that. He was even a bit distracted all morning. Couldn't really settle to work. Thought Bert was looking over and smirking. Maybe not. Can you imagine? Nervous about lunch with a kid like that. Who was about to be his supervisor. No, no. Team leader.

The lunch left him exhausted, worried, and bitter. Now he knew what all Bert's sneering was about. Stuart had done him no favors putting him in Chet's team. And the company had done itself no favors promoting or even hiring the little shit. With his blond hair and white teeth. And smile.

He started by talking nothing but sport. The fucking Patriots. As if this would prove what a great guy he was. He knew Peter loved sports, blah, blah. Well, Peter hated football. He hated the Patriots. After about twenty minutes of this shit Peter asked him what he thought about Ken Singleton. That shut him up. Dumb bastard. But at the end of the lunch. This is maybe two thirty, mind you. He starts to talk about loyalty and Peter's problems. Loyalty? Problems? Oh, yes, Chet understood about slowing down when you got older but experience was important and, of course, the company valued his experience so much. Sure they did. Then he got to the crunch. He could arrange things so Peter got fewer claims than other team members and maybe not the biggies. Was he out of his toothy mind? The biggies were the only ones with any interest at all and even they held precious little. And as for speed, he had just been proving that he was still as fast as anyone. Well, proving to himself. So he laughed. And Chet said that he didn't really understand where this was going so he would spell it out. Chet cuts him a break and he does Chet a favor. In fact, two hundred favors. Monthly. In cash. What, is this serious? It sure as hell was and maybe he should realize that with his record and a couple of reprimands, he was on very thin ice. Thin ice indeed. But nothing a bit of understanding between them couldn't cure. Chet then stood up, turned to Peter and suggested he might like to pay, and walked out.

Peter was numb when he went back to the office. Where did he turn? Chet was right about the reprimands. He was hardly likely to be supported against a newly promoted set of very white teeth. Bert was smirking when he got back. What did he know? Nothing about the money but he was probably happy to drop Peter in the shit. Bastard.

Peter left early. Went home without checking the computer. Didn't even stop for a drink. Must be eggs and bread at home. Maybe he should telephone Cheryl. No, not tonight. He had to think. He couldn't settle to reading. Remembered that Schoenfield would have had a chat this afternoon so he turned on the computer to read the transcript. There it was. It was over. Prince Fielder was going to Detroit. Made sense, they needed a first baseman who could hit. Cabrera was crap. What were they thinking, Cabrera has one position. First base. Fielder has one position. First base. So as of now they have two of the best hitters in baseball and one position. Maybe they have heard that Selig plans to introduce two designated hitters to improve offense and increase revenues. It didn't really matter; Fielder wasn't going to the Nationals. Maybe he should call Rizzo up. Tell him to get on with his real job now. Center field and the bench, Mike. Go for it. Just think of all the players still available. Whoops, they're all gone. Asshole.

*

Peter awoke early with a dry mouth and headache. Nothing to do with beer this time. He was unsettled by the meeting with Chet and unsure what to do. There seemed little sense in talking to Stuart who was leaving for new challenges in a week. And no sense talking to his new supervisor because that was Chet and Chet was the problem. He could just pay up. The thing about that was the fact that it was unnecessary. At his best, he was more than able to keep up with the work. At his worst he did so little that he hardly kept up with a reduced load. The real point was that he was being threatened with a type of blackmail. True, he had stepped over the line in passing on work. And it was true that he had made some mistakes when things were at their worst. But that would only lead to dismissal if he was not doing his job now. And Chet was the person to judge that. How did the toothy bastard ever get the job?

When he got to work Bert was already at his desk grinning. Peter went over to speak to him, but thought better of it. Nevertheless, he heard Bert mutter, that things would be a bit different now. Did Bert think he was going to go halves or something? He went to Stuart. Asked if maybe he could have a word about the new team. But Stuart had no interest whatever. Got to realize that it's not really my thing now, whatever I suggest will just be shelved until next month. Next week, really. But he put his hand on Peter's arm. But I know what you mean. I was fooled at first, but I think he is a real problem. Looks the part, but there is something about him. I thought I was doing you a favor. Giving you a new start. Not putting you with Michele. I knew you might take advantage of Zainab, so I thought Chet was your best bet. I am just so sorry. Try to keep your head down. I think he's nasty. And Bert seems to think he can influence him. Believe me, Bert will not be able to handle Chet. Different league.

Peter couldn't even get interested in baseball. The bars were full of Patriot fans anyway, so he went home to read all about what was happening. Which was nothing. He almost missed the Prince Fielder rumors. Laughed when he read about Rizzo and Boras. Made it sound like big, bold Mike put his foot down. Mike, you were used. When did you ever sign a big name from Boras without paying triple what anyone else paid? You have the same relationship with Boras that Marilyn Monroe had with Jack Kennedy. Only she was pretty. Why not go hard after Jackson now. Scott needs you. Trouble is, you might get him. God, he should have called Cheryl.

*

The next morning when he got to work and turned on his computer there was a long email from Marianne. All about Cheryl really, except it was also a bit about Peter. A lot about Peter. Marianne seemed genuinely upset. Really quite sad. Almost as if she didn't really want to dislike him.

Marianne probably meant well, she always had a thing about talking things through and explaining and saying what you feel. He knew it was all a load of shit but sometimes he would let her talk and he would now and then say something about trying harder and she would sigh. And sometimes ask if he had listened. Which he often hadn't. He remembered when Bowden was trying to get Teixeira how she had gone on for nearly an hour. And they didn't get Teixeira in the end. Waste of time. Typical Boras trick that. Price went up for the Yankees, Nats end up with Dunn. Dunn had been all right in his way. Made Zimmerman realize that he had to learn to throw the ball properly. Now they had LaRoche because Fielder did a Teixeira on them. Still, a year or two of LaRoche was no bad thing. Better than nine years of Fatboy Prince. As one of the pundits said; there was no one to set the table for him. Amen.

Marianne felt he really had to try to contact Cheryl. Said she was very upset. She was over the worst now but still bitter that her father had not even contacted her. Well, what about Arnie and his welcoming message? How was he supposed to deal with that? Cheryl was the one who had a miscarriage and Arnie gets all aggressive. Asshole. Best to keep the family happy, though. Better call Cheryl. Maybe tomorrow. He emailed Marianne back. Didn't say anything about Chet, just that things were a bit rough at work. Hoped she was well. That sort of thing. Didn't ask about Frank.

Brad Lidge! Way to go, Mike. Let's look at things here. Needs: center field, bench, left-handed bat. Strength: bullpen. How do you do it? Now is the winter of my fucking discontent bubbling over. Mind you, Lidge is probably a good signing. Senseless, of course, one year of a veteran when they aren't contending and could give a youngster like Mattheus the innings. At least it looks like Rizzo is going to the office again, sifting through the coffee grounds and such.

Zainab gave him a sad smile as he left the office. Asked about Chet, said he looked shifty to her. Well, yes, a bit. He'd have to give that some thought. Not tonight, maybe phone Cheryl. Need a drink first.

*

Friday again. Bleak weekend coming. Worse than Super Bowl weekend was the weekend before the Super Bowl. Why they had to wait two weeks was beyond him. Well, not really. Tied into television revenues. Another chance to see a Brady drive for those he missed it the first seven hundred times. He should have called Cheryl. He should talk to someone about Chet. Who? He should smash a computer into Bert's grinning face. All this and more. And there wasn't enough work to keep him going. And Bryce Harper wasn't named number one prospect. Not that he cared. He preferred prospects like Espinosa who had to work at it. Like Lombardozzi. Like Peacock. Like Milone. Like Norris. Like Cole. Fuck the Nationals. Fuck weekends. Fuck Arnie.

He may have an awful head-ache, but all that beer at least meant he didn't want to get out of bed until well past noon and by then it was just about time to head out for more beer. He mentally took stock of his life. No center fielder, no wife, no relationship with either of his children, crap basement apartment, his job was diabolical and set to get much worse starting Monday, and all Rizzo could think to do was add arms to the only strength the team had.

Rizzo must have a thing about set-up men. Everyone was a set-up man. Lidge was now the set-up man, to go with the best set-up man in baseball and Rodriguez who had the best stuff and could be a set-up man and Burnett who was a lefty set-up man. Maybe they should bring back Tim Burke, he was the best. Until Clippard. He was something. Until they made him a closer. Think he had a house full of adopted kids.

It was great that so many young ball players re-cycled the nation's wealth into good works, only a pity the government never thought of it. I suppose when you have all of Afghanistan to conquer, looking after your own is a lot to ask of congress. A bit sad when athletic kids out of college with their millions are more caring than fucking congress. God, he felt awful. Was it Zurich people went to when they felt this bad? Little cocktail and zap. Who the fuck cares who plays center field?

Christ, remember Claude Brochu. Who cares who plays third base for the Expos? Had he never heard of Tim Wallach? Who cares, well not Selig or his puppet Brochu. But he cared and so did the other eight Expo fans left in the world. Might have been easier for Selig to just hire some Ukrainians to shoot us all. Maybe drive over us in their black SUVs. Then no one would care who played third base for the Expos. Imagine an owner who never heard of Tim Wallach. Fucking Brochu.

No beer. Walk to the library. Walk to the common. Maybe go to the bookshop in Cambridge. The one that sells second hand books for more than they cost new. He would telephone Cheryl today. Later. Maybe even Barney. Maybe go over to Marianne's and try to explain. Maybe not. Fucking Frank. He picked up his cell. No charge. That's okay; he would take a walk first.

By the time he got home there was plenty of charge on his cell phone so he dialed Cheryl's number. No answer. He was relieved. Then disappointed. Dialed again and this time left a message. Just dad, hope everything is fine and I will try again. Felt better. Even if he forgot to try again, at least she knew that he was thinking about her. Because he felt a little better, he decided to try Marianne. No, could get Frank. So he sent an email. Just to say he had telephoned Cheryl to wish her well. Wow, not so bad. He even tried Barney. Got Bobbie. Fuck off, Peter. He hated that woman. She sounded drunk. Always drunk. He decided to go out for a drink.

Checked the phone and computer before bed. No messages. Except from Mike Rizzo. Poor baby working 15 hours a day, seven days a week. Always looking to improve the team, it would seem. Great work, Mike. A decent PA with a copy of Baseball Digest could have picked up a couple of has beens coming off two bad years each. As for the big trade, well if you give up enough you might just pick up the best leftie available. Especially if he walks batters by the cartload and has make-up problems. For your information, Mike, make-up problems do not refer to eye-liner. That's all your hard work to improve the team. Six months of toil.

He hated people who bragged about how hard they were working. A sure sign that the job was beyond them. I mean, fifteen hours a day, seven days a week for six months to sign Mike Cameron and Mark DeRosa. Thank god he didn't move to a six day week or we could have signed Manny and Felipe Lopez. Still if he is working that many hours it might explained why he can't use real words in real sentences. Poor bastard's exhausted. All this we are quite comfortable with what we've got but we are always working to improve ourselves so we are even more quite comfortable with the guys we got and I am working several hundred hours a day to get comfortable by comfortablizing the positions in which we need to incrementalize our comforting procedure. Christ, Zainab should be GM; at least she speaks fucking English.

*

Checked for messages first thing. Marianne was glad he had talked to Cheryl. Didn't realize Cheryl hadn't answered. Barney had sent a text. Sorry about Bobbie but maybe it is best to leave us alone. Sure. Nothing from Cheryl. At least that was a relief. He put on his coat and went for a long walk. Had breakfast out and bought dinner to cook. Tomorrow was the big day. New team in operation and Chet was going to join them as of Monday even though it was still January. Pretty radical for an insurance company, that, I mean a month is a month. Needless to say, Rhonda would have to wait until February 1. You can push radical ideas only so far. He was going to have to think about what to do with Chet. He could just cough up the money, of course, accept the easy life. Ask Marianne to up the allowance pending the divorce. Hell, she could afford it and even now he was making out just fine. Saving quite a bit because the apartment was paid six months in advance. By Marianne. Including the deposit.

Hell, she could afford it. Frank was on big money. But still, Chet was a shit and he hated to give in.

Cafardo was his usual lucid self. Said the Nationals will be interesting. There's commitment to journalistic courage. Still, he writes about Boston, not Washington. And he's alright, really, always something to see about baseball, nothing on vinaigrettes. Mind you, I like Kilgore, can't really complain. And Zuckerman despite his tendency to be a bit enthusiastic. I mean, there only the fucking Nationals.

7. The New Team

Chet was in the office bright and early. Had organized four desks together in a group so that Chet and Bert would face Rhonda and Peter. When Rhonda arrived. Chet was all smiles, of course. Just one of the team sort of shit. Like being on the Pirates. Peter had to choose whether to sit opposite Chet's teeth or Bert's sanctimonious smirk. He opted for Chet. Went to start work, opened his computer and looked at his stack of paper claims. There was about an hour's work. What's this? Chet looked at him and winked. His heart sank. All day with nothing to do but watch Chet smile and Bert smirk. No chats on Monday and the only thing being discussed was Ray Oswalt who the Nats should have waited for. Kept Peacock and the others. Even now Oswalt for two year would be a better gamble than Prince for nine. Trouble with being a fan was attendance was less of an issue than winning. Or gradualizing the incremental developmental nature of our personnel in their respective comfort zones or whatever shit Rizzo was up to in today's fifteen hours. Rizzo could send some work over to him, pay him two hundred, and get home for dinner. He could sign Rick Ankiel for him maybe. Rizzo's wife could be pissed if he showed up for dimmer. I'm really quite comfortable with the vitamins now in play but think we should incrementalize an adjusted position whereby I get a steak instead of this fucking awful meatloaf. Darling. Certainly dear, I'll just speak to Mr. Boras.

He looked over at Zainab. She was looking back with a small but friendly smile. Stuart, you have wrecked my life. Of course, Stuart was off to his new challenges today. Poor bastard. Probably had as little to do as he did. But didn't have to fork out two hundred bucks. The trouble with sitting in a tight little group is it became noticeable if you left your desk ten times a day but even more noticeable that one member of the team was doing almost nothing. He waited for Chet to get up to go to lunch. Followed him to the elevator and approached him when they got out. Told him he could handle a lot more claims in a day. Didn't need any special treatment. Please, just treat him like everyone else. Chet smiled. Waited until they were on the street. Looked to make sure no one was listening. Listen, you drunken piece of shit, we got a deal. You may not like the deal but it is the only deal on offer. With your record, you're lucky to have job but you open your fucking mouth once, just once, and you're out of here. And you even mention this to me again and we've got a problem. Or you do. Called unemployment. Two hundred every month promptly on the last Friday of the month. Now ain't you lucky because all we got in January is Monday and Tuesday so you aren't due until the twenty-fourth. Let's hope you keep your job that long, I got plans for the money. He gave Peter one of those toothpaste smiles, said how much he enjoyed talking to him, and quickened his pace so Peter was left in his wake. Well, at least it was definitive. There was no way Peter was giving that bastard anything. There had to be something he could do.

He had nothing to do in the office but sit and worry. He worried more about his job than he did about the Nationals. He didn't even bother to check the baseball sites until the evening, which was just as well. Nothing. Last year the bench was Ankiel, Nix and Hairston and all they could say was how weak it was. So they replace it with DeRosa and Cameron. Wow. And center field was a disaster, so we replace Bernadina with, wait for it; Bernadina. Oh, and leadoff, big change there. No longer Ian Desmond. Whoopsie, made a mistake. It is Ian Desmond. Still, at least Werth will have a better year now that he will bat sixth, where he's comfortable. Didn't I say? He has to bat second where he is uncomfortable.

Remember, Desmond bats leadoff, so it's either Werth or Vidro and Vidro left ten years ago.

He missed Vidro. Came up with Vlad, or maybe a year later. Sort of followed Vlad through the system. Thing was, Vidro loved the Expos and Vlad did not. Great player Jose. Until the knees went. Fucking artificial turf. Build a decent stadium and people like Dawson and Vidro might have played a few more years.

So tomorrow was another day. Just like today. Nothing to do and precious little happening. He would follow the Schoenfield chat and stare at Chet's teeth. And think about how he was going to deal with him. He fell asleep but was awake by three in the morning. He tried to read a bit. But he was enjoying Wolf Hall and reading now would spoil it. And as for that Art of Fielding, well, right now reading something that was heading towards a happy ending was impossible. No chance of that in Wolf Hall.

*

Not sleeping meant he was at work early. With nothing to do. Chet just looked at him when he arrived. Because they were alone. No need for pretense. When Bert came in there was great fellowship all around. He thought he was going to be sick.

Bert was enjoying being the blue-eyed boy. Might have expected him to be bitter about not being a team leader but Chet had won him over. Brilliant management, treat one like a king and the other like a piece of shit. And demand money from the shit.

Peter agreed with Schoenfield, Nationals should have found just an ordinary fly chaser for center; anything but Werth. They spent all that money on him and he had a crap season. This year is not 2013, it is 2012 when Strasburg finishes after 160 innings and Zimmermann and Gonzalez establish themselves while Harper matures into the second coming of the Babe. Or Jose Guillen. Whatever, they aren't built to win this year, so you give your most expensive player a chance to redeem himself. Maximize his comfort zone incrementally by conceptualizing the concept of being comfortable in the concept where you had more than incremental comfort in your previous comfort zone. To put it in Mike speak. To put it another way, let the poor bastard bat sixth and play right field which is what he did when he played for the Phucking Phillies.

Christ, he hated the Phillies. Went way back, that. They reminded him that Pete Rose once played for the Expos. He didn't hate the Reds for Pete Rose, just the Phillies. And now they seemed to ruin every Sunday for him. And for Lannan. Rizzo wants lefties to pitch against the Phillies. After Lannan's remarkable success, he could see that. We are always looking to improverize performance wise against those teams that pulverize us score wise. Like the Phillies and the Marlins.

He tried Cheryl when he got home. Answer machine. Didn't leave a message. Went to sleep early with Wolf Hall open beside him. Woke at three again. Trouble with staying in and reading, he was getting into a cycle that left him four hours to kill in the morning and the bars were shut. He would make a real effort to discipline himself tonight. Go out and get drunk and come in after midnight like a normal person.

He was first in again. He had no work again. Rhonda was next to him. The new woman. He was all wrong about her. She was very young. Very pretty in a non-beautiful way. Sort of dark-eyed and short-haired and shy. Looked like she was terrified. He tried to talk to her but she was too nervous to really have a conversation. She was obviously dressed for the occasion. New outfit. All business. He felt sorry for her. Wanted to put his arm around her and tell her not to worry, it was a shit job, don't take it too seriously. She smiled when he offered her coffee. Do they do herb tea? Christ, they'd kill her.

Chet flashed his toothy smile and Bert grinned his smirky grin, but neither did much to help Rhonda settle. He waited until lunch when they had gone and then he turned to Rhonda and took her through the ropes. She was an innocent to the slaughter here and was in tears when he offered to help. He had taken her through the basics by mid-afternoon and quietly checked the two claims she had worked through. Told her he was not busy just yet so between the two of them, they would easily keep ahead of the game until the busy time.

When he got home he had a simple dinner before settling into the baseball news. It had been a very pleasant day, helping Rhonda, and now he could relax. Nice to see Livan had a job. He was better to be an icon in Houston than a fifth starter in Washington. Go on Livan, give 'em hell. He loved Livan. And he liked Lannan but the guy was an idiot to go to arbitration. Rizzo seldom lost and looking for a big raise after what was only a decent season, hardly spectacular, well; it was plain dumb. Leave him with a bad taste and likely to mean his job goes to Detwiler. Bad move.

Went to bed thinking about how he could help Rhonda tomorrow.

*

Got to work early again so he would be there when Rhonda arrived. Had both their paper claims stacked and he had worked through more than half before she arrived. Told her to just do the ones he had done and they would see if they agreed. Meanwhile, why not transfer copies of the electronic ones to him as well. By the time she went to buy him a coffee, he had finished half the electronic claims and suggested that she do a few of the ones he had completed. It was pretty clear to him that the only claim she should have to do were ones he had already done. So there was no chance of her making an embarrassing mistake. He could easily complete all her work and all his and also train her. Whatever training she had already had was crap. She kept making mistakes. She kept weeping. He kept reassuring. Chet kept smiling. Bert kept leering.

He checked the rumors site; Lannan had finished second in his case. Now they were shopping him. Never cross the boss. But signing Jackson? He could only hope that they could not trade Lannan. With Gonzalez and Jackson in the rotation they would have the longest games in baseball. Worse than the Yankees and Red Sox. Maybe twenty to thirty walks a game. Manager's nightmare. And Rizzo thinking he is clever because he has the best farm systems. Sure you do Mike. Norris, Peacock, Milone, Cole; wonderful set of prospects. How did you do it? Asshole.

Back to work. Rhonda drying her eyes. Again. Bert smirking. Again. Chet showing off his teeth. Again. Maybe send him to Marianne. Bribe her to pull the fucking lot of them out.

By the time he got home and checked the news again, Rizzo had signed Edwin Jackson. There goes Steve Catty. Once Jackson and Gio start walking them, someone has to take the blame and it is unlikely to be Mike Rizzo or Davey Johnson. Good-bye Steve. Maybe Ben Cherington will hire you, if he finds a job.

Mike was obviously feeling sorry for poor Scott with his big name pitcher looking at three years in Baltimore. Don't you worry Scottie; I can use some of the Prince Fielder money and save you a bit of embarrassment here. Sure, just a year is fine in case he wants something better next year. And remember, if he's shit and can't find a job, I'm always here for you. Ah, no, I don't think Johnny Damon, not right now, let the Lerners get used to Jackson.

And poor old John Lannan. Had to settle for five mill just to watch what happens next. Mike doesn't plan to trade him, of course, never get too much pitching. Nothing like a fifteen man staff to strike fear into the opponents. Thing is Mike, way back when the Yankees and Dodgers and a few others use to stockpile pitching, they made a few rules. Option years and shit like that. Now the thing about pitching depth is you have it in the minors because you have good young pitching there with options left. To give you an example, even a shit team like, say Oakland, may have some pitchers almost ready for the majors but with options left. Guys like Peacock and Milone. Asshole. Ever think that if you wanted Jackson and Oswalt, you could have dumped Lannan for something mediocre in center, and kept the farm as best farm system in baseball which is now in California. Of course, Scott may not have liked it.

Wonderful press conference full of comfortables and including the fact that something else is trending in the right direction. I wonder what he's like at home. Martha, I see the kids' grades are trending in the wrong direction. I would be more comfortable if they did their due diligence, book-wise, and incrementalized their grades in a direction that might be seen as more positive. Or else I'll kick their asses out of my house. Maybe see what Scott has on the market.

And tomorrow was Friday. And it was Super Bowl weekend. The best thing about it being Super Bowl weekend was that by Monday it would be over. Unless New England wins, in which case it may never be over. Not here in Boston.

*

It had taken a decent amount of beer to get him to sleep last night but he still struggled into the office to organize the work for Rhonda. He had reviewed all her work from yesterday and completed several of his paper claims before she arrived. In truth, she was not doing well. The reason the work was so boring was that it was not demanding. You could cope with a brain south of mediocre but Rhonda seemed seriously challenged. For all her charm, Rhonda's future looked bleak. But she arrived all cheerful smiles. Peter, what would I do without you? She took a bit of time to get started and then, just before ten, she smiled and left to go to the washroom. When she returned thirty minutes later, she smiled again and said she would just love a coffee, so he offered to get coffee. Bert said that he could use one and Chet made it four. That is, if you want one, Peter. By the time noon rolled around, Rhonda had done very little. At least she hadn't cried. And Peter had just about finished everything anyhow. But she should do a few just to make sure she knew what she was doing. But she gave him a lovely smile when she returned from lunch. Just after two.

There was no way he was going to face Super Bowl weekend sober. But he was in a rather more circumspect mood than he had anticipated. Shopped for some food, had something to eat, put some washing in. Drew the line at ironing. Then went out for a drink. Well, more than one. Avoided all the crowded bars. No time to be in a place full of sports fans. Anyway he needed to think. Rhonda had left the office talking to Bert. Big grins on their faces as they turned to say good-bye. Then they laughed as they got on the same elevator. Maybe nothing, but. Then there was Cheryl. He really should try to have a real conversation with her. And he should talk to Marianne about the divorce. She said that Frank wanted him to get a good lawyer just to protect himself. They would never try to cheat him. Of course not. Take the wife and house but not the money. Most of it but not all. Fucking Frank. Then there was Lannan. All right, he was shit on Sundays; especially if they played the Phillies, but he had been the best they had for four years. Except for Livan, of course. Scared of no one. Fast ball in the low thirties. Come right at you, would Livan.

Best thing for Lannan was a trade. He had it all worked out if Rizzo had the humility to listen. Lannan for Byrd. Then Cubs flip Lannan as compensation for Theo. Nats get a center fielder and Lannan gets to contend. The Sox are shit, but they contend. Not like the Nationals.

Rizzo bought himself a very short rope with Jackson. If they expand the wild card especially. Nats will be expected to be there despite the fact that there are at least ten teams contending and the Nats may be the tenth best. Even with Jackson. Maybe if you get a center fielder, Mike, but until then you are behind a lot of teams. Teams that don't walk people. Last year it was all this business of throwing strikes, so they bring in Gonzalez and Jackson. That should do the trick. What a mess. And now it was Super Bowl weekend.

Saturday and he required books. No sport on television, no sport bars, no newspapers until the Super Bowl was history. If the Pats lose, he could emerge from his cocoon maybe Wednesday, if not, maybe next weekend. Maybe make an exception for Cafardo. Hell no, he could read him on line. Couldn't risk a Boston paper this weekend. Or the New York Times. Maybe the Post. He would need a few books. And a few bars. Nothing like a broken marriage and a Super Bowl to increase literacy. And alcoholism. Not that he was an alcoholic like that dipso Bobbie. He often went a day without anything but a few glasses of wine with dinner. And maybe a beer when he got home. Or two. If you have to live where he lived and eat what he cooked, alcohol is obligatory.

*

Saturday dawned bright and early at noon. Rizzo was going to see where Harper was at developmentally in spring training. Mike, what you mean is that you have to evaluate his development. Not see if he is trending in the right direction devclopmentally. Read some Hilary Mantel. Learn how to talk. CBS think the Nats are going for it this year. Breakthrough in investigative journalism there. Jackson for 11 mill on a one year job does sort of suggest that it is not the long term they were thinking about. When will they learn patience? Christ, 2013 is not that far away. In 1994 it was, but not now. Maybe Selig plans to close down the shop again. Nah, Washington was his idea, bound to let them win the Series. Almost turn you into a Padres fan, that. Or the Twins. Except they play in the

DH slums. But supporting a team created by Selig and run by Boras is not exactly politically correct. Not like The Expos. God, he loved Ken Hill.

Fucking Super Bowl.

When he got home he felt sort of lucky to have found it. That sort of afternoon. At least he had found a few bars without televisions spouting on about the Pats. And it would be over soon.

*

Super Bowl Sunday. An exercise in avoidance. There were lots of coffee shops that were more likely to be hosting a discussion on Jackson Pollard than Tom Brady, so breakfast was not a problem. He opted for a Globe. He would dissect it, throw away anything that even hinted being about the Patriots before he even went for breakfast. He usually did that anyway. At his age carrying an entire Sunday newspaper around was foolhardy. Lucky Maine was there to provide paper for the New York and Boston papers. Nice place Maine, almost Canadian except it had a lot more guns. Cold and miserable nine months a year must make people nicer.

Oh god, Cafardo hinting that the Nats might still do a deal for Bourjos. Enough to make his day that. Best thing about the offseason is the hope it can provide. Here and there. For twenty-four hours maybe. At least he would have something to think about for the rest of the day. He could go home and write line-up cards in his head with a leadoff hitter, a center fielder, Werth batting sixth; shit, all the things he knew Rizzo should have been sorting out when he was trying to land Fielder. Or Boras was trying to land Fielder. Peter wasn't stupid enough to think the trade would come off. Not unless Bourjos was a Boras client and Depoto was an idiot. But for a whole afternoon he could dream. What with being Super Bowl Sunday, Dipoto may not even hear about the rumor until Monday. Might not shoot it down right away. Maybe there would be twenty-four hours to dream. He decided to go home with a decent bottle of red wine. No computers, nothing until Monday now. Who would have thought that he would be grateful for the Super Bowl, but it might give him Peter Bourjos for a whole day. Not quite a full season, but it was something.

*

When he got to work and turned on his computer he was shattered. He already knew about the Super Bowl. The Patriots had lost to a late drive. Brilliant. Except he hated the Giants. Always had. Went back to Frank Gifford days. Smug bunch of bastards. Always think they should win. Like the Patriots. Why couldn't the Bengals win the Super Bowl? No, the shattering thing was Rick Ankiel. Signed to play center field. He loved the idea of Rick Ankiel. Supposed to be a gem of a guy. Great story coming back after his pitching woes. Peter had been keen that the Nationals sign him for weeks. Months. But that was before Peter Bourjos was mentioned yesterday. Not that Bourjos was really coming or anything; it was just that he needed more time to dream. Just a day or two, for Christ sake. If Ankiel had waited this long, surely he could have lasted until, say, Wednesday. By then all the Super Bowl shit would be history and he would be ready to think about spring training. Never mind, Ankiel was actually a good signing. And they still had Lannan. Lannan had been as effective as Jackson over the last four years, and he had been half of the pitching staff. With Livan, who was gone. Pity they couldn't trade Chien-Ming Wang. But he was such a great story. What's wrong with a rotation of Wang, Lannan, Stammen, Livan and Zimmermann. Bring a little romance into the team. Maybe trade Strasburg to Billy Beane. Or just ask Boras what he might like. Boras must be the least romantic figure in baseball. Maybe after A-Rod. And Jeter.

Rhonda came in with a coffee for him. She asked if they could talk. Sure. What do you think about Peter Bourjos? But he was polite. He remembered how she was on Friday, though. She was weepy again. Apologized for behaving so badly on Friday. Said that Bert and Chet had asked her to go for a drink after work and they both were just awful. Well, frankly, they are just awful. But he said nothing, just told her to keep her head down and ignore them as much as she could. He would help her as much as he could and maybe she should talk to Zainab or Beryl. Zainab was one of the best and smartest in the office, while Beryl was just comforting. Like a grandmother. He didn't add that she was bordering on senile. Probably had been for thirty or more years. Sometimes he felt guilty that he had passed claims to her. She was so slow, anyway, and had often had to stay late to finish her work. And Peter's.

Rhonda wanted to tell him about some of the things Chet and Bert had said but he warned her to be quiet. Firstly, he didn't want to know. Secondly, he didn't really care. And thirdly, the less she spoke about it the more likely she was to keep her job. At least until she got pregnant. Couldn't say that, but it was true. Let Anna be your beacon. She may well have landed someone in the private office class. Lots of talk, lots of giggles, and precious little work.

He shouldn't moan about Anna, she still favored him when handing around claims. And Beryl. She went easy on Beryl. He had noticed that. Anna was kind. Triumphant about her new guy in the executive suite, but kind. The bigger they are, the nicer they are he thought.

Then there was Chet, who had just arrived late. Teeth everywhere but noticeably cool to Rhonda. Classy guy this team leader of theirs. Within the first week he has tried to extort money from one member of his team, tried to get into the panties of another, and befriended the biggest creep in the building. And struck out. Three strikes. Bert never befriended anyone, he was just a creep. He wasn't paying the extortion. And you didn't have to be a mind reader to see that the panties had held firm on Friday night. Trouble was, Rhonda was really not all that bright. Learning the job would take a moron half an hour; anyone with bordering on average intelligence ten minutes. Just look around. Morons. Except Zainab. And him, but he was a special case.

He spent enough time sorting out Rhonda's work load that he hardly heard any Super Bowl chatter. Just enough to know that the all-forgiving New England fans thought it was time to trade Brady and fire Belichik. For a city that suffered the curse of the Bambino so stoically, they could be a little hard on the Patriots. So what.

Rizzo had shaken his post Prince paralysis and signed Ankiel and Teahen in the last two days. What a marvelous bench you have built, Mike. Forget Nix, we got Teahen. And replaced Ankiel with, wait for it, roll of drums; Ankiel. Still, at least he has a pulse. Hope he read Cafardo. Nothing on that rumor. Peter Bourjos. Even he would give up Lannan for a legitimate center fielder. Rizzo can be strange. Maybe holding out, want them to throw in Pujols as a make weight. Especially as he missed out on Fielder. Wonder if Pujols and Bourjos weigh as much as Fielder.

Still best to skip the bars tonight, maybe Wednesday. Spring training slowly asserting dominance over the Super Bowl. Christ, he hated cooking for himself. He also hated going out to eat by himself. He also hated grabbing a burger in a bar. Wonderful way to lose weight. Being sick helped. He was like a pregnant woman these days; sick most mornings. Christ, should phone Cheryl. This time he tried. Let it ring a few times then cancelled. It would show up as a missed call and she could make her own decisions. When you thought about it, his children didn't exactly give their deserted father a lot of support.

Rhonda may not be the brightest of sparks, but she was good for the office. There was a collection of slobbering men around her this morning when he came in. He shooed them away and organized their day. Explained that it was best to do this without Chet around. Or Bert. He gave her back some of her work. Wrote a few notes. Things like, would she like to look at this again and are you sure about the ratio here? What he could have written was how the fuck can you make mistakes like this with a fucking computer to help you? Maybe not. Not yet. Anyway, Chet was down on her so he wanted to help her. He suggested they both come in half an hour early every morning until she was more comfortable with the work.

An uncomfortable day to say the least. Billy Beane rewarded for fleecing the Nationals with a longer contract than Albert Pujols. Maybe Lannan should get Brad Pitt to play him in a movie. Sure to win arbitration next year. Maybe George Clooney would do it. Might go and see the Clooney movie. Not Moneyball. Crap book; crap idea in the first place. I got this great idea, draft fat kids that have great statistics for getting walks at second rate colleges and find someone to write a book about how clever I am. Revolutionary stuff, drafting shit. Christ, Billy, Baltimore has been doing it for years. Maybe someone should write a book. Who would play Angelos? Maybe Meryl Streep. Thinks she can play anyone. Why not Peter Angelos? Or Duquette, she could do that. She sure as hell would think she could.

Schoenfield was depressing. He was coming around to Schoenfield. Took some hits today for not predicting the Cardinals would win the World Series. David, David, be careful. Never knock the Cardinals. Everyone loves them. Must go back to the Gashouse Gang or something. Maybe Stan Musial. Supposed to be a great baseball town. Maybe go some day. Watch the Nationals thrash the bastards. Schoenfield shot down the Bourjos rumor. Not even a rumor, just Cafardo trying to cheer him up because of the Super Bowl. And it sort of worked, but there is nothing left on the shelves now that Rizzo traded all the colored glass beads for his leftie starter. Rumors have to start somewhere, so he would back Rizzo for starting this Bourjos shit. Maybe scare someone who has spare center fielder in the Nook Logan mold to come calling. Lannan and Solis, maybe chuck in Lombardozzi and Hood and they should be able to get someone who doesn't have a bad limp. Maybe get Morgan back. That would force Werth into early retirement or suicide or something and save millions. Creative management. Someone call Michael Lewis, great book in this, Brad Pitt would be wonderful as Rizzo.

God he hated work. Rhonda was now talking to Anna in a corner and half the men in the building were casually standing around like it was natural to stand near the women's washroom and discuss putting up shelves and how much beer they drank. Anna came over with some claims. He got a couple, Rhonda got fewer and Bert got a bundle. So did Chet. And Peter got a wink. Good old Anna. And she had diplomatic immunity now that she was sleeping with the private office. Find someone for Rhonda, Anna, because she needs a fast track to the pregnancy ward. Claims are not her field. Anna leaned over him, nice smile, bit of cleavage. Asked if his wife understood him. Said if she did, he should treasure her because he was the only man over thirty in the building whose wife understood him. And she giggled. Of course, his wife did understand him, which explained Frank.

Oh god, this cheered him up. As he was about to leave he checked rumors and Boras was now hiring staff from Rizzo's office. Not only can't you have Fielder, you can't have Gluvna either. Why are you doing this to me Scott, you know I have been good? Because I can, Mike. Because I can. Christ he wouldn't even need to drink himself to sleep tonight. This would see him through the evening. Better have a drink to celebrate, though.

*

Rhonda said it was like getting her math assignments back in school. She always got everything wrong then, too. He hoped not this wrong. He was philosophical about it, though. Zainab had said that he was simply wonderful the way he helped Rhonda and Anna went out of her way to reward him with a glimpse of cleavage on a regular basis. Nothing too overt. He would avoid a coronary. But he was happier at work. Despite Chet and Bert. He could easily do all the work of Rhonda as well as his own and help her learn. Showed you how little was really done in the office.

He avoided a coronary talking to Anna but not later when Law published his report on prospects. Twenty-first. Top last week, twenty-first today. Mind you BA's ranking was before Beane raided the store, but even so; either Law was an idiot or Callis was. He would back Law any day on that one. Better cook, maybe. Maybe not. It was all about self-promotion. Beane, Boras and Law. Sounds like a sit-com. Make it Beane, Boras, Law and Selig and it would be a sit-com.

Thing about prospects was that if you take the top twenty from any team, even Tampa, and maybe five or six make it as regulars, maybe one or two with impact. So having the top system but having no one in the top twenty-five prospects is a contradiction. With Harper and Rendon, the Nats have two potentially high impact players. Rendon has the injury thing, of course. Having ten high ceiling guys who are just out of high school counts for shit. Which is why Beane has Cole and Mike has Gio. Much as he hated to support Rizzo while he continues to annoy people over this center field thing. Not everyone is annoyed, of course, not Bill fucking Ladson with his Werth can cover center field horseshit. Rizzo can do no wrong for him. Look who's in left, Bill, a first baseman. One who can hit, mind you, but there is no golden glove in Morse's outfield future. And if Werth is in center it is because there is a rookie in right. A promising one, but a rookie. Great arm, so when the ball rolls slowly to the wall, he will hold the hitter to a triple. Way to go Bryce. So we have a right fielder in center who might cope if he wasn't expected to cover for inadequacies in left and right.

Of course, the real trick to running a good minor league system was to over-hype the prospects and then trade them to Florida, whoops, Miami. Or Oakland. Oakland was always good for dumping a star for prospects. Like Gio. Christ, maybe he's good. Maybe the reason Scott wanted Gluvna was because of what he did hyping Peacock, Norris and Cole. At least it's a good sign that they went to Oakland. Billy Beane building a new last place team to take to San Jose. Then he would make some remarkable moves, get more attention, finish last and hope to hell his ten year contract had an escape clause. Asshole. Boston and the Yankees had the best organizations, forever developing great young players that didn't make it, but had the decency to not make it somewhere else after having been traded for Adrian Gonzalez or Roger Maris or something.

After lunch he corrected Rhonda's homework again and quietly passed it back to her. Christ, she was dumber than Rizzo, poor kid. Bet she'd have got a center fielder, though. God, he had forgotten to check to see Law's top prospects. Law being Law, Harper would be maybe ninth, just behind the cheese soufflé. Likely spoil his weekend. What a stupid idea, how could anything spoil weekends that were as fucked-up as his? Do your worst Keith, baby, Harper the only Nat at ninety-six and five recipes in the top twenty. What a baseball mind.

Well, he was wrong. A grand total of two Nats on the list. Nats missing Gluvna already. Need more hype. He watched Law make his little speech. Really wimpy little guy. Looked like he got bullied at school maybe. Would explain the way he treats people on his chat. Peter had been bullied a lot at school. Not being athletic and then later the pimples and his father being such a wimp and things. And when Bryan wasn't there anymore, it got really bad. It was pretty unpleasant, but life goes on. Look at the way he had recovered. Drunk, underachieving divorced parent estranged from both children. One of the few real fights he had with Marianne was when Barney was being bullied. Asked him what to do and he had told him. Two ways, first was to just take it. Second was to help the bullies find someone else even weaker to bully. That's it, two ways. Marianne went ballistic, but she was wrong. Peter had chosen the first way and was relieved at the time that Barney chose number two. He hated the thought that Barney would go through what he went through. God, this was depressing. Was he thinking maybe he could convince Bert and Chet to bully Rhonda instead of him? He needed a drink. Settle him down.

*

It didn't help his peace of mind to read that Gio Gonzalez would be the number two starter partly to slot him between Strasburg and Zimmermann because if he was number one there would be four consecutive right handers. Jesus, he missed Goessling. Work it out Pete. It's called a rotation. It goes round and round. If there is only one lefty, he pitches every fifth game and when it is over, there are four right handers. In a row. Anyway you cut it. How could a team contend with guys like that writing about it? Shift him to the Orioles. Sort of thing that could keep you awake.

*

Friday morning and after correcting Rhonda's assignment and sorting out the day, he was really left with little to do. Try to guess who Super Chef nominates as the Nationals' sleeper prospect. If he chooses in their top ten, it should be Taylor. If he goes outside it maybe Rick Hague or Jeff Kobernus. Not likely to be a pitcher. Strasburg aside, Law is not high on the pitching. Fridays were so awful. Sick of the week. Scared of the weekend. And Rhonda was becoming more popular by the hour. Well, she was attractive but with her stunning mathematical ability she needed all her time to calculate claim adjustments. Unless she let him do it. Bert had asked Rhonda if she had thought of working in group insurance and then leered like it was funny. She probably didn't know all the group grope jokes and the stupid one about the gang in group getting a bang out of their work. Bert was a shit. Still, Rhonda's best hope was likely marriage. Follow Anna's lead. Sort of sexist to suggest it.

God, an email from Marianne. He hated to read it in the office. Always made him feel worse. Mind you, it would be a challenge for Marianne today. Making him feel worse. One good thing. Girls' lunch today Rhonda had said. She was invited. Anna, Beryl, and Zainab. He knew why they organized that. They were really great women to do that for Rhonda. They'd give her the clues. Wouldn't make her smart but could make her careful. Felt better. Opened the email. Frank and her would like to drop by Saturday about noon. Sign some papers. Well, that did the trick. Then, by the way, have you tried the kids lately; both going through a bad patch. Not his fault. They reject him completely now what is he supposed to do, call to say he loves them. Despite the fact that they think he's a shit. Trouble is, he did love them. Other trouble was, they did think he was a shit. Worst thing was, he was a shit. Typical Marianne email. Depressed the hell out of him. Nice to suggest noon. More or less saying that, as you will be sick and hung-over until at least 11:45, we would like to do it at noon thus preserving our afternoon. Sweet, that.

Zainab passed his desk on the way back from lunch. Patted his hand. Said she admired him. What? No one had ever admired him. Then Beryl had walked by, tried to speak but just sort of coughed or something. Then Anna. Big kiss. A few minutes later Rhonda came in and asked if there was some things she could take home. Just things to help her get a better handle on the job. He felt sort of stupid. I mean, what the hell.

And he was right about Michael Taylor as well. Pretty easy choice. Must be Gluvna building him up. He will announce he is becoming a Boras client next week and be traded to Billy Beane in Spring Training. So it goes. Weekend coming. Shit. Marianne coming with the papers to sign. Shit. With Frank. Fucking Frank. He actually felt pretty good. Jake's and a movie. Yeah. Jake's and a movie. Maybe the Clooney thing on the Common.

*

Well, George Clooney was a better father than he was, that was for sure. Maybe he would try the telephone again. Maybe after Marianne and Frank. Maybe they would answer this time. Decent film, I suppose. A little touch of Chip Hilton plays daddy. Mind you, Chip would have got it right first time round. With a gosh and a smile. Good old Chip. An example for us all.

The morning brought a touch of guilt. At least there was no hangover to combat, other than the feeling that he was a failure as a father which had hung over him for as long as he had been a father. With good reason. But today he was damned if he was going to feel sorry for himself. Shower and shave. Ironed a clean shirt, then ironed a few more for the week. Cleaned the place. Who would have thought a basement apartment could hold that many empties. Oh, well, rubbish will be collected soon. He hoped. This recycling shit exposed him, no hiding the bottles with kitchen scraps. Maybe he should go out and find some jam jars to mix in. Make him look a more complete person. He even vacuumed the place. Dusted. Dusted, for Christ sake. Who the fuck dusted? Should have used the vacuum after he dusted, but no one's perfect. The dishes took some time. Funny how things form a crust like that.

Fucking Frank. Always the lawyer. Now read these carefully and you should get a legal opinion. We want to be fair but we are the other side in this. Frank, you'd be the fucking other side in anything for me. Bet you support the fucking Red Sox. Well, Cherington has done jack shit while Rizzo has at least revamped the whole rotation. Gave up a bit, but the guy is trying. Not like your fucking Ben Cherington. A lot of talk about the do nothing Sox. They need Lannan, maybe Ellsbury and Pedroia would do it. We'd chuck in Craig Stammen maybe.

They were only there for an hour. Tried to be nice. Had some coffee. Smiled when he told them that he had hoped to bake something but there just wasn't time. Asked about work. Agreed to pick up the papers same time next week without actually saying that it was to make sure they got them back because he was so unreliable. Mind you, they had a point. Then, just as they left, the hand came out; please try to phone the children, for your sake as much as theirs. Please. My sake, every time I try either Arnie slams the phone down or there is no answer or Barney shrugs and hangs up. How do you shrug on a fucking telephone? He looked through the papers. Real bastards, those two. How could he hate people who were that fucking generous? Must be rich. Both of them. Fucking Frank.

After signing the papers and setting them aside he would go out for a drink. No sense annoying them, so he would wait out the week but by signing them now and placing them on top of the cupboard, he would know where to find the and not have to mess around signing them next Saturday. He went for a long, thoughtful walk, pensive rather than morose he told himself, knowing he was lying. What with Marianne and Frank being so decent and the Nats still not addressing center, who wouldn't be depressed? Saw a couple of projected line-ups in the paper but they all got it wrong. There was absolutely no possibility that DeRosa, Cameron, Ankiel, and Bernadina would all be there on opening day. What a joke. An entire bench of outfielders. Maybe include Xavier Paul and not carry a second catcher. These guys call themselves experts. Still, he liked Kilgore. And Zuckerman. He missed Goessling a bit because Kerzel wrote as if he would rather be writing about something else but he would just knock something out in ten minutes before he goes to the toilet.

He ended up walking until it was time to cook dinner, so missed out on his drink. When did he ever prefer cooking dinner to going for a drink? God, he was getting old. And boring. No, he wasn't getting boring, he had always been boring. Decided he had better go for at least one drink and that Lombardozzi really needed a year at AAA and this guy Blanco should be on the team. Like the guy at MASN suggested. God weekends were boring. Like him. Maybe phone the kids tomorrow. Like Marianne said. Maybe she would have told them to answer. Who knows? He liked the idea of Lombardozzi. Shame to send him down. Shit.

*

Sunday morning he woke up too early. It was getting light but still, far too early. Another wonderful day ahead. Maybe phone the kids. Shit no, why not drive out to Burlington. Roads are nice and clear. Why not? He hated the telephone and worst that could happen, well, maybe he shouldn't think about the worst that could happen. Anyway, he sort of enjoyed driving with the radio. PBS or maybe the classical music. He never listened to classical music at home, not without Marianne to choose it, but he liked driving to it.

He liked Burlington; it had been home for so long. He walked around the center which changed without changing much, somehow. Church Street still pleasant but the market square has had a touch up or two. Stopped for coffee and a read of the Globe. Maybe he could retire here. Meant to be a nice place for older people. Trouble is, he hated older people. Like him. He mostly hated younger people too, so maybe it didn't matter. Might as well stay in Boston and hate people. Boston wasn't bad. At least it didn't have a fucking Pumpkin Regatta. He walked over to the Community College and then down to the lake. Lake Champlain always looked better to him in winter. In fact Vermont was a winter place for him. Always preferred it in winter. Except for summer evenings watching the Lake Monsters. He went back to the Vermont Pub and Brewery for lunch. Lucky to get served. Over-rated probably, but still fun. He liked their burgers. Everyone did. Maybe not when you are alone. He walked back to the lake and along the front. Then back to the car. Should he phone Cheryl first. Maybe. Maybe just surprise her. Maybe just go home. Home, shit, what a laugh, his basement. He decided to take the newspaper back to the coffee shop and think about it.

*

The light was fading when he drove past Cheryl's house. Didn't stop right outside. Sat for some time, kept looking back. He finally got out and walked to the house, stopped, then past it, then turned and walked back. When he stood outside it a second time a curtain moved and he saw someone briefly. Cheryl, for sure. No turning back now, so he went and rand the bell. Nothing. Rang again. Then a third time. Still nothing. Their car was there. He shrugged. Got back in his car. Better go; get part way home before dark.

Could have been Arnie in the window. Or his imagination, maybe.

*

On Monday Rhonda was there before him. In fact, he had almost forgotten their agreement and had to take a cab to work. Even then he was only there twenty minutes early. Rhonda was impatient. Not in an unhappy way, she was just dying to show him what she had done on the weekend. Firstly, she had completed all her homework but, more importantly, she had written out all the instructions he had given her. It looked like an old-fashioned decision table; full of boxes and if this do that and things like that. But she had it mostly correct. He looked at it. It was pretty impressive. Thing was, he could tell her what to do but she obviously needed this diagram or whatever she called it. She did have one or two questions and marked a few things in pencil but, well, it was way better than anything he could have done. And he told her so.

Rhonda looked at him. Do you really mean it? I mean really mean it? Really?

He then looked at the work she had done on the weekend. It was all done correctly. She smiled shyly and said she had just used the diagram and it all just worked. Funny thing is that I hardly have to even look at the diagram anymore.

He asked her if she would mind if she showed the diagram to someone because he thought it was so good. You're kidding? I mean, don't make fun, I know I am slow. No, no, this is terrific. But who should he show it to. Certainly not Chet. He decided to take it to Zainab.

Rhonda was anxious to get working with her new confidence. He felt sort of useless again, without her work to do. She even asked if he minded if she did a few of his claims because she wanted to make sure she really understood. Would he check them? Sure, but they were all done perfectly. Oh well. Gammons had a hopeful little article. Billy Beane signed Cespedes, of all things. No money in Oakland and now they shell out for Cespedes. Four years, by then Oakland may disappear to San Jose. Last thing Billy needs is to show up in San Jose without his star center fielder who will by then have moved to left and still be chasing slow curves. Billy strikes again. Gives you hope for Rizzo. Maybe Beane out-stupided him.

Before he went home he had Rhonda clean up her little pencil marks and gave the diagram to Zainab to look at. She was such a nice woman, she promised to do it that evening.

Tuesday morning he didn't arrive the half hour early. Rhonda looked pretty disappointed. But it was hardly necessary. She said the morning sessions were the only nice thing about the job. Sweet, that. They agreed to meet just for coffee from now on. He felt sort of silly. Like a silly old fart. Well, he was. Not that it was anything like that. In fact she told him that he reminded her of her grandfather. She had really loved him and was heart-broken when he had died.

Amanda Comak did a nice little piece on signing the likes of Edwin Jackson. He agreed with her, good deal for the Nats. She was actually a bright woman. He didn't bother much with the Times, but at least when she wrote something, there was some sense to it. Not just a space filler. Mind you, even Kerzel cheered him up today. Maybe giving up Norris was not such a big deal. Some steady youngsters coming through at catcher.

Work was particularly boring. People avoiding accidents. Needed harsher winters. More slippery surfaces and fires to keep him busy. Collapsing roofs and ceilings, that sort of thing. Especially now that Rhonda was keen. At least Chet the Teeth and his pet Pekinese, Bert, were lazy bastards so they picked up some extra work there. Bert used to be really good but maybe Chet preferred him useless. They sat and giggled together like a pair of school girls. That was sexist. Like a pair of basketball fans. Celtic fans.

He promised to see Zainab in the morning about Rhonda's diagram. Stopped at The Junction on the way home, but his heart wasn't in it.

*

After his coffee with Rhonda and another one with Zainab and then talking to the pair of them, most of the morning had gone. Chet was furious and spoke to them. Sorry, didn't realize we were so far behind. Especially as our desks are clear, as you can see. What an asshole he was. Zainab wanted to present Rhonda's diagram to the Claims Manager. Charlie whatever. Anna's guy. Why not? Zainab was pretty enthusiastic, Said he had done a remarkable thing with Rhonda. Well, not really, but her diagram was okay.

Nothing much in baseball. When the big story is who might sign a Cuban eighteen year old, well, not much going.

Got home and checked the computer again. Nothing really. Email from Marianne saying Cheryl had contacted her. Marianne said he was to be understanding. Hard to be anything really. What was he supposed to do? Send an email to Marianne and ask her to forward his understanding to Cheryl and Arnie? He decided he didn't want the Nats to sign Soler. Might as well see if Goodwin worked out. He had a bad feeling about Eury Perez. And about Hood.

Work was impossible. Sure Rhonda was bursting with enthusiasm and Zainab was full of the new diagram. But there was nothing much to do. Except look at Chet's stupid smile and hate him. And Bert. Well, at least Bert didn't smile all the time.

*

Had to happen, of course. Cancer and brain tumor. But it was awful. The first really great Expo rookie. What a system they had built. All those great outfielders. No centerfield problem when you got the Hawk out there. Christ, think of the Singletons and Folis and Wallachs that passed through. But The Kid was the first great rookie. And now he was gone. Fuck it. Guy wanted to be an Expo. Went to the Series with the Mets but went to the Hall as an Expo. Played when they were in Jarry Park. He'd seen him hit one out of there. Need a drink tonight. Maybe two. Locals would be full of Varitek and Wakefield. Will they, won't they. Who the fuck cares about Varitek. Carter was a real superstar catcher.

*

By the time he got to work on Friday it was far too late to have coffee with Rhonda. He knew she was disappointed. But he had to drink a few toasts to Carter. Found a few guys in The Junction who remembered him. In fact one of them had seen him play in Montreal. They all liked the Expos. How about that?

There was always a bit of affection for the Expos in Boston, really. Maybe because they were no threat. Other league and all. And never really made it. Never went to the Series. Fucking Rick Monday. And Selig. 1994. Expos were a cert. Fucking best team ever. Maybe Ruth and Gehrig's Yankees could have given them a game. Maybe.

*

Friday. Nothing. AJ Burnett going to Pittsburgh. Now that is big news. Poor old Pirates. Right up there with the Cubs this year, fighting it out for last place in baseball's worst division. Something to think about on the weekend. He hated weekends now. Maybe he always had. Frank and Marianne coming over again. Noon again, to make sure he would be up. Hopefully Cheryl would not be on the agenda.

He went home and watched Beltway Baseball from Thursday. Pretty hopeful really. When you compared the presentation to local television it certainly lacked an edge, but that's what the writers should be doing. Making you hopeful. Even when the team is crap. Christ, what a job it would be in Pittsburgh. Even with AJ fucking Burnett. Amanda Comak reminded him of Zainab. Why, he could not say. He liked her, though. Those three kids on Beltway Baseball maybe lacked pizzazz of ESPN and the music was dreadful, but they understood about center field and leadoff and wanting to bat Werth sixth and all the right things. Hope Rizzo was watching. Probably trending away on the telephone. Listen Billy, we got this guy trending better by the day so maybe you could send us a center fielder for him. His name? Yeah, just a second, written here somewhere.

*

Saturday morning he went out and bought some fresh rolls for Marianne and Frank. Brewed some decent coffee and put out some raspberry jam he had bought in the coffee shop. Organic shit. How the fuck can jam be organic? And who cares? Well, Marianne, actually. Maybe Frank as well. Still, he would show them that he could lead a decent life. Even if he couldn't.

Marianne and Frank were late. Not very late, but it surprised him as it was not exactly Marianne's style. She was always a pain in the ass about punctuality. If he was three or four hours late for dinner, she would hardly speak to him. I'll bet she never got that angry with Frank. Big lawyer. Big deal. When they did arrive, the first thing Marianne did was ask about Barney. Had he spoken to him this week? This week. Last week. Previous week. When the fuck did he speak to Barney? More to the point, when did Barney ever speak to him?

Barney had telephoned Marianne very early this morning to say god knows what. Something about maybe going away for a bit something about not worrying. Seems Marianne had been worrying ever since.

Nothing causes worry like being told not to worry. People should know better. Mike Rizzo telling everyone he isn't worried about centerfield. Can't be so stupid that he isn't worried about center field. I mean, Benadina? Cameron? At least Rick Ankiel can play the position. Well, Cameron could too if he were only twelve or so years younger.

Marianne was still going on about Barney. And Bobbie. Had he heard anything? Oh sure, things go a bit funny and Bobbie would almost certainly phone him to spill her guts. Drunken bitch. At least Marianne didn't mention anything about his visit to Cheryl. Or his non-visit to Cheryl. Frank was silently nodding while Marianne continued to worry on behalf of all of them. He joined Frank. Nodded away in sorrowful silence. Great bonding moment for him and Frank,

Finally they took their signed papers and buggered off to worry somewhere else. Gary Carter is dead and all they can think about is some stupid telephone call Barney made at dawn. Probably drunk. At least Barney was probably drunk. With Bobbie it would be a certainty. Probably too drunk to telephone. Or answer the telephone.

This was no time to be worried about family. Spring training was just around the corner and it required his full concentration. There were always endless rumors at this time. All bullshit, of course. Most team were largely set by now but it did not stop rumors about trades, about rookies about to make the team, about players being out of options and on the block. Good stuff for the press. And the fans. Zuckerman was manfully trying to create a story a day. Leaving the wife and kid for a few months to write about baseball. Stick to it Mark, kids are a pain. Older they get, bigger the pain. And watch out for lawyers called Frank.

The doorbell rang. Well, the doorbell sort of hummed. Must do something about it. Maybe call the landlord. Ask for a rent reduction as all his friends come around and he can't hear the bell. Which was humming continuously now. Christ, uniforms. Now what? Seems Marianne might have been right to worry about Barney. Cops weren't so much worried as pissed off. A bit stupid to be pissed off at him because his son didn't answer the telephone. Wouldn't say what was wrong except that they had no reason to think Barney was dead or injured or anything. They just wanted to talk to him. He didn't say anything about Marianne. They probably talked to her already. Didn't mention Bobbie, either. Last thing anybody needed was Bobbie to worry about. Even cops need some consideration.

While he was talking to the police there was a call on his cell. Marianne, probably. Must have been there first. He really had to get back to spring training. And to The Junction. Or another bar. Any other bar. Looked like a long night.

*

The police were back in the morning. It was worse than he thought. Hit and Run and there was a body to think about. A dead one. God, Barney, what have you done? Police were pretty unhelpful. Suggested Barney had done a runner after hitting this old guy. Someone had seen the car and had reported it. God, Barney. Marianne was on the phone. What could he say? Best to go out.

He checked the computer before he left. Mike Cameron retired. Well, one less crap center fielder to worry about. The righty of the platoon is gone. More at bats for someone. Rizzo will deal with it. We're trending to using just two guys outfielderizing the defense. Maybe use DeRosa and Morse. Lot of range there. Then we could back up first with someone to get all those bad throws from the left side. Christ, Barney. Shit. Shit, shit, shit.

Jesus, Jesus must have arrived in camp. All the press had their little Jesus Flores article this morning. Big news, back-up catcher arrives in training camp. Would prefer to be top dog. Say, how about that? The way they can winkle out the big stories. Man, the Expos had some catchers. Not just The Kid. He was the greatest, of course. Right up there with the greatest ever. All enthusiasm and confidence. Best damn hitting catcher around. Could hit and run with two strikes. Not a Nat in six years could hit like that. And a catcher. Good defense, too. Computer is full of him throwing out one guy or another. Mike Fitz was good, and Fletcher. But there was only one Gary Carter. Then the disappointments: Colbrunn and Laker. And then the Nats and Bowden: Lo Duca and Estrada. Shit. Oh god, Barney. Not manslaughter. Surely not. Turn yourself in.

Bought a Globe, Cafardo was all upset because some of the Red Sox got bigger salaries this year. Pretty unusual stuff, Nick. Not as if salaries aren't trending up, though. Get a grip. Story in the Globe on a hit and run. Two in the morning, Saturday. Old guy. Dementia. Out in his pajamas. Bare feet. Oh, Barney, turn yourself in and let them sort it out.

Got home before nine. There was a reporter there. How do they do it? He lost his temper. Stupid that. Can't do Barney any fucking good by that. But the reporter was shit. How does it feel to hear your son has killed a defenseless old man? Fuck you. And there were messages from Marianne. On the cell. And an email. Please call. No way. What good would it do? You have Frank. Fucking Frank will sort it out.

8. Spring Training

Word gets around. God, he hated Chet. Didn't know you had a son. Strange business. You must be feeling terrible. Why don't I just keep bleating on about it so that even if you don't feel bad now, you soon will? Anything I can do, just let me know. Let's keep it top of the office agenda for as long as it takes to drive you out of here.

Zainab came over mid-morning and just touched his arm and left a coffee. Nice woman. And Rhonda was terrific. Just softly asked him how he wanted to play it. She could understand it if he wanted more work to keep his mind off things but if he preferred, she was now comfortable enough to take the heavier workload. And she was. It was a miracle. Good for her.

Anna was the best though. She leaned over Chet's desk and just said the two magic words. Fuck off. Gave Peter a real lift. And even Beryl gave him an encouraging smile or two. So he felt better. Took time to check the computer. Fucking Rizzo. How the fuck do you regress someone? Must come as a real relief to Lombardozzi that Rizzo has no intention of regressing him this year. Apparently he has no plans to digress him from the infield to redress the imbalance caused by the depress caused by the retirement of Mike Cameron. Fucking regress him. Shit, Mike. Even Bowden speaks better English better than that.

Lombardozzi must have been scared that the Nats were going to sign Fielder. Take his spot on the roster. He's been eating his way into the Fielder figure he thinks they must have wanted. I mean fifteen pounds. You are supposed to be a lean and mean middle infielder. Not the second coming of Miguel Cabrera.

Hey, have to admire Detroit. Balancing their infield like that. With Cabrera at third it is less likely to tilt to the right. Mind you, it could sink. No chance of small ball over in Detroit.

Great city, Montreal. Not a baseball town? No shit. Naming something after Gary Carter. Maybe they should re-name Dominion Square. Trouble is with all the militant French they will have to call it Cartier Square. Place Cartier. Or Place Gary Cartier to distinguish it from Place Jacques Cartier. Like the streets named after Bishop Mountain. Poor bastard had two streets named after him. Rue Montagne and Rue de l'Eveque. French wouldn't countenance his real name. Not that a fucking Bishop should have anything named after him. Maybe a condom. Bishop Condoms for real protection. Fucking fruitcakes, the French. Mind you, when he used to go to Montreal he loved it. Maybe go back. Nice fruitcakes. But fruitcakes.

He had regular emails from Marianne. Let's stay in touch. If one of us hears anything, get in touch immediately. God, Barney, Barney, what have you done? Then, late in the afternoon; an email from Barney. Holy fuck.

Dad, about what you said to the newspapers. It was great of you. Don't try to get in touch. I need to think for just a day or two. But anyway, thanks.

What the fuck had he said? What the fuck had they printed? Likely had no relationship to what he said. He slipped out to find a newspaper. The article accused him of defending murder. No wonder Barney loved it. But he read it. Apparently what he said was that the newspapers were totally irresponsible and he had no intention of talking to them, which he was obviously doing at the time. Must have been drunk. And he said that they hadn't the brains to distinguish a terrified kid from a real criminal and that if anyone really wanted to talk to Barney more compassionate reporting might be a start. Shit, not bad. Did he really say that? Maybe he wasn't drunk. He was sure angry. He remembered that.

No bars tonight. Best to be at home with the computer on and his cell phone. He owed Barney that. Christ, Barney, talk to someone. He emailed him. Just to say he was there. You know, won't help much but maybe it might. A little.

The morning paper gave a few more details about the accident. Hit and run, late at night. Early in the morning really. So what is an old guy doing out in his pajamas? The newspaper made it seem like this somehow made the old fart even more innocent. Sweet old man out for a stroll in the middle of the night cut down by crazed driver. Mentioned that the car sped away but no suggestion it speed into the accident. Why not give Barney a break? Maybe the old guy was drunk? Or demented?

Trouble with all this Barney stuff was that it interfered with spring training. He would love to go down to Florida one spring for about five weeks and just wander. They say the back diamonds are the best. Not formal and everyone still thinks there in for the World Series. Must be wonderful. Imagine having the sort of talent that lets you earn a living that way. Not that they could possibly earn what they do. He remembered Karl Malone saying how people didn't realize how tough it was, all the nieces and nephews expecting presents and such. Poor Karl, should have sent him a few bucks. Asshole. What could you expect from a basketball player? Funny how some sports personalities are less lovable than others. Bonds and A-Rod. Then there are the Gary Carters. Place Gary Carter.

Great idea. Maybe one day a Tim Raines Boulevard. Chemin Larry Linz. Almost hit .200 one year, did Larry. Sure could run, though. Like Eury Perez.

Work was a drag. Bert asked him how the family was doing and Chet snorted with what might have been a laugh. And Anna spilled a coffee down Chet's back. Gosh, you gave me such a start. What was so funny? I am so sorry about the coffee. Was it hot? And it has ruined your shirt. And your suit. And even some on your tie. Clumsy me. He loved Anna. No wonder Charlie whatsit fell for her. Heard he was legit. Divorced but okay. Two young kids, though. Anna would likely bring the total to a respectable four. He could see Anna wanted children in manageable numbers. God, how was Barney getting on? Marianne was emailing often and sounding more distressed each time. Hate to have her drilling my mouth just now. She was probably checking her email and phone between each patient.

Today was the hospital watch in Florida. LaRoche is healthier than he has been since puberty. DeRosa thinks he is but can't remember that far back; Ramos would rather play baseball than be kidnapped. Such drivel but it was all exciting because it was spring training. Even Marrero feels good. Can't walk, but feels just fine.

The evening lasted forever. Went to bed after midnight and lay awake until god knows when. Marianne telephoned. Several times. Many times. He didn't answer. Fuck it, let Frank deal with it.

*

190

He picked up a newspaper on the way to work. He was becoming addicted. Morning and evening additions. Nothing on Barney. Good or bad? Hard to say. Let's say good. Couldn't bear the sports. All Red Sox. Well, Bruins and Celtics. No features on important people, like Bryce Harper and Ian Desmond. Christ, Desmond has to hit leadoff and all they talk about is tonight's games. Celts and Bruins both up for a sound thrashing. Let's hope so. And Boston got jack shit for Theo. Well, what did they expect? Guy needed a change and was offered the earth, so he went. Maybe they don't drink beer in the Cubs' dugout.

Big news today is Edwin Jackson is going to hold the ball differently. That should make the difference. Amazing stuff. From that distance he wouldn't know if there even was a ball in his hand much less how the fingers were on the seam. Bonds claimed he tracked the spin. Probably did. It's the steroids. Funny, Bonds takes a few pills to make himself a better person and he's mud. Tim Raines snorted so much coke he didn't know if he was in left field or in the toilet and he's loved. Except by the guys who vote for the hall.

Terrible the way the writers all write the same story. Lombardozzi getting fat one day. Kerzel, Zuckerman, Kilgore all right there to watch him eat. Get a comment or two. Then a day of health reports. By all of them. Then Zimmerman's contract and Ryan Mattheus throwing smoke in February. They might as well share out the work. Everyone does two stories a week and share them around. Probably it is what they do anyway. Maybe not Zuckerman. He is so fucking conscientious. Glad he's not in claims. Little enough to do as it is.

*

191

Another long night. No bars, no food, no sleep, no news. But the morning paper had some. Sketchy, but Barney was in custody. At least he turned himself in. Full confession. Oh god, now what? Likely put the poor kid away for life because he got scared and ran off. Shit, shit, shit. But, it was the right thing to do. How can he try to say he is proud of him without sounding patronizing? For that matter, how to tell him anything? Where the fuck is he now? Fucking Alcatraz? He got off the stop before his usual stop and telephoned Marianne. Thank god her line was busy. So he texted. I think he did the right thing. Things might still work out. Fat fucking chance really, but they could hope. Until the trial. God, he hoped the judge and jury didn't read the papers.

He thought work would be awful but Bert and Chet were silent all day. Sullen but silent. Zainab and Anna played it just right. Like they were pretty sick about it themselves but were putting on a cheerful front. Beryl took the trouble to come over. My husband was a reporter before he died. Bunch of idiots. Keep cool.

At least Rizzo seemed to be working on a new contract for Zimmerman. He had worried that with Rendon coming, Rizzo might let it slip. Sort of deliberately but making it look like he was crushed. The whole situation could regress his well-being incrementally in a non-positive direction. Get him signed Mike. And come out and say Harper is going to Syracuse for the daffodil season, looks to join the big boys once the summer flowers are blooming.

The evening paper had very little. Barney had confessed. Swore he was not going fast. Swore he had not been drinking. Swore he had not noticed that he had hit someone. Then got scared. All made sense except the bit about not noticing. Apparently at least one witness saw the car slow to almost a stop and then speed away. Poor, scared bastard. He called Marianne. Talked for thirty minutes. Well, talked for one minute and listened for twenty-nine. Poor Frank.

He went to bed exhausted. Maybe it was the wonderful news that Ryan Braun had got off on a technicality or that Elijah Dukes was arrested for eating a bag of marijuana, but he just felt so good about the law. Apparently Dukes had been arrested dozens of times and drives without a license these days. System didn't bother to follow up. Presumably on the basis that if incarceration was supposed to be corrective, they were wasting their time with Elijah. Barney would probably get twenty years because some old fool walked in front of his car.

God, he should be concentrating on spring training. Moving the infielders around. Trying Rendon at second and Espinosa at short. Totally insignificant, of course, unless Jerry decides he needs a shortstop with power more than he needs a second great center field prospect. Maybe Dipoto feels Bourjos' youth gives him a slight edge over Wells and Abreu in left. Smart guy. But dreaming about Bourjos put him to sleep.

*

Nothing in the newspapers on Friday morning. He didn't miss the righteous indignation of the third estate. Their brave quest for justice would have seen Barney lynched by now. Free press. Shit. He arrived in the office early where Rhonda was already working. She smiled. Nice smile. Said she was missing their morning tutorials so was glad to see him. Coffee? She had been working on her process diagram, could he just have a look? He knew what she was doing, of course. She really didn't need him to tell her what a useful teaching tool she had created. She wanted him to be a bit involved. Phony as shit.

Transparent as shit. But he loved her for it. And it worked. Until Chet arrived and was more sullen than yesterday. At least those fucking teeth weren't on permanent display. When Rhonda absented herself to go to the washroom, Chet turned to him and reminded him it was almost the end of the month. Pay goes in today. He expected his two hundred Monday. Actually due Friday but he was being kind what with his family problems and all. Tuesday at the latest. Peter had pushed it all to the back of his mind. Tried to forget. What with Barney and all. But the Chets of this world didn't work that way. He looked down. Said nothing. But he wouldn't pay. God this was a lousy spring. And yet, and yet. There was Rhonda. And Anna. And Zainab, Zainab was wonderful. He would get through the day. Get through the weekend. Maybe hear some good news about Barney. Maybe not. Maybe Dipoto would realize he was a bit depressed, send Bourjos to the Nats for Roger Bernadina.

In the evening there was nothing. No news from Barney. No news on Zimmerman except that there were persistent rumors that the deal was getting close. Rizzo not happy about a no-trade clause. Never know when Billy Beane might want him or Scott tells him to unload and play Rendon at third to go with the other Boras clients. Lannan's not long for the team. Wrong agent. Lannan is supposed to get the third spring start. Another week in the fold.

God, Frank better do something with Marianne. She must be on speed or something. Phone, email, email, phone.

*

Shit, Saturday morning and the first thing that hits him is Zuckerman reminding him that Zimmerman gave the Nats a deadline for the new contract which has passed with no signing. Nothing from Rizzo, nothing from Barney, several thousand emails from Marianne as well as all the missed calls. Time to go out. He actually enjoyed going out to the local coffee shops for breakfast on a weekend. If only he didn't have to read Boston newspapers. Barney made it, Zimmerman did not. Shows a certain lack of judgment. The police continuing with questioning and have yet to press charges. What the fuck? Poor kid confessed. Probably deciding whether they can do him on murder one. Then send him to Texas for execution. Bastards.

This thing with Barney was really screwing up spring training for him. When he turned on the computer there would be a dozen emails from Marianne and none from poor Barney. So much going on right now and he could hardly enjoy it. Gerardo Parra would be a decent addition. No way is it a Lannan for Parra deal, but there still could be a way to work it. Some of the fan comments about the deal were a bit stupid, like where would LaRoche go? First maybe? This thing about Harper starting in the bigs was just crap. Not going to happen. Put Parra in center, Werth where he belongs and batting sixth and worry about Harper getting a game in June. No one prepared to wait until 2013 except him. This lot needed half a century of the Expos to learn something about patience. Still, nice to dream about Parra. Maybe not Peter Bourjos, but who is? Well, Mike Trout, which is why Dipoto should cut us a break. Roger Bernadina is a legit fourth outfielder whereas Bourjos would just be an embarrassment. Of riches; but an embarrassment. Maybe do a deal straight up.

Callis is really high on Rendon. And Callis is pretty good on prospects. Short on shit literature and cracking eggs for omelets, but good on prospects. Says Rendon is a bit small, well then, look at second. Espinosa would understand. Or maybe move to short. Desmond would understand. Whatever? Rendon still a long way away. But the big news is that Zimmerman is likely to sign long term. Between him and Rendon maybe they could work out a rotation; each gets three months a year on the DL. Of course, then they would probably both want to play in the Series. Christ, Davey's got problems there.

He went for a long walk. Took his phone. Never know. Well, he knew Marianne would phone, but he kept hoping for Barney to call. Rotting in a stinking jail somewhere. All those stories about innocent kids being thrown in cells to get beat up and raped and stuff like that. For Christ sake, he has already confessed. No need for the rubber hose.

Sat and looked through a newspaper. Not much. Just another mention on page three hundred of section fifty-one to say the police were pursuing their investigations and that a man was being held but had not been charged. Christ, get on with it. Police probably didn't want to charge him so they could do their questioning routine. The Wire's done nothing for police tactics. Cops probably out getting drunk and leaving Barney to sweat it out with the thugs in the cell block. Poor kid must be terrified. Time the cops learned a little compassion. Media drove them to play this horrible role and Barney would be the victim. Most cops would be plenty more tough than Barney. Plenty of nurses, too. Even nuns would be tougher than Barney for fuck's sake. Mind you, nuns were probably pretty tough cookies. Had to be hard to be such heartless shits. Shuffle the orphans off to wherever for a few pennies in the poor box then force the poor into a few hours prayer to get the pennies. Scumbags. And Barney goes to jail when all the priests and nuns run around being righteous. He hated the fucking church. Bugger an urchin. It's god's will. He was a fine, compassionate priest if it wasn't just the one little fault. He ruined the lives of every boy in the choir. We could hardly hold that against him. God this Barney thing was getting to him. He was becoming slightly unreasonable. All he could think about was what might happen to Barney in the cells. Not really the nuns' fault. Not when you calmed down and thought about it. Went to the library and asked about a book. Needed something like Stieg because he would not be able to concentrate. Woman recommended Jo Nesbo. Neighbor of Stieg's.

Walked home. Turned on the computer. Nothing from Barney. Zimmerman contract getting closer. Who fucking cares? Well, he did. He just sometimes forgot when he was frustrated. Jo Nesbo didn't help much. Too much violence. And perversion. Sells books but hardly does worried fathers any good. And he hadn't even had a drink today. Nothing to eat, either. He fell asleep just before he should be getting up. And Marianne made sure he didn't sleep in. Christ, Marianne, Sundays were long enough without this. Had he heard anything? Yeah, fucking telephone woke me up. No, nothing from Barney. No, nothing from the police. No, he had not seen the paper. What? Released. Maybe as early as today. He was up. Time to get a paper.

Well, what a day this was turning into. Six more years of Zimmerman. Great move. One of the very best. And how can you help but love the guy wanting a no-trade contract. Loyalty, nothing beats it. And such a great player. Great for the team.

And then this thing with Barney. That was something. Released this morning. Can I stay with you for a few days, dad. Sure, sure. Yeah, mum will be a bit hysterical and you know, with Frank being so bloody calm. Drives me nuts. Don't want to go home because of the press. I'll explain when I get there. Can we meet at The Junction? So there you go. Good start to Sunday. Told Barney to meet at the coffee shop opposite The Junction. They would have a meal and a bottle of wine later, but first some coffee and something to eat. He would get some food. How far was he? That close? Already. Good, good. No, he wouldn't tell Marianne. Just tell her he had an email to say he was out and fine and he would get in touch.

So the story came out and it was sad. The police had broken Barney in thirty-six horrible hours. Bobbie had been drinking. As usual. They had an argument and she took the keys and went off in his car. Her license was already suspended so when the guy walked into the side of the car as she was turning a corner she panicked. Kept on about how no one saw her and then later about how he could get away with it because he had a license. And also he wasn't drunk. She just kept crying and shouting and calling him a coward until he finally agreed.

The police had more information than they let on. They knew it was a woman behind the wheel. They knew she was alone. They even had a decent description. They had gone to his neighbors and by the time he confessed, they knew pretty much what had happened. Right down to the drunken argument that several neighbors had overheard. But they didn't let on. They left him hungry. He was cold. He was crying. And finally they broke him. Real 1984 horseshit. Take Bobbie. So they laughed. Laughed in his face when he cried and said it was Bobbie. Think we didn't know that, you schmuck. You must be as pussy-whipped as they come. Drunken bitch got you eating out of her hand. Or something. Or somewhere. And then when they brought her in and he was still there and she spat at him and called him a yellow piece of shit.

But the chief had been decent in the end and he gave Peter the credit. Said he had read the newspaper. The bit about fear turning scared kids into criminals. Your dad is a wise man. You should fucking well pay some attention. Anyway, making criminals wasn't his job. Should lock him up forever. Lying, obstructing justice; all that shit. Caused lots of problems. Which was crap because they knew all along; they just wanted to watch him break apart. Still, chief cop said he might want to thank his dad that he's free. So now he needed a bit of time. Maybe just a week or so. To think. Then he would talk to his mother, but not yet. Then he would have to get sorted. His boss was a good guy. Gave him some leave. Told him to dump the bitch. Damn right.

So dinner was pretty nice. Really nice. Good old dad saved the day. How about that? He hardly remembered what he said but he felt pretty good. Nice to have dinner with his son. Share a bottle of wine. Coffee. Then a second cup. Make up a bed on the couch. Barney pointed out it wasn't necessary to be uncomfortable as the couch pulled out into a real bed. He hadn't noticed that. Good old Marianne. Or maybe Frank.

*

They were both up early. A little self-conscious what with being really close last night. When really they had never been that close. Not for years. Maybe not ever. Barney said he would just hang around. Maybe buy a paper. Maybe go for a walk. He'd do dinner. Could he borrow a few bucks? Maybe a hundred or so?

Going into work was strange. He should have been prepared. Anna hugged him. Rhonda hugged him. Not Zainab. Not her thing, but in many ways the soft touch on the arm was even better. Beryl sort of kept looking over and smiling and then, after maybe fifteen minutes came over and said she was so glad things seemed to be working out. Bert just scowled. Then Chet came over. Showed his teeth in a horrid grin and said it was nice to know his son was a sap rather than a killer and, by the way, the money was now due. Like by noon.

Peter turned to Chet and told him to fuck off.

What?

You heard, fuck off.

You saying you won't pay.

I'm saying fuck off.

You got til noon, then I go to the corridor suits.

I'd go now, if I was you, might as well. Waiting isn't going to help.

The day was slow after that. Spring training went on without him. Some nice things about Zim. About the pitching, too. Gonzalez and Purke, as well as Strasburg. There seemed to be some real excitement around. Great stuff. I guess. Somehow he mostly thought about dinner. With his son.

As he left the office Mr Roberts spoke to him. That was Charlie's last name, Roberts. Anna's guy. They needed to talk. Tomorrow. Urgent. How about ten o'clock. Chet had kept his word, it seemed. Shit.

But it didn't spoil dinner. Peter got out his only ever baseball card. Did Barney know that Gary Carter hit .293 in 1982? Almost 100 RBI's. Barney laughed.

Did he remember how they bought the card? On holiday. Peter had bought it for Barney when they were out together and Barney had left it in a restaurant and Peter had gone back to find it. And never given it back. You know dad, I never gave a shit about Gary Carter. Yeah, I know, I know. Dad, I had been a Star Wars and Star Trek freak and we're on holiday and I'm about to finish high school and my father buys me a baseball card. Jesus. Barney didn't even know that Gary Carter had died. Prison life. Lose touch. Never mind, Barney had dumped Bobbie. After she dumped him and spat in his face, of course, but still, she was history.

*

Christ it took a lot of useless analysis for Schoenfield to decide that the Nats had a lot to do to catch up with the Phillies. Tomorrow he'll maybe see if the Astros have caught up with the Cardinals. Based on solid statistical analysis, the Astros are shit. Based on a quick glance, they are shit. Based on a quick glance, the Nats have untried pitching, a mediocre offense and no fucking center fielder. Spend some time with the kids, David. And Law took the trouble to point out that Zimmerman and Rendon both have histories of injuries. Thanks, Keith. No one had noticed that. But if Werth's contract is your benchmark, Zimmerman's is pretty user-friendly.

*

Breakfast with Barney was a bit strained. These things never work. Not really. Sure he needs support, but really he needs to sort out his life. Get rid of Bobbie. Get to work. Get a life. He talked about Bobbie a lot. Embarrassed. Embarrassed because he knew the relationship was crap and embarrassed because he couldn't get out. Was it the sex? Not even that. When she was sober she was not interested and when she was drunk she was a slut. Anybody's. Used to really humiliate him. Call him inadequate. Go off with some guy they had met in a bar. Come back in a day or two. Often a bit beat up. Say things like at least the guy was a man. He never hit her. Wanted to, but never did. Christ, how did he stick it that long? Sorry, dad, not your problem, is it? Not really but then, sort of. Must go to work. See you tonight? Maybe.

*

The wait at work was a very long hour. He saw Stuart go in. Came out and wouldn't even look at Peter. Then Chet. Came out with his teeth on display in a surly grin. Then it was Peter's turn. Morning Mr Roberts.

Hey, call me Charlie. We've been together a long time. Blah, blah. One of the best, blah, blah and more blah, blah. Then came crunch time. We are offering early retirement. Like as of now. Suggest you take it. Two warnings. Mistakes, a few big ones. Passing work to colleagues when you got behind. Covering up. Really not much choice.

And if he refused to retire? A damaging inquiry. Do nobody any good. Chet felt very strongly. Stuart backed him up.

Well, Chet' a piece of shit. Just ask around in your inquiry, which I am sure will be very fair.

And Stuart is a coward. New opportunities in group underwriting my ass. You know he's shit-scared. So what now?

You want to make it hard, it can be hard. Will do our due diligence. You get to be suspended until Friday. Come in Friday late afternoon. Find Chet was right and you go. Flat-out fired. Reduced pension and benefits. Check out the health care you get as a retiree. Be sensible.

You know, some days I just don't feel sensible. Do your due diligence and I'll see you Friday. You'll support Chet. So what? At least when the next guy complains you'll remember today. Know what? I'm faster than Chet. Faster than Bert. Michele is faster, but Christ. And Zainab, she's the best. Then me. Had a bad patch and you give me Chet. But Chet is shit. You work for the company or you work for Chet?

That's totally unnecessary.

Maybe. See you Friday. And he left. He knew he had blown it. At least he could have had a full pension. Better health care. But somehow that was like giving up. And that due diligence shit. That's what Rizzo did on every fat veteran looking for a job. Manny, Ordonez, all those guys. Imagine, he was the Vlad of claims adjustment.

He made many stops on the way home. Hated going back to see Barney like that. No need to worry. Little note. Time to go dad. Time to make it on my own. Thanks for everything. I'll telephone on the weekend. Mum too. I'll be fine. You too.

He dragged himself to bed but not before the gods of pitching struck down Solis. What is it about the Nats? Maybe Tommy John was a virus. Yeah, I was struck down by Tommy John when I was twenty-three. Made a full recovery but not before my wife and kids caught it. Kids are fine but Sally will never pitch. Not in the bigs. And Peter will never adjust another claim. And Chet would smile his toothy smile at some other poor bastard.

Reassuring to go to bed knowing Rendon is impressing Adam Kilgore. Well, you can be sure this little nugget is leaked from on high so Adam will write about it. Today it was Tyler Clippard day. Rizzo must call all the beat guys into his office and tell them to write about somebody who is feeling a bit blue. Maybe good old Charlie Roberts is calling in the insurance press to write an article about him for tomorrow's claims journal. Good old Peter. Great in his time. Sort of the Livan Hernandez of claims. Fat and slow. And gone. How are you supposed to sleep at a time like this?

*

Well, if he had a job, he would easily have been on time. Woke before dawn so he would have plenty of time to worry. Telephoned Marianne. Not about Chet, about Barney. She was definitely very cool; obviously hurt by the fact Barney had come to him. But she was okay. It was a good time to call her as she had an appointment in five minutes. Always the professional. Now there was nothing to do all day but wait for Rizzo to trade for a center fielder. Maybe go out for breakfast. Relax like it was a Sunday. Of course, he hated Sundays. It could work.

*

So there will be another team in the playoffs this year. Two more if you counted the American League. Maybe help the Nats. Maybe help Rizzo focus on center field. Can't go to the Series with Bernadina in center, Mike. Look bad in the papers. Yanks favored to top Nats in seven due to weakness in center. Lose your job over shit like that. At least you won't lose it because some toothy shit wants two hundred lousy bucks a month for nothing. Well Lo Duca. And Estrada. But those were Bowden days.

Nice little thing about Cherington. Says Valentine will decide if Iglesias will make the team. The way it works Ben, is you make the decisions. You talk to Bobby and then you say 'Well Bobby, that's pretty convincing so we'll do it your way' but you don't announce in the press that you have decided to let Valentine run the whole fucking show. For two reasons. Firstly, it wasn't your decision that he run the whole fucking show because if you had any say, that is the wrong decision; and secondly, try to keep up appearances for the next job application. Got it. Asshole. How did Cherington get a job like that when couldn't even keep a crap job in insurance? Shit.

And the Nats apparently weren't even in the running for Fielder. Bronze medal went to Angelos while silver went to the Dodgers. Maybe Rizzo wasn't an idiot. Still, he had no center fielder. Dierkes said it might take Zimmermann to get Bourjos. Don't do it Mike. Get something cheap and nasty for a year.

*

Woke to a miserable day. Cold and damp. No job and no inclination to go out. Thought about the extra playoff place. Must help teams like the Nats. Some purists were against it but either you go back to two leagues and the champions play each other in the Series, or you expand the playoffs and see it as a different sort of competition. Like basketball and hockey. Which were crap.

Not much going in spring training. Little things about Tyler Moore and Rafael Martin and all the other nice guys that will not make the team but Rizzo wants to get a mention so they feel they have been noticed. Mattheus is another one. Must be tough on the youngsters. Dying for someone to break a leg or fail a drug test but have to keep saying how happy they are just to get a chance and they will keep working and things have a way of falling into place. Sure they do. Ask Matt Chico. Ask Kory Casto. Still, they get a chance but basically it is a marginally more competitive field than insurance.

Tomorrow seemed far away. Not just in time. Another planet. And the meeting on whatever planet it was on, would be late afternoon. That was to help the riot control police quell the unrest when he was officially fired, presumably. Could be crowds gathering with placards already. Should have paid the two hundred. At least for a month or so. Give him time to plan. Hated to think about it.

Hated thinking about Harper and Strasburg. What if they were crap? So hopeful. After the seven years in the wilderness. Harper apparently doing everything right. Model citizen and all. Imagine, a baseball team again. Nothing like the Expos, but at least they might be competitive. And he'd have all day to follow it. Every day, all day just as shitty as today. Something to look forward to. He decided he owed himself a night in The Dorchester. Trouble is, Bruins are playing New Jersey. More like a brawl than a game. Check the computer first; see if the Nats traded Lannan. Disgrace if they do. Best pitcher they had. Other than Livo. Hey, an email. Barney. Thanks dad. I'm going to be fine. You were great.

No big deal. But nice of Barney, that. He decided to head over to Kendall Square. See the silent film that won all the awards. No car chases or explosions there. Even without beer that had to top the Bruins. Fucking hockey.

9. Conflict Resolution

They would just assume he would arrive straight from a bar, stinking of beer. Why disappoint them? He would start in the Junction and work his way north slowly. He had hours, should be perfect. They might as well be happy with their decision. A touch of I told you so to make them feel good about themselves. Bring out the white in Chet's fucking teeth. Checked the computer. Four emails. Christ, he'd never had four emails in his life.

Marianne: Barney called. He said you have been terrific. We all appreciate it.

Cheryl: Barney's with me. You saved his life, you know.

Barney: Hi dad. With Cheryl and Arnie and I'm fine.

Anna: Anna? Christ. Anyhow, Anna: We're all behind you and everything will be fine.

What the fuck?

Who are all behind him? And why would everything be fine. He checked the baseball. Still no center fielder; so that wasn't fine. He had better get to the Junction quickly before another email arrived.

But he didn't go to the Junction. He had coffee and read the Globe. He even read about the Bruins winning in overtime. Fucking Bruins. And he walked. And walked. And he arrived just in time for his appointment. Anna was still there making a fist and smiling. And Zainab, looking shy, like she might miss him. Rhonda, waving her chart. Even Beryl for chrissake.

Good afternoon Mr Roberts.

Come on in Peter. Sit down, sit down. Say, good to see you again. Look this has been unpleasant. More for me than anyone maybe. Learned a lot. I hate situations like this.

You hate them.

I know, I know. Terrible for you. Of course it was. I'll be honest. Don't repeat anything you hear this afternoon outside. I'll deny it. But I'll be honest. Thing is, Tuesday we took the decision to dismiss you without protecting your benefits. Easy decision if you check the file and talk to people. People like Chet. And Stuart.

I'm so glad you found the decision so easy.

Wait, wait, there's more. Much more. See, I have a little thing going with Anna. You know that. Everyone knows really. No secret. Both free and single. Well, I'm divorced. Anyhow, Tuesday night she just about throttled me. Real angry. Told me I was a shit and she didn't go out with shits. Christ, we were talking marriage. Still are, thank god. Anyhow, she says I needed twenty-four hours to think. I figure, humor her. Wait and then do it. So I agree. That's when Ms Potter starts. Wow. She is something. Never said dick until this week. Saved it all for me. Thought she'd kill me at first. Then thought maybe just a sound beating. In here with your mate Rhonda and that beginners' manual you had.

Wonderful stuff. Just wonderful. Then in here with Ms Rappaport to talk about Chet and Stuart. Hey, go easy on Stuart. He's weak and useless, but not a bad guy and when I called him back he was relieved to let it all come out. Then she brought in Michele Bremner to talk about Chet and Bert. Then she was back with Zainab Rappaport to unload on Bert and Chet big time. Then Michele on her own again. God, those guys were really socking it to you. Never should have got away with it. I blamed Stuart at first, but then thought about it. My fault. One hundred and ten per cent. That Potter woman was right about that. Bad management is the fault of the managers. I should get my fat head out of the sand. Say, she is something.

Anyhow, see you Monday. Little re-organization to do with Chet and Bert gone. But you'll manage. Get you training someone new. They say you're brilliant at training.

He was speechless. Stunned. Who the fuck was Ms Potter? Michele supported him? Shit.

They were waiting for him back down the corridor. Zainab smiled. Anna cheered. Michele just told him that he was the only man in the office who never once mentioned her sexual orientation. Rhonda kissed him. And at the back was Ms Potter. Of course.

Beryl, I don't suppose you're free for dinner tonight? Or maybe tomorrow?

You know, Peter, I believe I am.

That night he didn't check the baseball reports. Why spoil the day? Fucking Rizzo still wouldn't have sorted out center field. No fucking sense of occasion.

*

There was a lot to think about on Saturday morning. He hadn't checked the computer so that was where to start. Purke and Rendon had both played at least an inning without suffering career-threatening injuries. Another great victory for the Mike Rizzo scouting team. Purke may last another start or two before Tommy John virus and Rendon will probably stay relatively healthy until they need him. And Harper showed his maturity by going 0 for something. Great day as the Nats beat some college freshman team by a whisker. Mind you, might have been different if the college boys had been to spring training.

Nonetheless, wasn't spring training wonderful? Hood looked great, Taylor looked great. Fucking Martin looked great, a fifty old refugee from the Mexican leagues. Everyone looked great this week. That surely is the benefit of not playing real games. Astros think they're off to the Series. Someone's bubble bursts today as the Astros play the Nats in a winner take all game.

No important emails. One offering him Viagra and one suggesting penis enhancement. With Viagra, penis enhancement may be a reasonable option. What the hell. Thought of emailing Barney. Or Cheryl. Or Marianne even. Or phoning. Just to say he still had a job. But as they never knew that he was about to lose it, it seemed a stupid thing to do. Nice to still have a job. A lot to understand there. Beryl explained a bit. Said they had met and decided that they just weren't having it. They being Anna and Zainab and Rhonda. And Beryl, of course, leader of the pack, apparently. Didn't really like to admit it but it sort of came out.

He enjoyed the dinner. Not a very communicative woman but it was all very nice. Because he had a job. Not sure quite what the job would be as there was only half a team and no team leader and Charlie had said they would shake things up a bit. But a job. He knew he needed that. And his friends. Zainab and Anna and Rhonda. And Beryl. Imagine that. Beryl leading the charge.

Reality struck. The Astros eliminated the Nats and have a clear path to the Series led by Livo who took the time to make his old teammates look stupid. It was Rizzo and Johnson who were stupid, of course. Must have re-assured them to see Jackson throw almost a tenth of his pitches for strikes. Oh well, spring has just started. Maybe Lannan will look good. Trouble is, look good and you're gone; look bad and you're in the pen mopping up. Poor Lannan. Deserved better. Like Livo.

Nice to read that Prince is happy in Detroit. Christ, maybe they should start talking extension soon. Of course, Boras doesn't look to do extensions. Talk is that Detroit needs a pitcher. Maybe if Lannan does well. Shit, Detroit could do a lot worse and Lannan deserves something like that. Show Rizzo his ring next year and ask him where Edwin Jackson is now. Manny needs a left fielder over in Cleveland. Maybe they could send him Bernadina. If ever a guy needed a new start that's him. And Manny might be good for him. Why not. Left fielder who can fill in a few games in center. Not a bad job. If players leave the Nats, nice to see them do well but in another league. Like the American League Western Division. Or Houston. No one would begrudge Livo a good year. Hell, even if he is a money launderer. I'll bet he does that with style. All-timer, that guy. Up there with El Presidente and Woodie Fryman. Funny how he didn't feel the same about Steve Rogers. Fucking Rick Monday. Thinking back to the early Expos put him to sleep. Nice and peaceful. Back when there was a touch of real romance in sport.

*

Wow, ten o'clock. Hadn't slept like that for a long time. Maybe back when he was being breast fed. Maybe. Not that his mother would have breast fed him. Maybe Bryan. God, Bryan. Still, it was never his fault. It was an accident. Better get out of bed, no percentage thinking about it. He enjoyed the local coffee shops. Coffee and the Globe. Nice start to a Sunday. For a man with a job. And a nice little apartment. Even if it was in a basement. Shit, not basement so much as lower ground floor.

Cafardo was very reassuring. Nats still in on anything resembling a center fielder. Scouting Bourjos, Jones, Parra, Bourn, and maybe Richie Ashburn. Don't touch Ashburn, Mike. He's an ex-Phillie. Anyway, I think he's dead. At least he was a Phillie when the Phillies knew their place. Finished last. No, fifth or sixth. Pirates were last. Always. Things sure changed in Pittsburgh. Cafardo again took the time to tell us that Ben was leaving all major personnel decisions to Bobby while he decides who cleans the toilets in the visitors' clubhouse. Doing a great job, Ben. You can take comfort in the fact that if the Red Sox finish out of the play-offs, Valentine will finally admit how much he has depended on you throughout the year. Maybe do it in Japanese. Well, tough. I've got a job of my own to think about.

He called Marianne. Just to say Barney seemed okay. Sort of pleased him to be the one passing on the news. She was pretty subdued. Cheer her up Frank. Hell, it's only been a few weeks. Maybe he should call Cheryl. Nah, don't push it. Maybe go to the movies. Good idea. Except it was all explosions and shit. Unless it was animation. Dr fucking Seuss for Christ's sake. Maybe back to Ken Burns. Or Kurosawa on DVD. Throne of Blood. Maybe Hidden Fortress in honor of Barney. Maybe Rashomon. Under-rated gem, that one.

Spring training is wonderful. Lose gazillion to fuck-all and all you get is optimism. Strasburg was great despite this losing thing, Harper legged out a hit and is yet to get the fucking ball out of the infield in the air but looks a cert, Gorzelanny a bit rusty but feels superb while allowing umpteen runs and not getting anyone out. Who wouldn't love spring training? Well, maybe Peter if Rizzo doesn't find someone to play center and save Werth's so-called career. Wow, crushed twice by the worst team in baseball and it is seen as a sure sign that the Nats are bound for the Series. And he had a job.

*

He entered the office on Monday feeling more nervous than he could possibly have imagined. Exactly how did it work now? A two man team. Two person. Him and Rhonda. Should have checked the computer before he left. Hated to do it just yet. Not with things having changed. If they had changed. He spoke to Rhonda about having a very low profile and proving they could do as much work as the team used to do when there were four of them. Got a few smiles and winks. Tried to look cool. At about eleven Charlie Roberts came over and asked him and Rhonda if they could make a short meeting first thing in the morning. Down in personnel with Dolly Parton. Well, he actually gave her the correct name, which was Holly Patton, but women with big tits called Holly should never dye their hair blond. Even if they are managers. Anyway, everyone was a manager in personnel. He and Rhonda would be there. Anna walked by a minute later to tell them she had told them everything would be fine. Which she hadn't, but with looks like Anna's, you concede the point.

He spoke briefly to Zainab. Apparently Rhonda's chart was somewhere in the building. Maybe Charlie's office, maybe Dolly's. Good news maybe. Beryl looked over and smiled a few times. What a nice woman she was. For a geriatric. Make a good grandmother. Apparently she was a grandmother. Five times.

They easily kept up. He knew enough to extract the computer claims for Bert and Chet. There was also a small mountain of paper claims, maybe more like a hill. All done by quitting time. He had not looked at the baseball sites once. New resolution. Anyway, what happens on a Monday that can't wait until evening?

*

The trouble with the Nats being so much better was that all the talk was about Harper and Strasburg. Maybe Zimmerman or Zimmermann or even Gio Gonzalez. But there was a time when guys like Jamie Carroll and Livan Hernandez were real heroes. And last night Miguel Batista was pitching for the Mets. Few people remembered that he was an Expo. Way back. Maybe even in the eighties. Writing poetry and pitching. Great swingman. With Gil Heredia they would have been just the thing for Davey. Long or short relief. Even a few starts. Heredia went down but Batista goes on forever. Even brought fans to the game. To watch Miss Iowa, but still. Passan at Yahoo sees Harper as maybe an A-Rod clone. Great. Let's be obnoxious. Cheat a bit, maybe go off the base path to bump a pitcher. In the Series for all to see. Called it being competitive. More like being an asshole. Full time. Can't win with a team full of guys like Batista, but who wants a team full of A-Rods. They should trade Harper even up to the Twins for Jamie while they have the chance. Trouble is, Espinosa plays second and he's okay. And Carroll doesn't do center field. Probably give it a shot, though. That sort of player.

Now that they were rid of Chet and Bert, Rhonda and him were getting through more work than ever. Team of two. Lean and mean. Way back he once went to watch a four man softball team crush a local team. Full team but they couldn't handle these four guys. Pitcher, catcher, first and deep short. Could have managed with two because the pitcher was that good. Needed the other two for hitting. Like him and Rhonda. Lean, mean team.

The meeting with Dolly and Charlie was pretty brief. Could they just keep at it for a week or so? Just the two of them. Anna was instructed to take it a bit easy on them but they would get as many electronic claims as the full teams. Just pass a few to Zainab's team. You know how to do that do you, Peter? They all laughed politely. What a wit good old Charlie was. Seems they were making plans. Dolly said they hoped to make a new training team. As turnover was a problem, they had to train quite a few new employees for claims every year and they thought Rhonda's diagram was the key to making it work better. Called it Peter's diagram, but he corrected her. Rhonda smiled. Never said a thing. Well, Peter hardly spoke either. Wanted to say that if they wanted less turnover, hire uglier women, but decided against it. Still a fucking marriage factory. Had been and always would be. Maybe best to adjust. Like Dolly said.

Of course, not all that happened in spring training was positive. LaRoche nursing a career-threatening twisted ankle and Morse pulled a muscle somewhere and may be out for a few years. Probably has a golf date. He was back to the computer at work. Trouble with being so efficient. He actually wanted to leave the baseball until he got home but he couldn't stare at Rhonda all day. Even with the odd break for Anna. Good night for the Junction. God, the Nats won another meaningless game. How will they cope? And Bryce Harper got another hit. If he played for anyone else he would need to be taken down a peg.

Not much talk about baseball in the Junction. Decided to go home early. Largely because Frank was there. Peter was no psychologist, but there were tell-tale signs that the early romance had been tempered by the incident with Barney. Did Peter ever see her get that excited? Well yes, whenever he was more than five hours late for dinner. Frank had some growing up to do. Still sitting there when Peter left. He was going to be late but he had a few hours to go before he even approached the record.

*

The pleasure of going to work had worn off after two days. Even with Chet and Bert gone, it was still a crap job. Nice that he felt a little more secure, a little more wanted, even a little more liked. But it was a crap job. Enough to drive a man to drink. Or back to drink. Looking back, he maybe drank less when he was really depressed. He used the drink to help him sink. What a useless bit of insight that was. Hardly likely to stop him going out tonight. Now Frank might stop him. The

Last thing he needed was to bond with Frank over alcohol induced depression. So he decided he would try a film. Must be something on over on The Common. He asked in the office. Fucking Star Wars again. No chance. Had enough of that with Barney. Someone suggested Hugo. Why not give Scorsese a chance. But animated 3-D? Someone else suggested Woman in Black. A thriller. Beryl piped up that she had seen the play. In London. London asked Zainab, when was that? All got out of hand. Ended up going to China Town and then to see Woman in Black with half a dozen women from the insurance industry. They offered to pay as he was their date. Sort of funny. Paid himself, of course. Sat beside Anna. Kept glancing down. Well, you would. Beryl on the other side. Not so tempting. Nice woman though. Then a drink afterward. Just Beryl and Anna by then. It was fun. He hated to admit it. No lawyers. No dentists. No doctors. Just insurance people. All boring as shit. Like him.

When he checked the computer later he learned that the Nats bullpen was over-powering and that the rotation was living up to expectations. Failing to mention the astronomical level of the expectations. So goes spring training. Sort of like daffodils, cheerful but inclined to fade as spring progressed. Right now, however, the Nats were solid favorites for at least a hundred wins. Phillies would be lucky to stay close.

And the Nationals were looking at Bourgeois from Houston. Solid addition if they could get him for something like Maya, but that seemed very doubtful. The idea of a right-handed hitting center fielder to complement Ankiel was a decent idea. Brett Carroll was getting great reviews. Rizzo pumping the newspaper guys up to make him feel good about Syracuse. Made a great impression, Brett, off you go and I'm sure you will be back soon. Next in line after whathisname, Bryce something or other. We'll see. With all that pitching, maybe they won't need an outfield. Just play with six men. Hell, that softball team won with only four. All in the pitching.

What's John Lannan done to deserve this? Being shopped again. All things being equal, which is a stupid thing to say as all things have never been equal and never will be. All things being equal, Peter would back Lannan for more wins than Wang, Jackson, or Strasburg. Not to mention Detwiler. Count on him for 180 innings and an ERA below four. That translates into thirty games in which you have a chance. Hope he goes. Somewhere good. Beats fucking Rizzo in the seventh game of the Series. Maybe not. Depends on whether Rizzo is still with the Nats. Get a center fielder, Mike, and you might last a bit longer. Until Bryce signs with the Yankees. By the way, Mike, let him play in Washington before June and he's one year closer to those bastards. Remember, he's a big head. And you're an asshole if you don't send him down. Get Bourgeois and keep the ego in AAA until fucking November. Let him watch the Series from your box.

*

Thursday everyone was talking about the movie. Had to admit it was a good idea. Now they were saying they should do it more often, maybe make it a once a month thing. They asked him. Didn't like to say that by mid-April he would have probably committed suicide if fucking Rizzo didn't sort out center field, so he just smiled and asked why not? Shit, can't hurt. Beryl said that maybe not always a horror film but he had an impression that she loved the scary bits. In a funny sort of way. She was okay. Not exactly Anna, but okay.

Jackson was the next coming of Walter Johnson today. Crushing Houston in spring training is not a great moment in sport but, if you are the Nationals, maybe it is. Detwiler was brilliant. Nice that, because he liked the idea of Detwiler finally making good. Use him in relief. Sure. Wang gets injured, or even once Strasburg is finished his innings, there he is, ready and waiting. Except that, the more he is ready, the more likely poor John Lannan is to be dumped. Of course, if he is dumped to the Reds or Red Sox or Tigers, it could be wonderful for him. But to be dumped by a team that has never finished above last place, while seldom finished above last place. To be dumped by them, that's insulting. Especially if you were their best pitcher. Especially for one year of Edwin Jackson so Rizzo can help his old friend Scott create a better market for his pitcher. Mike, repeat after me, years come sequentially with 2013 being designated, pre-ordained even, to be the next in line after 2012. And to be followed by 2014. I tell you that in case it might help you get a feel for the sequence. Now the Nats will be decent in 2012, but not ready to be really good until 2013. And maybe 2014 too. Won't that be nice? Except your fourth starter and your fifth starter were on one year contracts and if they do well, they're off. Boras' rules. And you will have traded a really very decent lefty who you could have controlled for 2013 just for the pleasure of watching Wang break down and Boras get even richer. Asshole.

No wonder he dropped in at the Junction on the way home. Ran into Frank. Christ, guy looked awful. Marianne sure can pick them. Mind you, at least Frank was rich. If your husband has to come home stinking of beer, he might as well have a pocket full of money. He stayed and had one with Frank, but he was a boring shit. Poor Marianne. Far as he could recall, her last husband was a boring shit as well. So it goes.

Friday meant weekend was coming. He dreaded weekends but maybe there would be an email from Barney. Or he could call Cheryl. That last email was quite hopeful. He might ask Beryl if maybe she wanted to go for a walk and something to eat on Saturday. Or Sunday. Maybe a movie. Maybe not. She was a bit old and boring. Like him. Like Frank. Now. Poor Marianne. Poor Peter, he might have to find an alternative to the Junction what with Frank sitting there moaning all the time. Marianne had tried everything to get Peter to stop going to the Junction all the time and now maybe she had finally succeeded.

Nice to see Strasburg pitch reasonable but not brilliantly and the Nats lose. Stopped the dynasty talk. MASN has now hired this guy Dan Kolko who seems young and enthusiastic. Just hope someone explained the difference between 2012 and 2013 to him.

Saturday dawned entirely too early. Whatever happened to sleeping in? Used to be he could sleep until noon. Even without beer. Now who he would be awake the same time on Saturday and Sunday as on work days. He blamed Frank. Fucking Frank. He should stay out of the Junction. Find his own place. Now he had maybe sixteen hours to kill. Walk, library, walk, computer, walk, eat, try to save first beer until evening. Maybe late afternoon. Maybe with lunch. An early lunch. In a bar.

He should have asked Beryl if she would meet him on the weekend. If only to stay out of the bars. Mind you, why should he stay out of the bars? In fact, his problem was getting into the bars. They didn't seem as attractive as they used to. Fucking Frank. But he was not the only problem. He got more pleasure going to a bar when he was supposed to be somewhere else than when he had no place to go. Like now.

Lost in the euphoria about Bryce Harper was a nice little paragraph about the stint by Craig Stammen in today's game. Another gamer. Like Lannan. Seems Lannan is bound to go and Stammen likely to end up in Syracuse. Just so Boras is happy. Eleven fucking million and Lannan just to keep Boras sweet. And now Prince Eater has condescended to announce that he was intrigued by the thought of playing for the Nationals. Sure you were. At least being depressed about Lannan and Stammen helped get him to a bar.

*

He hoped Rizzo found time in his twenty odd hour day to read Cafardo. The bits about why would they play a perfectly good right fielder out of position in center. Mind you, the solution offered was shit. Harper should be in Syracuse, not center. Even if it meant Ankiel and Carroll platoon. Read Ankiel and Bernadina might platoon but Bernadina won't be in Washington come April. Had his chances. Shame, though.

No Frank in the Junction when he went for lunch, so he stayed for dinner. Got home and realized he had not turned his phone on for some time. Forty-two missed calls and seventeen messages. Thank god for the delete all button. Checked the computer to see what happened to Gio before bed and took the opportunity to delete all his emails as well. Felt sort of cleansed.

*

Well it was becoming clearer what was expected at work. Nothing. He had so little to do he thought he might steal some paper claims off the others. But he had principles. They were just strange. As principles went. He dragged himself through the day dreaming of the Junction. Fucking Frank. Surely it should be enough to take Marianne without insisting on going to his favorite bar. And he needed something tonight. Work was much harder without people like Chet and Bert to hate. Even Michele was being civil. By her own standards.

Zimmerman was establishing the fact that the Nats will miss him when he goes down injured. Harper establishing his credentials for the DL. First cuts today. No surprises really except the guys cut were all probably stunned stupid. All of them chatter on about working hard and great experience and soon be back and grateful for the opportunity. Corey Brown must be pissed off to glory. Team's desperate for a center fielder and he hits gazillion then is the first guy cut. All part of Mike's master plan, Corey. Prefers to play right fielders in center.

At least Frank had the decency not to drink in the Junction. Nothing going there. Typical Monday. Boring as shit. Making it indistinguishable from six other days he could name. Went home early to read that Johnson was overwhelmed by Zimmermann's pitching tonight. Only half a dozen runs in a couple of innings. Looks ready for the big breakthrough.

God, he had missed calls from Cheryl, Marianne and Barney. And messages. All pretty much the same. Called but no answer, please call back. Not tonight. Maybe tomorrow.

*

Greeted in the morning with the happy news that he was invited to a meeting with Dolly and Charlie in the afternoon. More bullshit about Rhonda's diagram it seemed. Just the four of them. Nice and cozy. Maybe he would ask them what they thought of John Lannan. Maybe not. Rosenthal added his dime's worth to the trade rumors and dropped the suggestion that Ian Desmond's defense can be erratic. Guy who can spot that should go on to the journalism hall of fame. Christ, Ken. Slow day or what?

He had to admit he was a little bit pleased with the meeting. Much as he hated the idea of being pleased at work. Or anywhere else for that matter. He and Rhonda were their own little team and he would be promoted to team leader. Christ, the extra money would have been more than enough to pay Chet. Guy should have been more patient. So he was the leader for the training team and all new claims adjustors would start with two months in their team before being sent into the cruel world on their own. This should drive most of them out of the business. See what it did for Peter and they'll walk out on the first morning. Fuck it, why not be pleased. Steak and a bottle of Chambertin tonight. Maybe phone Barney. And Cheryl.

There was a message on his phone from Barney. Just to say that I am doing well, really well. Keep trying to reach you. Should phone. Just as he was considering, the damn thing rang. Marianne. What the fuck? Where's Frank?

Hey, Peter, you did a really good thing with Barney and I never said anything. Maybe I was a bit jealous. I don't know. Went through a bad patch, maybe. Felt unnecessary. Even Frank was fed up but things are all okay. Even with Cheryl. You should call her.

So he ended up having a family night. Talked to Barney and Cheryl. And Marianne, of course, but she wasn't family really. Not now. Fucking Frank. Didn't tell anyone about the promotion. Really more of a change than a promotion. Shit, a bit of a promotion. Anyhow, no big deal.

Jackson was marvelous tonight. Which is to say he was roughed up. Wonderful. Spring was like that. Pitchers all over the place but never felt better. Hitters are shit but never felt better. Morse, Ramos, Bernadina and Ankiel are all injured but never felt better in their lives, Zimmerman is the concern. Mashing the baseball. Getting ready for the DL in April.

*

People at work congratulated him on his promotion. So it was a promotion and not just a switch. Must be. Anna gave him a kiss and she was sleeping with Charlie so he must have called it a promotion. Strange sort of pillow talk that. Hey, you know the old bald geek in claims, smells of beer amongst other things, well, gave him a big promotion today. Team leader. In charge of one other person and maybe a trainee from time to time. Hope he can handle it. Might need some stress management training.

Poor John Lannan. Tigers are interested. Shit. Guy pitches to contact. Tigers had the worst fielding team in the history of the game. Statues at the corners. Fat statues. Then there was Dimitri's brother sleeping in left. And if not Detroit, maybe Houston to keep Wandy Rodriguez company as a left-handed pitcher they didn't need because they were about to finish last in two different leagues over the next two years. Bud to Houston. Cheer up, look what happened in

Washington when they got those draft picks. Lannan better go to Boston. Join the beer and chicken club.

And tonight Strasburg got clobbered. Bet he never felt better

*

He hadn't really bothered with Zainab much so he brought her a coffee in the morning. She smiled her smile. Glorious smile. Said she thought that he had become a snob now that he was a big shot. Or maybe he only had eyes for another woman. Christ, was she flirting? Did Pakistanis flirt? Well, British Pakistanis maybe did.

Chien-Ming Wang lasted almost three innings. Thank god they didn't trade Lannan. Poor Chien-Ming, how unlucky can you get? You know with him it is likely to mean the 60-day. Probably need Tommy John surgery on his fucking knee. At least there will be none of this never felt better shit tonight. Maybe no chicken and beer for Lannan. He's pitched well tonight. Like the others. Clobbered, no command but felt great. Get clobbered and swear you feel wonderful, John. Impresses the hell out of Johnson.

*

What with his new promotion and all, Peter felt obliged to ignore baseball during the day. Zainab came over. Asked if he had ever watched Scorsese's film about George Harrison. He wasn't a great Beatles fan and he wasn't a Scorsese fan either. In fact, he was pissed off when Zainab told him that Scorsese might

226

be a really nice guy. Shit. Another romantic illusion down the drain. But he took the film and was polite and all. It was Zainab.

Beryl walked over and saw the cover. Loved it, she said, but preferred the one on Dylan. Scorsese and Ken Burns, both great. What the fuck? What's a grannie like Beryl doing liking Scorsese and Dylan and stuff? Anyhow, if you looked at what was on in the movie theatres, Harrison was a god bet.

It was a good evening. When was the last time he had a good Friday evening? Probably back on his mother's breast. Except he was damn sure he never spent any time there. Stark thinks the Nationals are oozing talent. Wang may only miss a season or two with his injury. Lannan less likely to be traded, Red Sox look like crap, Andy Pettitte going back to the Yankees at age ninety some odd. A night to lie in bed and dream. Lombardozzi creamed Sabathia. And, of course, Gonzalez and Stammen were impressive. Gonzalez taking several hundred pitches in his three innings and Stammen striking someone out as he got clobbered. Neither ever felt better, it would seem. Maybe they are learning to love being crap. Like the Pirates. Christ, the NCAA tournament has started. Glad he avoided the bars. Fucking basketball. Spoils spring training.

*

Saturday was a fine day so he walked over to watch the planes take off for a bit. Why was taking off more exciting than landing. To watch, that is. Being on the things was equally terrifying either way. Maybe taking off was worse, because once you were up there you fucking well had to get down. Somehow. And then when you were taking off to go somewhere, there was landing and then the return trip. Marianne said he spoiled holidays but he was so scared that they seldom went on any, so he could hardly have spoiled them.

Ended up in the library and started chatting to the woman behind the desk. Christ knows why. Anyhow, he ended up with a book about the Panama Canal and the Scorsese thing on Dylan. Great, they lend out films now. And CDs. Next it will be small ensembles and maybe a small theater group. Do Hamlet in the evening. Put you to sleep. Bound to work. Fucking Shakespeare.

Zimmermann pitched well and felt wonderful, unlike all his colleagues who get pummeled and feel wonderful. Never succeed with that attitude. Christ, this Harper thing was getting serious. A lousy double in a tied exhibition game and he's back in the headlines. Now a center fielder. Sure Bryce. You can do it all. Cover for Morse in left. Play center. Oh yeah, conduct city tours for visitors to Syracuse. Washington press keeps trying to hide the fact that he's an obnoxious little shit. Like A-Rod.

*

Sunday was gorgeous. He kept thinking about George Harrison after watching the Scorsese thing. Walked and walked. God knows where he eventually had breakfast. Must have been late because it was beer and a burger. Not that conventional a breakfast. Well, not that unconventional either. Not for him. Not on a Sunday. Harrison expressed ideas that were completely annoying. Just the sort of thing to make you a complete asshole. Which he wasn't. Or didn't seem to be. Maybe Scorsese just liked him. Zainab was right, it was good stuff. A lot of it, mind you. Over three hours. Ringo Starr came across well but not McCartney. It's okay to say something meaningful, Paul. No one will dislike you or sue you or anything. Ringo was great. Nice combination of intelligent and witty. Then there were Clapton and Lennon. Assholes top to bottom. Clapton should be shot. Great musician, maybe just cage him and let him out to sing a song once in a while. Once in a very long while.

So after his late breakfast there was Cafardo. Comforting stuff. Lucchino is such an asshole. I only interfere when Cherington doesn't do exactly what I tell him. So far I have been very impressed and I gave him two biscuit just last week.

Cafardo's right about Lannan. Detwiler has more value. But Mike wouldn't give him to Houston when he wanted Bourn so he's not going anywhere now. Not with Strasburg being shut down in August. Works quite well, Detwiler fills in for Wang until he overcomes his injury, maybe in 2020, and replaces Strasburg in August and then he's ready for 2013. Which, as you will recall, Mike, is the year of the Nat.

Nats playing Detroit again. He had a soft spot for the Tigers. Ever since they signed Fielder. Best move the Nats made this winter. And now they have Xavier Nady. Not that there is anything wrong with Morse or LaRoche or Ankiel. Always part of the master plan to put them on the 60-day. So they could play bridge with Chien-Ming Wang. Nice for them. And Jackson on the mound. Nice short game. Maybe ten hours.

Stopped for a drink on the way home. He had seen the Quencher Tavern before. Never impressed. It was just that it was quiet and not crowded. And he did not want to hear about basketball. The best thing about the Sweet Sixteen is that after eight more games there would only be eight teams. Best was when they were down to none. Just imagine if every basketball team that ever was, was atomized. Painfully. Assholes. So this old guy talks to him in the bar. No idea of etiquette maybe. Peter didn't encourage him. Just said he wanted a quiet drink where no one was discussing NCAA basketball. That should shut him up. But no.

Yeah, know what you mean. Shitty game for bigheaded freaks.

Exactly.

Mind you soon be over. Baseball's not so bad. Except maybe here in Boston.

Exactly.

Yeah, I still follow it a bit. Not like the old days.

Exactly.

Miss the Expos, I do.

Exactly. Hey, what the fuck?

Used to love that team before Selig sold them down the drain.

You liked the Expos?

Sure, you must have heard of them. Played in Montreal. Before they moved to Washington. Not the same now really but I still sort of follow them. Their general manager is a bit of a schmuck. Too close to this player agent called Boras.

So Peter had a long afternoon and evening of the Expos. Jem only came to the place Sunday afternoons and maybe once in mid-week, usually Tuesday or Wednesday. Just for a quiet beer or two. Couldn't take much more. Imagine that. An Expo fan. On I Street. In Southie. Been to Jarry Park. Wait until he tells……tells…. what the fuck? Who cares?

By the time he got home Edwin Jackson had thrown several thousand pitches, two of them for strikes. Felt great. Great outing for him. Everything's great. And Chad Durbin made a big step forward, pitching as badly as everyone else. Felt great. Great outing. Pity there is no place for him. Fit right in.

Bryce Harper sent to Syracuse after striking out four times. Good move that. And he will play center field. Great, take all the time you need to learn the position. So now we have Ankiel in center and if LaRoche is out for the season having Tommy John on his bunions, Morse will be at first unless he needs Tommy John on his back. Looks like a great year. For the doctors. Again. So we have Ankiel in center and Bernadina in left. Christ, what an improvement over last year. Enough to wreck the weekend.

10. Redemption

God what did they want this time? Another meeting with Charlie and Dolly. Can't get any work done. Not that there is any work to do. Meeting all set for tomorrow at eleven. No, no need for Rhonda this time. Just toss around a few ideas. Get his input. When has anyone ever wanted his input? So with it being a day off for the Nationals and nothing much going on at work, he had a long time to think about what ideas to toss around with Dolly and Charlie. Came up blank really. Ideas? In insurance? In claims? Not this century. Not last either. Have to go back to John Hancock or something.

Took the long way home. Via the Bistro, and the Junction and maybe one or two others. Telephoned Barney. Told him about the meeting. What the fuck? Why not?

Say that's great, you know you were in a rut and a bit of responsibility will do you good.

You think?

Phoned Cheryl. Mostly listened. They had started adoption procedures. Everything rosy as shit it seemed. Still, it was good to hear her so happy again. And Arnie had answered and he had been polite and even pleasant. Didn't mention the promotion. Let them have their moment. Not really much of a promotion. Not like having a child. He would tell them when he went over for dinner at the end of the month. Barney would be there. Could be okay. He liked Burlington.

What with no game the few pieces about the Nats were mostly about Harper. You could almost feel sorry for the poor kid. MLB site had an article saying the Nats had an impactful bullpen. Sounds like Rizzo is getting to them. Guy goes to university for a dozen years. English major. Post grad in journalism. Tells us the Nats have an impactful bullpen. Jesus.

*

Peter was a bit nervous going into the meeting. What could he say?

Are you looking forward to your new responsibilities?

Yeah sure?

Do you thing you can handle it?

Yeah, sure.

Brand new concept for us?

Yeah sure?

Had a few problems in the past.

Yeah sure.

Think we can do anything about the turnover? I mean, other than you and Ms Potter, maybe Ms Rappaport. No one stays.

Yeah.......but then he realized he was being asked a serious question. Not just being polite sort of thing.

Anything we can do to attract more stable staff?

Look, claims is what it is. Quite boring. A lot boring. Live with it. We do. I mean me and Beryl and Zainab do. Because there is nothing else for us. But young ones, hell, why would they stay? Anything interesting comes along, there out. Got a brain, they move to something better. Got a body, they get married. Simple as that. Your real solution is a quick training program so new staff are useful quickly. Screen them so that the promising ones are discovered early and send them somewhere better; maybe actuarial work or something. Give the younger ones a social life. Let them get married and out. They become pretty useless if they stay too long. Except for the ones like me who become resigned to their fate. So let them have their movie nights and club visits and darts nights or whatever and be prepared to let them go. We can train two a week forever. All it takes with Rhonda's program. A week maybe. No need for two months. They are ready to get married and move on in two months. And if they move on, the new ones are just as cheap because training should cost next to nothing. The ones training probably do more than the bored veterans. And often happier because everyone will let them know that they aren't going to be there long. By the way. Should move Michele. Can seem sullen, but she's a whiz. She could be really good in a more demanding job. And Zainab. Under-estimated because she looks foreign.

Dolly looked a bit shocked. Charlie had his mouth open. Say, that's good, Peter, good stuff. Leave it with us. We can talk again. Soon. Real soon. Shit, he should have shut up sooner. Like at the beginning of the meeting. He tried not to look at the others when he returned to the office. Zainab asked if it went well. Beryl hoped he had spoken up. Anna hoped he'd blasted the idiots. God, he wished he could go home. Via the Junction. No, the Quencher tonight. Might run into Jem.

But no Jem and the Quencher didn't have much going for it without him. The Junction was full of basketball. And Peyton Manning. Christ, they hated him in Boston. Soon be hating him in Denver. Guy's washed up. Not that he cared.

Why does Kansas need two center fielders when the Nats have none? Really piggy that. And what did Houston get in return? Presumably the Royals' top five draft picks or something and they can't be named yet. So Houston is subscribing to the Rizzo system. No center fielder. Must be looking ahead to the 2013 draft, maybe 2014 and 2015 as well. Going all out for a hundred losses. Maybe Kansas will send Lorenzo Cain over to The Nats. Nice gesture. Look, we got this new guy, Jason Bourgeois is his name. Houston just sent him here for free, more or less. Something about tanking early. Anyhow, maybe you could send us a relief pitcher from Potomac or something and at least Lorenzo will get a game. Nice kid. Tries hard.

Boswell did a nice thing on Harper in center. He liked Boswell. Any friend of Ken Burns was bound to be okay. And Shelby Foote. Wonder if Boswell got to meet Shelby. Burns probably only used Foote in the baseball film because he was so wonderful in the Civil War one. Christ, it had been years since he had read Foote's Civil War volumes. He had almost forgotten who won. Boswell thought moving Harper to center was a good idea. Well, really, so did Peter. He just didn't like to let on. Rizzo might get complacent. Stop looking for someone.

Oh, oh. He must have gone a bit far. This was a bit scary. Could he please be ready to present his ideas a bit more formally at a meeting next Tuesday? Slightly larger group, maybe half a dozen. Let them know what he needed. Maybe just a screen for power point. Would he bring his own laptop, or just a USB stick? No more than about twenty minutes. Let them know down in personnel on Monday. Just buzz Ms Patton.

Christ, he had never presented anything in his life. Maybe once or twice. In high school. Without fucking power point. Without anything. Big posters; paper things. Shit. Shit, shit, shit.

And then Anna came up to him and asked wasn't it exciting? Oh sure. And Beryl came over with Zainab to ask if it was true. Is what true?

You know what, don't be silly.

Definitely a night for the Quencher, but no Jem. So he moved on to the Junction. Assholes. Fucking Red Sox. Fucking Bruins. Fucking basketball. So he went home and read about the Panama Canal. Christ, some people died. No one cared, so I suppose it didn't matter. Teddy wouldn't get away with it now. Killing Muslims is one thing, but dying in the jungle on a works program……no way. Well, maybe. Most of them were foreign. Who cares? This guy David McCullough was a good writer. Might try the Brooklyn Bridge one. Or re-read Shelby.

How was he going to make a presentation? And Johnson didn't help his sense of doom. I mean, if Harper was going to be a center fielder, then it made sense that Lombardozzi had to become the leadoff hitter. So why mess him around with him playing left field. Why not catcher? Make him a true utility player. Poor bastard was in no position to say no but I bet he'd like to stuff his outfielder's glove down Johnson's throat. Let the guy play infield. He does second well. Assholes.

Power point. Jesus.

He wished Lannan got opening day but that was absurd. Just romantic. But why not Zimmermann? He was their best last year. Shit, what difference. Strasburg seemed a decent kid. Marginally more humble than the budding center fielder.

*

He could hardly face anyone in the office. Power point presentation. He didn't have a clue. And he hated to ask in case they realize what a jerk he was. Maybe Zainab. No, even she would be shocked by his stupidity.

At least Charlie had given him Rhonda's chart back. With some notes she had made. He spoke to Rhonda. She was full of good wishes. But at least she was supportive. She would make clean copies on her computer tonight and pass them to him on a USB. He wished to hell he knew what to do with a USB. Sort of like a UFO? Well, it was for him.

Maybe Rizzo would get one of the Royals' center fielders. Take his mind off it. Shit. Shit, shit, shit. Fucking Rizzo.

On the way home he stopped in a computer shop. Asked about USBs. What size? They all looked pretty small to him. Exactly the same size. Said it was for a power point presentation.

One?

Well, so far.

How big, though?

Maybe three pages.

Three pages? Won't need all that much capacity. Think 32 gigs should handle it?

He could see he was being laughing at, so he walked out. No big problem. Three shops down he bought two USBs. Nothing big, just for a few presentations. They were cheap enough. Took them home and stuck them in the side of the computer. Even wrote a few pages and managed to save them. Power point? Shit. Then he had an idea. A good one. Barney was a whiz. So he called Cheryl. Asked about the adoption. All that shit. All going fine. Still hoping to see him April 8. Barney will be there.

Then he phoned Barney. Really looking forward to dinner at Cheryl's. Blah, blah. Say, not around anytime this weekend, are you? Great, because I have this power point presentation at work and wouldn't mind going through it with someone who's really sharp. Blah, blah. No, no big deal. New post really. Yeah, in training. Yeah, bit more money. Saturday morning would be great.

Now to see how the Cardinals man-handled the Nats. Gio lacking command. Injured players all in hospital. Lombardozzi catching. Zavier Nady batting fourth. Playoffs for sure.

Well, well, all good stuff. Gio feeling marvelous and Davey feels that his team is just where he wants them right now. Pity they lost 9-0. Assholes. At least they solved the problem of getting men on base. Who gives a shit? Why even bother getting men on base if Morse and LaRoche are injured and Harper is in Syracuse. And Ramos is hitting close to zero. Just break your heart if Desmond and Espinosa were on base. So why bother.

*

He loved Rhonda. First thing she did when he came in was to hand him a USB. So he fumbled his out of his pocket.

Mind if I look?

He did really. He knew he hadn't a clue.

Peter, these notes are great but would you like me to sort them out as a presentation and we can look at them again?

So after lunch he sort of met with Zainab and Beryl and Rhonda to look at the presentation. They all commented and suggested changes here and tweaks there.

Well, all but him. Then they all agreed it was looking really smart. Down to six pages. They all agreed, that was plenty; short and sweet. Two pages of background, three describing the proposed process, and a summary. Short and sweet. Fifteen minutes at most. Then Zainab told him that he had done a really good job. Sure he had. Bought his own USB stick and spent five minutes on some notes and then turned it over to the support team. They all got a cup of coffee and were smiling and chatting. Decided it was time for another film night next week. Beryl suggested they go to see The Artist at the Landmark, Kendall Square. Said it was a lovely little theater. Some of them had not seen it yet and even he had to admit it was worth a second look. So Wednesday it would be.

He was quite exhausted by the time he got home. All this power point shit. He was almost looking forward to going through it with Barney; maybe not tell him that it was all the work of his colleagues. Not lie or anything, just ask what he thought without talking too much about copyright. Made himself a bacon sandwich and a cup of coffee and turned on the computer. Coffee on Friday night. What was going on here?

Nice to see the Nats had solved their offensive problems. Scored a run today in what was their tenth game without a win. Lost 5-1. Rest easy, Mike is in control. Says he is really comfortable with the team. Well, he would be. He's been with them for a few losing seasons now. Get used to that sort of thing. Zimmermann said it would have all been fine if he had pitched around their number eight hitter to get to the pitcher. Comforting to know that one of the Nats' great starting pitchers is talking about avoiding the number eight hitters in future. Great year ahead.

*

He had almost forgotten that being a father had a good side. Barney was terrific with him. He had brought some real croissants, the kind that crumbled because they were flaky but not hard. Looked through the presentation and was complimentary. Terrific stuff, dad, short and sweet. Then asked about some of the facts. Encouraged Peter to emphasize the marriage thing.

Look, dad, if people are using it as a marriage brokerage, so what. If you can train them in two weeks, you only need them for a few months to get your money's worth. No sweat. Bring it into the open. Talk about it. Then he asked Peter if he knew how to get from the USB to the screen.

Easy as anything, you toss it to someone who looks important and ask if he or she can get it set up while you look through your notes one last time. Then, when they are done, you go through the slides with them one by one. Hell, there are only six. Then just make sure you can go forward and backward if you want. And ask for the bloody stick back when you leave. Barney kept laughing when he talked about the women in the department and the things like group grope and looking for partners. Kept saying, use it, use, it. Good stuff. These guys will appreciate a smile.

Peter asked if maybe they should go to lunch together. Sort of like a father and son. Maybe a bar or something. Not me, Dad, I am being careful. Tell you what, how about China Town. Tea with lunch and maybe a movie. Peter knew Barney was weird so suggested they try the Landmark.

Say, great idea, Salmon Fishing in Yemen is on.

What the fuck? But he enjoyed it. Going to lunch and a movie with his son. Oh yeah.

Pity the Nats spoiled the day. I mean, the Orioles, for Christ sake. Have they no decency? No pride? Jackson must never have felt better because he hardly threw a strike except for one that Wieters knocked over the wall. He may have had a nice day, but he needed the Junction. Maybe just one or two.

*

He decided to have an exciting Sunday. Out for breakfast and Cafardo then maybe go to the Quencher later to see if Jem showed up. The way the Nats were going it took a certain amount of will power to stay sober. Thank God for the NCAA tournament. Made the beer taste worse. Then again, where was the joy in staying sober? Then again, where was the joy in being drunk? Perhaps he was beginning to get a bit pessimistic; lost his lust for life. And everything else.

Telephoned Cheryl. Why not. She is my daughter.

Had lunch with Barney.

Yeah, I heard. We're dying to know how your presentation goes and how this new promotion works out.

Things get around. You know I'm terrified. Never done anything like this before.

Dad, you'll be fine. Just keep it short and sweet. Ten, maybe fifteen minutes. And, make the buggers smile. At least once or twice.

It was a dreary day so he spent a few hours with the Panama Canal. Funny how the complete lack of regard for human life becomes romantic after a century or so. Yeah, sent them into the disease riddled jungle. Dropped like flies. But made men out of them. Well, the few who survived. Great book, though. Shame to finish. Except Shelby was waiting. And he would get the one about the Brooklyn Bridge out when he returned this one. Time for another coffee and Cafardo. Hope Jem is in the Quencher. Sort of hoped he and I could maybe see each about. Talk about baseball.

Doom. By the time he left for the Quencher the Nats were already up by five runs. Nothing worse than letting them think they were actually good. One or two blowouts won't hurt but this is no time for a winning streak. Then there was the Cafardo thing. Casually drops that the Angels are interested in Jordan Zimmermann. Great idea, sell the farm for Gonzalez because nothing is as important as pitching, then ship your almost best starter to Los Angeles where he can be near his friends Brad and Tom and Derek and AJ.

Cafardo had decided that Cherington was on the way out. Discussed the positional battles on the Red Sox and came down for Valentine in a very strong 'Ben you are an idiot' sort of way. Mind you, he was right. Play the glove at short and the bat at catcher. Not exactly as if Saltalamacchia was a defensive wizard. Back the kids. Unless they have a big mouth. Like Harper. He needs a year in Syracuse. Maybe more.

He opened his heart to Jem. Jem laughed.

243

Nothing matters in spring. Hell, one or two blowouts were nothing. Either way. Okay, nine or ten blowouts weren't even that big a deal. Spring training. Enjoy it. We're still tied for the league lead. Hey, anyway, next year is the one to think about. This year is just to get the pitching ducks in a line. Jackson and Wang won't be hard to replace because Detwiler is there and Lannan is a decent starter. And if he goes, look at the fifth starters available right now. No problem. And Rizzo won't let Zimmermann go unless he gets Mike Trout or something. Guy's done a great job really. Had a few breaks with the draft, but Morse and Zimmermann and Storen, well, he's done some good things. In his job, all you can hope is you make more smart moves than dumb moves because you have to make moves. Sometimes you just catch bad breaks. Look at Madson over in Cincy. Poor bastard. And as for Harper. Going to be great. Cut him some slack. He's a kid. What were you like at that age?

If Peter could remember correctly, he was a weirdo wimp with no friends. Who sure as hell couldn't play center field.

He really enjoyed Jem. A bit soft on Rizzo maybe, but decent guy. Had some great Pascal Perez stories. I-285 with his Pascual change-up and checking the runners from between his legs. Fucking Yankees. He was never going to thrive in New York. They didn't care. Poached him and wrecked his career. He needed Felipe. So did his brother Carlos, the leftie. Weird but wonderful. Did nothing in Los Angeles. God, it was great to talk to a real fan. Fassero and Martinez. Best one two they ever had. Except El Presidente and Pascual. Jem said that would only be so if you only include the Expos. Strasburg and Zimmermann could beat it. And with Gonzalez and Detwiler, well, I'll bet Philadelphia is thinking about them already. Jem was so optimistic. Refused to admit they would all need Tommy John surgery by April. Laughed it off. Not very realistic in that sense, but still great to talk to. He left after just a few beers. Jem was like that. Just a couple. Too old for marathons. They agreed to meet Tuesday evening. Just for a few.

*

He was the center of attention on Monday morning. It started with his early coffee with Rhonda. Are you ready? Let's see the slides. Looks great. Keep it short and sweet. Maybe ten, fifteen minutes. This is really exciting.

Then Zainab. Then Anna. Then, in the afternoon, Beryl came over.

You know, Peter, I'll bet you are finding this pretty stressful. Why not just come back to my place tonight for a quiet dinner. Nothing fancy. Not late. No untoward advances. No discussions about work. No basketball. Just a chance to relax a bit.

How do you know I hate basketball?

Intuition. You never let on. Why I'll bet everyone thinks you hate baseball and love opera.

Zainab came over. Going to dinner with Beryl is a great idea. Take your mind off it and you two have a lot in common.

Me and Beryl?

Yes, of course. She hates the Red Sox.

It was a nice evening. Beryl did hate the Red Sox. Called the whole New England obsession with their image as childish. Nothing wrong with being a fan but how could they possibly believe their supporters were somehow special and more devoted. Her husband had thought like that and he was an asshole. And his friends were all assholes. Except Beryl called them fools, but he knew she meant assholes. He'd met people like that. All over Boston. Assholes. Beryl said they had the same sense of entitlement as religious groups. Like Christians. Thought they were special. Still, she said, Red Sox fans weren't as deluded as Christians. At least they finally won the World Series. She was glad her husband hadn't lived to see it. He was boring enough without that. Reported local news for the Herald for thirty years. Can you imagine? Took being parochial a bit far. And his newspaper friends. Assholes, all of them. Except she called them fools.

And when he got home the Nats had won again. And Lannan was going to be the fifth starter and not be a Tiger. And Bernadina did well. Bernadina had signed as an Expo.

Bring on the power point.

*

Peter looked at his watch. The entire presentation had taken six minutes. Five minutes and forty seconds. Short and sweet. Sure. He didn't know he could talk that fast. Everyone was very polite. Said thank you and all that. Offered coffee. Said it was all very interesting. Blah, blah. They mostly looked like they missed

Chet. And Bert. He had wanted to say a lot more but somehow, nothing came. Not after the six minutes. Five minutes and forty seconds.

He tried to look cool when he got back to his desk. His friends were polite. They could see he was crushed. They sort of stood off together and sent Zainab over as spokesman. Spokesperson.

It must have been very intimidating for you but don't you worry. We all saw the slides. The ideas were great and you got it all down to just six slides.

Sure, short and sweet.

No sense saying more if you got the point across. Don't worry. If they cannot see the merit in your proposal it's their problem.

Zainab was something. He hardly thought of her as a foreigner anymore.

Rhonda took him to lunch. Told him it was time he tried vegetarian. Noodle soup. Not bad. And kept him from doing something stupid. Like too much beer. Mind you, there was no meat in beer.

As he left the office Charlie came over. Shit. Shit, shit, shit. Well, he wouldn't be fired. He was pretty sure of that.

Say Peter, you gave us something to think about today. Great work. Concise. Short and sweet. Meeting next week to discuss where we go from here. Holly's office. Same deal; ten o'clock Tuesday. Bit of a follow up but no need to prepare anything unless you have some new ideas.

New ideas. He hardly had any old ideas. Except maybe about options in center field. Christ, the only real idea was that chart. Which was Rhonda's.

He almost forgot about Jem. By the time he got to the Quencher, he was getting up to go. Stayed for one last one when he came in. Nice of him. And the Nats had won again. A real winning streak. In spring training anything is possible. Lannan and Bernadina both mentioned in dispatches. He loved the old guard to do well. You watching, Bryce? Jem kept laughing at him. Told him he probably stilled wanted the dinosaurs to make a comeback. Take over Yosemite or something. Well, why not? Jem asked if he was following the fuss with the Red Sox.

You know it's supposed to be the GM who gives a vote of confidence to the manager, but here in Boston it's the manager saying he is happy with the GM. Shows where the power lies. Or at least where Valentine thinks it lies and he's probably right. Bunch of assholes. Except Jem called them idiots. Cherington won the shortstop skirmish but Peter figured Valentine would be the last man standing. Not necessarily, Bobby's too clever and people get tired of his act. Has a short shelf life. Cherington may not be the pussy people think he is. Hardly likely to get that job just for being a dingbat, now is he? He liked Jem but he could be a bit too easy on people. Like Cherington. And Rizzo.

When he got home he found that he had missed some calls. He didn't really want to talk to anyone about his presentation. Felt a bit foolish. Six minutes. So he just texted replies to Barney and Cheryl.

Went just fine but I doubt anything will come of it.

And went to bed where he didn't sleep. Six fucking minutes.

Things were back to normal with the Nats. Shutout and Gonzalez lacked command. Steve Catty replaced as pitching coach by Mark DeRosa. Mark, you'll have enough to do playing third base, leave the pitchers to Steve. He did just fine last year. Mind you, last year he had some great ones. Miguel, Livo, Lannan. Even Zimmermann was on board last year. Now he has a clubhouse full of potential. Poor bastard.

*

Woke up to find that Stan Kasten was a Dodger. Him and Magic Johnson. At least the Johnson in Washington knew something about baseball. Fucking basketball player. And Kasten. Mr Smooth. Did nothing in Washington. Sorry, sorry, Stan. Of course you did. Loved the way you stuck with Bowden. Great loyalty. Little Jim will be on the phone today looking for work. Selig hand picks another owner. Asshole.

Wednesday was going to be film night again. He didn't really want to go but could hardly back out. Some of the others were really looking forward to it. Beryl had told him that she needed to get out a lot more and she had enjoyed it. Even though they were all boring insurance drones. Might keep his mind off the presentation. Six fucking minutes. Not even that.

And it was fun going to the film, even seeing it for the second time. At least he spoke longer in his presentation than anyone did in the film. Maybe he could do a silent presentation next time. What next time? He went for coffee with Beryl afterwards. Just the two of them this time. They went for coffee but ended up having a drink. Just one. And agreed that if it was a nice day on Sunday, it would be nice to meet and walk on the Common then go to the Paramount for a late breakfast. Nice woman. Careful, Peter. She's a grandmother.

Poor Cheryl. He could have been a grandfather by now.

Christ, he had a date with a ninety year old woman. Shit.

At least Jordan Zimmermann seemed to want to throw strikes. Him and Henry Rodriguez. Imagine Rodriguez being the poster boy for throwing strikes. Funny how he liked Jordan Zimmermann so much more than Gonzalez or Jackson. Or even Strasburg. He liked Zimmermann and Clippard. And Stammen.

Xavier Nady looks like a great acquisition. Going for a hat trick on TJ surgery. Not even a pitcher. Nats should start Tommy John Anon. Hello, my name's Xavier Nady and I'm a johnaholic. Hey, great to see you Xav, never alone. Not here with the Nats. We all fucking well have it. Hope you can still play cards with us in Florida. Should manage with just the one arm. Yeah, we all go down for re-hab. Send out hopeful bulletins in September. It's a real gas.

Still, Zimmermann pitched well.

*

Not much doing in the office. Other than discussions about silent films. Look, it's not a new idea. Used to do a lot of them way back. Then they brought in sound. It's only recently that they realized that sound was killing the films. Christ, what would Hollywood do with no explosions or screeching cars? Could be wonderful. Like in the comics. Put the sounds in a bubble. Show the explosion and have a bubble across the screen that said 'BANG' in lurid red and purple. Then a few gunshots: 'Kapow, Kapow' but in smaller letters. Then one of these deep throat kissing scenes they are now so fond of doing: 'Slurp, slobber'. Real breakthrough in cinematic art here.

Nats are now working on their DL. Most teams working on their twenty-five active player rosters but Rizzo has his annual twenty-five disabled player list to complete first. Then try to find a few active ones to play the actual games. And Zimmerman and Flores haven't even gone down yet. Give them time, they have a week. Should have signed Eric Bedard, he wouldn't let you down.

More disaster in Florida. Jackson pitched brilliantly, Nats won two games in a day, LaRoche played. Everything is rosy. Can't last. At least Ankiel is getting on board. And DeRosa. DeRosa is new but Ankiel should know better than to say it is nothing serious. Nats don't do 'nothing serious' injuries. Frank Jobe or nothing. Shit, when your outfielders are getting Tommy John, you know it's an epidemic. At least Nady had it done before he came to Washington. Or at least he had the first two done. Looks like he will make the team. Two TJs, what's not to like? Fucking idiots. Must be some players out there without health problems they could sign. Johnny fucking Bench maybe. There was a player. For a non-Expo. Doesn't even limp. No Gary Carter, but decent.

Got home to a ringing telephone. Just Marianne. Don't forget to call the kids, there looking forward to seeing you next week. I heard about your promotion. Isn't it wonderful? Obviously hadn't heard about the post-promotion six minute

251

wonder presentation. Still, he called Cheryl. Why not? She wanted to talk about his promotion. Didn't mention the presentation to her. Why spoil it? Thing about getting one promotion in forty years, it can be taken out of proportion. Tried Barney while he was in the mood but had to leave a message.

*

Friday was a gorgeous day. He almost felt good about the weekend coming up. After all, Jem would be in the Quencher. Be sort of fun to hear him stay positive once the season approached and all the players checked into hospital. Then there was the date with Beryl thing. Christ, what had he done? Still, she was nice enough. And actually damn smart. Hated the Red Sox. Hated the whole Red Sox Nation thing. Hated the Bruins. Hated the Celtics. I mean, she was no fool. Must ask her if she hated the NCAA. The Dance. More like a Prance. Prima donnas. So they can jump. Big deal.

Rizzo announced that he was perfectly content to start the season with the team he has now. Well, that's nice. Maybe Detwiler can play center. Pitched well but Wang is on the mend and Lannan is the fifth starter. Platoon Detwiler and Stammen in center. Of course, they just stuck Ankiel on their roster. Must have been the fact that he is injured. Perfect fit. He owed himself some beer. And tomorrow night was Final Four night so he would be locked in his apartment. Had to do the heavy lifting tonight. Beer for supper.

*

He decided he should stay in bed Saturday. Was that really snow? Fucking spring. April Fool? No, that was tomorrow. Just shitty weather. No need to get up. He felt too sick to eat and Rizzo was not likely to do much to cheer him up. Always a lot of talk in spring training about guys out of options and trades to be made but the simple fact was that cutting down to twenty-five players was tough enough without picking up a few more. Even a center fielder. That was okay. Hell, if Jem could take it, he could take it.

He rolled over. What an idiot move that was. But he made the toilet. Just. Might as well get up. Final Four. No way he was going near a bar. A Shelby day. Bring on the peninsula campaign. Fucking McClellan could have been a GM. Do nothing. And claim to be brilliant. Maybe he needed some beer to help with the Civil War. Pretty awful war, needed something cheerful.

ESPN had a few things on the Nats. Apparently Davey Johnson brings experience to the team. He's over ninety years old, what the fuck do you expect, pre-pubescent toilet humor. Give us a fart joke, Davey.

Still the Nats are confident that this is the year. And the writers are equally confident that it is not. Fascinating. To humor the writers, Strasburg got creamed today and the only guy to hit well was Chad Tracy who's on his way to Syracuse.

*

Woke up to drizzle. It was a bit warmer than yesterday, but pretty awful. But at least he remembered to telephone Beryl to cancel their walk. Hardly got a word in.

Yes, it looks hopeless. Why don't we meet at the Gardner and then have something in their coffee shop. Unless you have a better idea?

He did, actually, get an early start on the beer before meeting Jem at the Quencher for a mid-afternoon beer so that he would be in a good mood for a late beer.

Nice, idea Beryl. See you there in about an hour.

*

He was a bit late by the time he got to Jem but Jem didn't seem to mind. He was in a good mood. Always so positive. Even about the Nats.

Where've you been? Did you know the Nats have already won?

That's impressive, must be the offseason. Never win on Sunday when it counts.

Hey things are changing. Even Espinosa got a couple of hits. You notice he's had problems.

Yeah, heard he had Tommy John in his left eyeball. Could hit from the left side but not from the right.

More or less. Anyone ever tell you that there is a cynical side to your nature?

So I've been told. Never guess where I've been while you waste your time worrying about baseball trivia?

Well, out in the rain for one thing.

Fucking museum. The Gardner. All that Italian shit.

Say, that Isabella, she's a girl with a past. Collected all sorts treasure in her day. One thing and another.

Well, try her bread pudding some day. No room for any beer.

You sure? My round.

Just the one. You say Espinosa got a hit?

I tell you, they're going to be good this year.

Well, mediocre.

*

Phoned Barney and Cheryl when he got home. Asked Cheryl if he could bring a friend next Sunday.

No, no, nothing really. Just a colleague who has been supportive.

Sure Dad. I hope she's over twenty-one.

Well, maybe. Just.

Don't worry. She's welcome. You and Barney and your new friends. We'll grill her about your promotion. And you can ask me how the adoption is going.

Jesus. Are things moving?

Have to wait until next week.

When was the last time he went to bed on Sunday without even reading Cafardo? No big deal. Read him in the morning. Fucking Red Sox supporter.

*

He was awake early so was able to catch up on the baseball news. Generally accepted that Valentine and Cherington were annoying each other but a few people now thinking that, as Valentine tended to be the bigger jerk, he would get the pink slip first. And Cafardo rated Johnson as a pretty good manager and Xavier Nady as a great late pick-up. Shit, all positive stuff. Jem must be affecting the ether.

He wasn't sure how to deal with Beryl. They'd had a nice time in a nice sort of way. Really, well, well, nice. And he had invited her for Sunday. Not sure why. Still, she was, well, nice. Bought her a coffee. Just put it on her desk. She gave him a nice smile for that. Anna giggled. Fucking Anna.

Charlie dropped by to remind him about tomorrow's meeting.

You know, you seemed really nervous last week and that presentation was about the shortest thing I've ever seen.

Yeah, well, short and sweet.

Exactly. Said it all in so few words and just five/six slides. Brilliant stuff. No wonder they all admire you down here. See you at the meeting.

Jesus Christ.

He decided to keep his head down. Really concentrate on his work. Too bad there was nothing to do. Except worry about the DL. All those who could still walk were on the roster as far as he could see. How can you have that many players injured before the first game is even played? At least they didn't play the Phillies until May. Noticed there was a Sunday game in that series. Nice. Maybe Wang will be back.

Nice for all those vets on non-guaranteed contracts. Until the middle of the month when Morse and Ankiel want a game. Then, there is Harper. Never know; he might want a taste of the Bigs sometime soon. Only decision is over the last relief pitcher, which will be Chad Durbin just so they don't lose him. Poor Stammen. Deserved better. Mattheus too. Tough having an option year left.

Great, Nats lost. Zimmermann is the losing pitcher and Bernadina joins the hospital contingent. Must be time to open the season.

*

There seemed far more concern at work over his meeting than with the Nats injuries. At least no one mentioned the Nats. Best thing about all these women was no one mentioned the Red Sox either. Or the basketball. Christ, who won? One of the teams beginning with K. Who fucking cares? Well, Kentucky. And Kansas. Well, both really.

He took a deep breath before going to the meeting. Did they say Dolly's office? I think so. Shit, shame if he missed it. Maybe not.

*

They were all waiting when he got back from the meeting. Of course, they had their mole in the suits corridor. But he liked Anna, so he wasn't upset that she knew everything even before he did. They said they had decided to all take him to dinner ton Thursday to celebrate.

Shit, he was only getting a cubicle. And the money was better than he thought it would be. But Thursday was Opening Day. Priorities.

Beryl told him not to be such an asshole, only she said fool. He needed a life. And anyway, it was an afternoon game; didn't he know how things worked in Chicago?

By the time he was able to turn on his computer again Chad Durbin was in Atlanta and John Lannan was in Syracuse. Syracuse. That's about as low as it gets.

Thanks for saving the franchise from complete humiliation over the last three years, John. We really love, admire and respect you. Think you are a real big league pitcher and a first rate guy. Now fuck off. We got this guy can do the job for only eleven million. Only he can't throw strikes. Throws balls at ninety plus, but no strikes. Shame, that.

Shit, who will pitch against the Phillies on Sundays?

Must have been a real tough decision for Durbin. Stay in the Nats minor league system with a prince of a guy like Mike fucking Rizzo destroying your career, or play for a contender with Frank Wren running a professional show.

Way to spoil my big day, Mike. He hoped Lannan would get traded to whoever planned to win the World Series this season. And the fucking Nats finished last. No, not last. Don't need any more bigheads like Harper.

At least Stammen was still there. For now. Fucking Rizzo.

*

That night he decided he really should telephone Cheryl and Barney. After all they were his children and keeping in touch was important. Started with Cheryl.

How are things going with the adoption?

I told you, Dad, you have to wait until Sunday. But I will say that we are really excited. How are you? And how is your new friend?

Just a colleague really. Helped me out a bit at work.

And how is work? Any more details on the big promotion?

Well not that big, but things are okay. I guess.

Now what's that supposed to mean? No more money. No private office? No secretary.

Well, sort of. Did get more money. No office, but a cubicle. And I will share a personal assistant with some asshole in another area. So I guess it' pretty good.

Just pretty good? Dad, you're such a jerk. It's terrific. Finally something to show for all those years.

*

Decided he needed beer. Changed his clothes first and before he was out the door the telephone was ringing. Barney.

Hey, Big Shot, you bringing the champagne on Sunday?

Well, it's just a bit of a different job.

Christ, Dad, sounds like you're a very small step from Senior Vice-President.

Well, I am being called Senior Training Officer. Stupid fucking title.

You bet it is. Don't know why you bother. Why not resign?

Okay. So I'm pleased. A bit.

He was exhausted. All this enthusiasm from the children was way over the top. He would risk the Junction. Surely even Red Sox fans wouldn't gloat over an exhibition win.

*

It was all a bit worrying at work. He was so used to the big crowded office. Even if the cubicle was right there on the side, it was different. Made him feel like an asshole. Like Stuart. In fact, Stuart's spare shows were still in the corner. Asshole. Please God, don't make me an asshole like Stuart. Getting through the day would be tough but at least there was Jem tonight.

*

Jem agreed with him. Sort of. What a terrible thing to do to John Lannan. But Jem figured the season would prove to be interesting.

For a change. You mean they won't be officially eliminated from the playoffs until maybe mid-May.

Maybe even later.

Shit, they'll have to make another movie about managing baseball. Rizzoball, think Brad Pitt would be interested?

About the Nats? Think about it, Peter. It would be called Borasball and he would insist on doing all the casting. George Clooney would be the lead. Don't know who would play Rizzo, but I do know one thing.

Yeah?

It would be a Scott Boras client.

He loved Jem.

*

He woke up early. Opening Day. Fucking awful. All the hope and optimism he had been feeling throughout the offseason was about to be crushed by the reality of actual game results. And he had six months of it ahead of him.

CPSIA information can be obtained at www.ICGtesting.com
Printed in the USA
BVOW041130071012

302329BV00007B/31/P

9 781475 158496